SIXTY M

A nail-biting race against time.

Five very different people.

Five very separate lives.

Sixty minutes to bind them for ever.

As the clock ticks away the minutes of a single hour on a July morning, the lives of five strangers come crashing together in a headlong rush towards an inevitable conclusion.

Tony Salter is the bestselling author of three previous novels – Best Eaten Cold, The Old Orchard and Cold Intent, the sequel to Best Eaten Cold.

He is also working on a series of illustrated children's books set in Norway.

He lives in Oxfordshire with his Norwegian wife.

ALSO BY TONY SALTER

Best Eaten Cold

The Old Orchard

Cold Intent

SIXTY MINUTES

Tony Salter

ETS Limited

Dawber House, Long Wittenham, OX14 4QQ

First published in Great Britain in 2019 by ETS Limited

ISBN: 978-0-9957977-8-9

For my father, Michael.

Prologue

The minute hand of the big clock pointed to the heavens, finally eclipsing its smaller sister.

There was a moment of stillness. A lull before the storm. The peace at the centre of a hurricane's eye.

In the middle of the huge hall stood a young man, one hand deep in his pocket, his clean-shaven cheeks shadowed by the massive dinosaur skull hanging above his head.

Less than fifty other souls were scattered about that great space, enjoying the sights of London and innocently unaware of the drama playing out in front of them.

Most, but not all, were unaware.

The young man's eyes flicked back and forth between the two figures who were approaching him from either side. Their mouths were moving, but he was unable to hear any words. The swirling clamour of the battle raging inside him filled his head and swamped all other sounds.

Time had stopped — a gesture of generosity offering him one last chance to change his mind — and, as the fear and strain took hold of him and squeezed, he started to tremble.

11:00

Jim

As he warmed his fingers on the fifth cuppa of the day, Jim looked up at the big clock. Only eleven. One and a half hours until lunch and then four more hours after that. And it was still Monday.

How had he ended up here? At his age? Going through the motions of this dull, pathetic, excuse-for-a-job. It wasn't how the master plan was expected to pan out. He was supposed to be winding down and choosing his own working hours by now. That had always been the idea.

Jim had always needed structure in his life. That was why he'd joined the army as soon as he was sixteen. Nothing was wishy-washy and uncertain there. You had to swallow a lot of shit, but you knew the rules and there were no surprises. The only downside had been when wife and kids appeared. It wasn't easy to keep the family on the straight and narrow while you were away on tour for months at a time.

But there'd been a plan for that too; Jim had known that mixing army and family would be an issue and he'd had his transition organised for years. Julie could manage to take care of the girls for the first ten years and then he would hand in his ticket. He'd have over twenty years under his belt and would be set for a decent pension even though he'd only be thirty-nine.

The other great part of his plan was that the army transition programme would fund the first year of his taxi driver training. It was a bit of a joke really, but if someone was offering a free handout, Jim had never been backwards about stepping forward.

He'd always wanted to be a cabbie; his uncle had driven a taxi for forty years and, as kids, Jim and his brother would often sit with an A-Z map book trying to catch out Uncle Don by giving him the names of tiny, obscure streets – little mews or cul-de-sacs which no-one would ever want to go to. They never managed to beat him. Not only did he know every street and where it was but, if they gave him two addresses, he was always ready to talk them through the route from one to the other.

'... go down Formosa Street and take a left on Warrington Crescent, down to the roundabout – great pub there – slight right up Sutherland Avenue, straight over Maida Vale to Hall Road. Follow that for a couple of blocks before taking a left onto Grove End Road. Just a short stretch before you take a left onto Abbey Road and drive over the famous zebra crossing past Abbey Road studios ...'

Don was a genius and Jim could still picture himself as a kid, wide-eyed and overflowing with admiration. That would something to be proud of. Something special.

It had been a good plan and, on the face of it, every piece had fallen into place like the delicate components of a Swiss watch, tick-tocking away in perfect balance.

But events had conspired against him – he still didn't quite understand how – and his perfectly constructed clockwork mechanism had started to lose time. It was only a few seconds a day at the beginning – fights with Julie, one or both kids testing his patience, traffic conspiring against him – but, year after year, it got worse. A gradual decline until that moment, two years earlier, when a sharp piece of grit found its way into the inner workings and the watch suddenly stopped.

In retrospect, if he'd been more flexible, more aware and less self-centred, he might have found a way to keep his plans together. If he'd left the army a few years earlier, things would probably have turned out differently. Maybe so, but he was sure about one thing. He would have found a way to fix everything if it hadn't been for that stupid, stuck-up, interfering bitch.

Even thinking about her made his chest tighten – it was as

though he was being squeezed by thick rolls of white bandage like an Egyptian mummy and his saliva was sour with shame as the panic and fear washed over him.

He dreamt about mummies sometimes; he was still alive but two tall thin men were wrapping him up ready to put his body into one of those massive stone coffins. The bands would tighten around his chest and he would begin to struggle for air, but they didn't stop or slow down, both bending over and working their way upwards turn by turn, carefully avoiding wrinkling the soft cotton, first smoothing it out and then pulling it tight. By the time they reached his neck and chin, the terror would be squeezing out of him like toothpaste; the next wrap would cover his mouth and nose and that would be it.

Jim reached into his pocket and took out an orange plastic pill bottle. Julie was right. He had to find a way to let this go. Shaking two capsules into his palm, he swallowed them with a gulp of lukewarm tea. He was still panting like an overexcited puppy and he wrapped his head in one hand, thumb and little finger squeezing his temples as he hunched forward, trying to focus on keeping calm. Easy to say, but so hard to do.

Slowly, steadily, he felt the bandages around his chest loosen, allowing him to breathe again. He took out a white cotton handkerchief to wipe the beads of clammy sweat from his forehead and imagined the strain he was putting on his body. This had to stop or it would kill him. He had to move on and draw a line in the sand.

Hassan

'Excuse me. This is my stop.'

'Oi! All right, mate. No need to shove. Where's the bloody fire, then?' The man reached out to grab Hassan's arm, snarling. He was tall and wearing a smart suit like a businessman or a banker, but the shine of his shaven head and his glass-blue eyes told another story.

Hassan twisted and pulled free of the grasping fingers. 'I'm sorry. I'm ... I'm ... late,' he mumbled over his shoulder as he stepped past and down onto the platform.

'They've got no bloody manners, have they?' The alpha male laugh followed him down the crowded platform, stuffed with

3

triumphant disdain. 'Wanker! Why don't you piss off back home? …
Tosser!'

Hassan didn't turn around. He gripped his bag with both hands, hunched low and weaved carefully through the heaving mass of tourists and office workers until he was safely away. Guys like that were everywhere back home, and he'd learned how to survive early on. Always avoid eye contact, keep your head down and, nine times out of ten, nothing would happen. If that failed, you were stuffed – there would always be more than one of them and the only hope was that they weren't either too drunk or too angry.

None of the other passengers looked up; they didn't want anything to do with trouble and he sensed a Red Sea parting around him as if to emphasise his toxicity. If Mr National Front decided Hassan was worth getting off the train for, there wouldn't be any help from bystanders. They probably didn't actually wish him harm, but he was definitely to blame for their discomfort and fear – just by being there.

He kept moving until he heard the hiss of the train doors closing accompanied by a now-distant shout of 'Fucking Paki'. His sigh of relief merged with those of his fellow passengers in an echo of the closing doors and the parted waters flowed back together as though nothing had happened.

It was only getting worse after the Brexit vote. Whatever eventually happened, he couldn't believe that people had been so stupid. Everyone liked to talk the talk about Britain being an inclusive society but it hadn't taken long for a whole raft of closet racists to show their true colours. The most depressing part of it all – from a very long list of depressing things – was that apparently his father and most of his friends had voted to leave the EU. Did they really think their lives would improve? That they would have a real voice in British democracy?

Hassan couldn't pinpoint exactly when he'd realised that his father was a stupid man. As a child, your father just "is". A Godlike figure embodying size, strength and infallibility, the idea of questioning your dad was as unimaginable as believing you could fly.

The cracks had probably first appeared during the second year of his GCSEs. His youngest brother, Omar, who'd been twelve at the time, had asked their dad to help him with his maths homework while Hassan was sitting quietly in the corner revising for his mock exams. He couldn't help listening in and it was as though he was hearing a familiar song for the umpteenth time but, by some magical wave of a wand, he suddenly understood the meaning of the lyrics.

The excuses, explanations and eventual grumbling exit were the same ones that he'd heard so many times, but it was only at that moment that he realised that his father didn't have the slightest idea how to answer the questions, but was too proud to admit it.

Once Hassan learnt to translate the language of bluster and self-deception which had played understudy to true wisdom for all of those years, he discovered example after example, both in daily life and in the secret pockets of his memory. His eyes were opened for the first time and he became alive to once-forbidden possibilities.

Cold drops of sweat were stinging his eyes as he came out of the tube station into the bright sunlight. It was always the same after an incident like that; the fear would rush in like hand-pumped Real Ale into a pint glass - two, maybe three, great swooshes – until he was full and frothing over. Adrenaline-fuelled impulses would then scream at him to defend himself or to run … run … run …

Experience had taught him that neither was the smart option. He'd tried fighting, but it made it worse every time; running seemed to evoke the hunting spirit of the wolf pack and was no better. The right choice – almost always – was to make yourself small, humble and weak. They got their victory, the ritual humiliation, and most of the time he could slink away unharmed.

In his secret heart of hearts, he hoped that he left them confused, their primal urges only partially sated, and with a lingering sourness in the roofs of their mouths which wouldn't go away. He didn't really believe that was true, but it was all he had.

His body would be in one piece but there was always a price to pay. He could feel it again – the effort of fighting his animal instincts had left him exhausted and as weak as he'd been pretending to be. And the shame burned him, a lifetime of insults and apologies building layer upon layer and towering over him in a constant reminder of his weakness.

He thought about whisky.

It had been almost two years now. He was proud of himself and grateful to God for helping him to crawl out of the abyss, but he still thought about whisky constantly. It had always been whisky for him. Most of his friends drank lager, but he'd never liked the gas and the bitter aftertaste. Ironically it was his father who'd given him his first illicit sip of peaty malt when he was seventeen, and that was it. He was enslaved.

The rest of his family weren't particularly devout but Hassan had still been brought up properly and had always known that alcohol was forbidden. In spite of that, and the many, many punishments, he'd never been able to help himself. His father's hypocrisy only made it worse.

Even now, the thought of that first mouthful made his knees shake. The smoky tang on the roof of his mouth, the awareness of money in his pocket and the anticipation of the warm comfort that he knew would fill him as he moved through the third double shot, and the fourth ...

It would be the comfort and companionship of a false friend and would never last but, for those few short hours, Hassan had always believed that it would be forever, and he missed it with empty, acid spasms.

South Kensington was as crowded as he'd been told it would be. There was money everywhere and dozens of gorgeous women dripping with jewellery and designer clothes. Clothes which left nothing to the imagination. And the cars; any one of them would probably be worth more than his parents' house. Insane. All links with the real world seemed broken.

After the darkness of the tube station, the late morning sunshine reflected off the white paving stones and floated blurred black inkblots across his vision. It took him a while to focus – paving stones were never white in Bradford – as he looked at his map and tried to recover his sense of direction.

He felt calmer. Stronger. The incident in the tube had shaken him badly, but he was safe out on the street. An alien planet, but the air was breathable. Apart from the rich people everywhere, there were hundreds of tourists from all over the world. He was just another visitor – blue jeans, bomber jacket, clean-shaven, short hair – he could have been Spanish or Italian. Just one of the crowd.

It was a big day for him. He was finally going to the Natural History Museum. He'd wanted to come here since he was a boy and now he was only five minutes walk away.

In his parents' house there had only been one book apart from the Koran – a battered old picture book about dinosaurs. Hassan had worn it out with overuse, the grubby cardboard pages splitting and peeling so much that the ancient sauruses were losing limbs and heads one by one.

One day, he'd been admiring the close-up, actual-size drawing of a Tyrannosaurus tooth, when his father had snatched the book from his hands.

'It's not right,' he'd said to Hassan's mother. 'Enough. The boy's obsessed and it's not normal. He should get out and play cricket with the other kids.'

And with that, his father had thrown the book into the fire. Hassan hadn't spoken a word for three days and never forgave or forgot that casual act of cruelty.

Shuna
'Mum?'

'What?'

'MUM?'

'WHAT?'

Zoe flounced into the kitchen wearing some sort of spangly tank top and the shortest shorts Shuna had ever seen.

'Mum, can I wear this today?' she said, tilting her head to one side like a cartoon owl and half-closing her eyes.

That attempt at coquettish charm might work on Zoe's father, but Shuna wasn't even slightly impressed.

'Don't be ridiculous,' she said. 'We're going to the Natural History Museum, not a party. And, by the way, young lady, I doubt very much you'll be wearing those shorts to a party either. Where did you get them? They're outrageous.'

The diva exit had started before Shuna finished her sentence – Zoe hadn't been under any delusions about the response she would get. 'I got them from Jenny,' she said. 'Everyone's wearing them. I think you actually want me to look like a freak.'

Shuna smiled at the disappearing back of her oldest and called after her. 'If you want to have time to go to Muriel's we have to be out of here in the next couple of minutes. Tell your sister to get a move on.'

Her smile sagged and she let out a soft sigh. The next few years were going to be tough, and she'd been foolishly hoping for another year's grace. There was nothing more annoying than the way people always said how things today were worse than they used to be, but surely she hadn't been that developed and precocious when she was thirteen?

It wasn't only the media and technology onslaught which stuck its grubby fingers into every corner of their lives. Living in a big city made a huge difference – Shuna had grown up in the country and her teenage passions and energies had been poured into looking after her horses.

But, if her memory wasn't playing tricks with her, everything really had been so much simpler back then. Coming from a rich family which owned a vineyard had helped, but they weren't exactly living a pauper's life in London, so that wasn't it.

While Shuna was growing up, boys had mostly remained in the background, even through high school – it was only after she'd gone to university that things changed. It was as though someone suddenly pulled back a big red velvet curtain and exposed a whole secret world which had been hidden from view. Wonderful, exciting and a little frightening, but she'd been nineteen by then and ready to deal with all the new experiences – good and bad.

And still nothing to compare with London – Stellenbosch was

only a small town, and the culture had still been very conservative in the eighties. It must be different now but, from everything she'd heard, the Afrikaans puritan streak still ran though every element of life and things hadn't yet changed as much as most people had been expecting.

She sipped her tea and wondered absent-mindedly if she'd ever go home again.

Zoe's mood was transformed as she bounced back into the kitchen, little Anna traipsing behind her like a miniature replica – same hair, same eyes, same nose, no-one could ever question that they were sisters.

'Here we are, Mum,' she said, all smiles and youthful exuberance.

Zoe's magical change of attitude could only have arisen because she was up to no good or she wanted something. One way or the other, Shuna knew she would find out soon enough.

'Good,' she said. 'Let's go then. We're meeting Dad for lunch after the Museum, but we've got time for a hot chocolate first.'

A hot chocolate at Muriel's Kitchen was their special "girls together" treat – extra-rich, dark, velvety chocolate, with a swirl of cream and two outrageously expensive pistachio macarons each. Shuna wasn't sure which of the three of them was most excited; the thought certainly made her stomach tingle.

There was a long queue at the counter of the cafe, but they were lucky and managed to steal a table from two smartly dressed old ladies who were paying their bill.

'What time are we back from lunch with Dad?' said Zoe as they sat down.

'About three I should think,' said Shuna.

'OK,' said Zoe.

'Why?' said Shuna, guessing the question had something to do with Zoe's bounciness.

'Nothing,' replied Zoe. 'Just asking.'

Anna lifted her hand to her mouth and giggled through her fingers. 'Zoe's got a date,' she said. 'She's going to see her boyfriend.'

'Shut up,' said Zoe. 'You're such a little moron.'

'Zoe!' snapped Shuna. 'You know I hate that word.' She found herself smiling through her irritation. 'A date, eh?'

'It's nothing Mum. Honest. I just had a message from Julie and everyone's meeting in the park at four o'clock for a game of softball. There's this boy who'll be there …'

'Does "this boy" have a name?' said Shuna, desperately trying to keep a straight face.

'He's called Spike, OK?' mumbled Zoe.

'Spike?' said Shuna, unable to control the squeak in her voice. 'What sort of name is that?'

Zoe had been practising her withering stare for months and was showing real talent. 'It's not his real name, Mum,' she said. 'Obvs!'

'Oh,' said Shuna, confused as to why that was so obvious.

'Look, it's something to do with the shape of his head when he was born. Everyone just calls him Spike, OK?'

'All right,' said Shuna. 'I was only asking.'

'Fine,' said Zoe. 'Now can we stop talking about it, please. You're both so embarrassing.'

'All right,' said Shuna. 'We'll drop it. Anyway, here come the hot chocolates.'

Dan

He'd deliberately chosen something easy to read – the final part of a Scandi-noir trilogy which had been his guilty pleasure since the release of the first volume. The writing was actually quite good and the plot and characters were compelling. Not an "improving" example of the literary art, perhaps, but Dan was finally starting to realise that the knee jerk worship of quality, literary novels might be an overrated pretension in any case. Anyway, if he wasn't improved enough by now …

The book was compelling and long-awaited but, despite that, the words refused to stay in one place. He pulled his glasses further down his nose and squinted without success; he must have looked like a demented gargoyle as he desperately tried to follow the letters around the page and he could feel the niggling approach of an incoming headache.

It wasn't going to work.

Dan sighed theatrically, closed his eyes and rested the open book on his lap. He knew that trying to concentrate for long was hopelessly optimistic. The thoughts running around his head wouldn't be silenced – how could they be?

He thought about Rachel. She would have that big, optimistic smile on her face as she explored Harrods, floor by floor, room by room. She'd been so relieved when he'd offered to come here and read his book while she shopped alone. It was her first visit, and she was loving everything about London. Harrods would be a highlight and, although she would never have said anything, he was sure she'd been dreading him spoiling it for her.

They'd been married almost fifty years and together for even longer. He tried to remember a single time when they'd enjoyed a shopping trip together. He suspected they never had. It was that whole Mars-Venus thing. He didn't want or need many things and, when he did, he went straight to the correct counter and bought them. What was the point in shilly-shallying around?

Rachel would go into the store with a purpose too but, for her, the whole in-out, bish-bosh, brushing hands of a simple, clean transaction was too crude and clumsy – a bit like sleeping with someone on the first night. Whatever kids today might think and do, Rachel would no more have considered that than she would have slapped a child or cursed in public.

For her, department store shopping was a courtship of sorts, a gentle and measured dance with defined pace and rhythm. There was usually no wavering from her final goal – she was a deeply practical woman – but she would pretend to be distracted at each step along the way. Trying a Kashmir sweater for size, allowing the make-up girls to tempt her with coral lipstick or French perfume, it was always the same and, if he was stupid enough to accompany her, he wouldn't be able to ignore his frustration at the pointlessness of it all.

It was the same every time and, without fail, he would sense his reserves of patience draining away like oil from a cracked sump.

And then, in a graunching of seized gears and pistons, he would ruin it for her; he would drown out the inner music of her dance and shatter her illusions in a screech of tortured metal. He didn't mean to, but something would always come out, some slightly sarcastic, vaguely patronising, marginally misogynistic comment that would inevitably lead to them both swearing to never go shopping together ever again.

As he sat on the hard bench, unable to read and dizzy from the spinning in his head, he sensed her absence like a missing limb. It was only a couple of hours though and he was very pleased he'd left her to shop alone this time. It had taken him fifty years, but he was learning at last.

Perhaps he should have made his confessions already, but there was still plenty of time and the picture of her marvelling at the extravagance of Harrods' food hall put a smile back on his face. Yes, there was still plenty of time.

The hall of the museum was huge. Dan guessed you could probably fit four basketball courts inside it and still have room for the cheerleaders. If you shifted that damn dinosaur out of the way, of course. He'd never been much into old bones and history. What had always interested him was the here-and-now, the people around him, the human condition. Endlessly fascinating, endlessly unpredictable.

He'd never been much of a jock either but he did like basketball. They'd made everybody pick a sport at school and, at over six-four, shooting hoops had been the obvious choice for him. Not that he'd been any good – not fast or accurate enough to get into any of the high school teams, and college basketball had already become semi professional by the time he went.

That hadn't stopped him from dropping in on the pick-up games around campus and he'd eventually found a group of like-minded and equally mediocre friends who he'd played with fairly regularly for almost forty years. Every year, he'd been a little slower and – depressingly – a little shorter, but it had helped keep the middle-aged flab away for long enough. He shook his head as he looked down at his bruised and liver-spotted hands. Those games were already tiny dots in the rear view mirror and gaining too much weight no longer seemed to be an issue.

There were only a few other people dotted around the hall and he looked around, hoping for a distraction. That old museum guard looked like a sour-faced S.O.B. sitting slouched in the corner. Did he have so much to be sour about? Maybe he did. Who was Dan to judge?

Since he'd retired, Dan had spent more time thinking about life and the nasty way it had of coming and biting you when you least expected it. He had also realised that it was important to be careful before you threw out accusations or judgements based on assumptions. It was the easiest thing in the world to do, but you never knew the true story lurking behind a life. In fact, he'd become more and more convinced that there was no such thing as a single true story in any case.

Valuable thoughts, almost approaching wisdom, and a shame it had taken until now for him to see things so clearly.

His phone started to vibrate. It was Rachel. He felt awkward speaking in the cavernous, echoing space, but couldn't ignore her.

'Hello,' he said, almost whispering as he hunched over.

'Hi darling, it's me.'

'Yes. I know. I can see that on the phone. How's Harrods?'

'It's amazing. I've just been to the food hall.'

'Something else, isn't it?'

'I've never seen anything like it. Not even in New York and definitely not in Toronto. And the prices! Do you know what they charge for a tub of Philly cheese?'

'Nope. But I bet it's a lot.'

'You'd better believe it. Three pounds. I only pay around eighty cents back home.'

'Well, that's how they pay for that building and all the lights I guess.'

'... And the other thing is that most people don't actually buy anything. It's full of people just wandering around looking at all the stuff.'

'Well, some people must buy things some of the time or there wouldn't be any point would there?'

'Huh. I guess so,' said Rachel, her voice suddenly sounding faint and far away. 'Anyway, how are you doing?'

'Oh, you know. I'm fine, I guess. Just sitting around reading my book. Looking at a massive dinosaur. How long do you think you'll be?'

'I'd love to wander around for another hour or so if that's OK with you. Then I'll swing by and pick you up at about twelve. Are you all right with that?'

'Sure. Don't you worry about me.' Dan's heart sank at the thought of another hour spent alone with his thoughts. 'I'm fine. You have a good time.'

'Thanks, sweetheart. You're an angel,' she said. 'I'll see you in a bit.'

'Bye, now,' said Dan, into an empty phone.

Nadia

The building was the same. Nadia stepped into the empty lift and pressed the button for the top floor. A new guy on security, otherwise nothing had changed. Why was she surprised? There was no reason for anything to change in such a short time? She was just tired, and it seemed as though she'd been away for ever. Nadia stared at herself in the mirrored lift wall. Make-up wasn't going to help – she looked as exhausted as she felt.

The sixth-floor corridor was empty – grey walls, smoked-glass doors and soulless art her only companions. The sound of her heels on the wooden floor was unnaturally loud, click-clack-echoing as though she was in a dream. She reached the end and knocked gently on the final door, before opening it and stepping into the room.

'Hi Nadia. Lovely to see you back.' The woman behind the desk greeted her with a glowing smile before pushing her chair back and standing up, arms stretched out wide.

'No need to get up, Sue,' said Nadia, much too late. 'Wow you are looking …' She stretched her hands wide.

'Huge?' said Sue, laughing and crossing her arms protectively in front of her. 'Whale-sized? Like a walking hot-air balloon?'

Nadia giggled. 'Yup. All of the above.' She leant forward for a closer look. 'Can't be long now?'

'Two and a half weeks … although I bet this little one's not going to be in any hurry. I finish on Friday.'

'I can't believe it. Last time I was in, you were barely showing.'

'Has it really been that long?'

'Feels long enough for that to be your second,' said Nadia.

'Birmingham not so great?'

'It was shitty … literally … and dull for six months; now all hell's breaking loose and I've got almost nothing to show for it.' She gestured at the closed inner door. 'He in there?'

'Yup. With Phil. They'll be done in a few minutes. Why don't you go ahead? Meeting room three. I'll join you for a coffee.'

'Thanks,' said Nadia. She put an envelope on the desk. 'This needs to go to Admin,' she said. 'Breach report.'

Sue looked up at her with sad eyes. 'James?'

Nadia nodded. Was her misery so obvious?

'I'm so sorry,' said Sue. 'I thought he might have been the one?'

'Me too,' said Nadia, 'but waddya gonna do?' She shrugged self-consciously and turned to leave. 'Goes with the territory, I guess.'

The meeting room was even more faceless and neutral than the corridor outside; cold grey walls, an unadorned white table and black Vitra chairs. Faceless and neutral, but very expensive and achingly cool. Maybe not the best use of the taxpayer's money.

Sue came in holding two cappuccinos but, before she had time to sit down, the insistent ringing of her office phone dragged her back out again. Nadia had been looking forward to a catch-up and instead was left alone with her thoughts, halfheartedly following the digital timestamp as it wandered aimlessly around the flat screen TV. The massive display dominated an entire wall and the white digits stood in stark relief against the dark, black, empty glass.

11:01 and no sign of the others. Nadia could feel the acid burn in her stomach – time was running out, she knew it.

Aside from the fact that her premonitions of impending disaster were well-founded, she knew that feelings of emptiness and despair were to be expected. It was always hard to jump back into the real world after an assignment and, in different circumstances, she'd have already been through a week of debriefing and adjusting – twice-daily psych consults mixed with an intensive programme of lectures and exercises.

Circumstances – the same ones which kept her focused on the minutes ticking away – hadn't allowed for that luxury, but she was struggling to remember why she was there and what she was supposed to be doing.

Events of the previous evening hadn't helped. She'd guessed things weren't going to go well and her gut feel was rarely wrong. Bloody James. Why had he decided to be so pathetically romantic?

After nearly a month of total radio silence she'd known there must be serious issues, but Nadia had been holding onto the hope that they were manageable problems. Since she'd left, the fact that she'd 'abandoned' him had been a consistent thread running through all of their FaceTime chats. Perhaps he'd decided to exact a childish revenge by not answering her calls?

That hope had evaporated when she found out that he'd paid a two-week penalty to move out of his old flat at short notice. That was completely out of character. James was a generous warm-hearted man, but both his mother and father had been accountants and he hated wasting money.

It had been almost dark by the time Nadia arrived at his new address and then he'd taken an age to answer the door. When he finally opened up, he stared at her without speaking, jaw clenched and eyes glinting black in the shadow of the doorway. There was no hint of his usual warmth and charm and he clearly wasn't pleased to see her.

'Hana!' he said at last. 'What the fuck are you doing here?'

Nadia knew then – or rather she'd thought she'd known – that he'd found someone else. It was the obvious explanation. Her replacement was probably inside the flat, stretched out languorously on crumpled sheets and wondering why James was taking so long to get rid of the unwelcome distraction.

'What am I doing here?' she replied, struggling to control the hysterical falsetto squeak in her voice. 'When I left for Melbourne, we were in a serious relationship … or at least I thought we were … you told me you loved me for Christ's sake. And then, three weeks ago, without any warning, you stop calling me, you ignore my messages, it turns out you even move out of the flat.' The well-rehearsed words tumbled out in a single breath and she gasped for more air. 'Did you think I'd just accept that and move on? If you wanted to dump me and didn't have the balls to tell me to my face, you could at least have sent me a text.'

Nadia could feel the rage building inside her in waves as she watched James standing in the open doorway, glaring at her as though she were somehow the guilty party. Her fists clenched and, if he hadn't opened his mouth to speak at that moment, she would have hit him, or the door, or both.

'How did you find my address?' he said, still looking at her like a complete stranger.

'What?' said Nadia. 'What?' Where had that come from? Something was really not right. 'I looked it up. What's that got to do with anything? Weren't you listening?'

'I heard you perfectly well,' he said, although he didn't seem interested in changing tack. 'Where did you look it up? I'm ex-directory everywhere. I made sure of it. How did you find me?'

'I don't know,' said Nadia, suddenly sensing the ground shifting under her. 'I don't remember.' Alarm bells were ringing in her head as she realised this wasn't about a lover's betrayal. He knew something. But how?

She closed her eyes and took a long slow breath. Her personal hurt would have to wait. 'OK. Can I come in?' she said. 'I don't want to have this conversation on the street.'

Something crumpled in his face and his shoulders sagged. He stepped backwards and held the door open for her. 'First on the left,' he mumbled as she squeezed past him in the narrow hallway.

She sat down on the brand new IKEA sofa and watched him pacing up and down.

'Who are you anyway?' he said, as he reached the fireplace and turned. 'Is your name even Hana?'

17

His surprise and indignation appeared genuine and the man she remembered was back. He was either a brilliant actor or there was nothing sinister to worry about. She needed to be sure though – the scenario was textbook and there was a process to follow.

Nadia looked at him, looked at his pleading eyes and allowed the sadness to wash over her for a few moments. However he'd found out, she could imagine the raw pain of betrayal he must have felt and she knew him well enough to know he would never be able to forgive her for that. She deserved to feel guilty for what she'd put him through … but was his pain worse than the burden of living a lie, of living many lies?

It was Sod's Law that they'd met while she'd been working undercover. Changing name a few months into a relationship was never a good option, and she'd been stuck as Hana Koury as far as James was concerned. If he could have been patient for just a little longer, she would have been able to explain everything and they might have had a chance.

As James continued to stare down at her, each of her false lives began to seem as real as any other, pulling Nadia into pieces like banners of smoke torn apart by the wind. She closed her eyes, marshalling her thoughts and reminding herself of who she really was and why the lies were necessary.

Necessary, maybe, but at what cost? Was it always going to be like this? Was this her life? She'd always known personal relationships would be complicated, but she'd be thirty-five in a couple of years and James had been different. For the first time she'd dared to allow hope to creep in.

'Sit down, James,' she said. 'Tell me what's going on. What's happened?'

'Aren't you even going to answer my questions?'

'I will … but first tell me why you're asking them.'

He slumped into an armchair and, when he looked at her, she could see tears in his eyes.

'Do you remember the last time we spoke?' he said.

'Yes. You called me at work, but I was busy and you said you'd call back later.'

'Do you know where I was when I called?'

'No. You didn't say.'

'I was standing outside your office door?'

'In Melbourne? You went to Australia?'

'Yup.'

Nadia could picture the scene. A cheap plywood door hiding a virtual office in some unassuming building in Melbourne's Central Business District, lights switched off and no sign of life. James standing there checking the address three times before calling her. He wasn't a big traveller. She'd told Admin there was no reason to worry about an unexpected visit.

'Ah,' she said, as it all became painfully clear. 'What were you doing there?'

'I wanted to surprise you,' he said. 'I went to your apartment first. Flat 17b didn't exist and your name wasn't on any of the buzzers.'

'I can explain,' said Nadia. 'At least some of it. First, I need to …'

'… I had to see you,' said James. 'I missed you so much.' He looked up at Nadia, tears now flowing down his cheeks. 'I was there to propose to you. How stupid was that?'

Nadia hadn't known what to say. This kind gentle man had loved her and wanted to marry her. He'd travelled to the other side of the world to tell her. She'd loved him as well, but all she'd been able to do was lie to him. And she was going to need to lie some more.

Completing the security breach report had taken almost two hours, but Nadia was sure there were no loose ends. By the time the boys from IT had worked their magic, Hana Koury would never have existed.

She was jolted back into the present as the meeting room door swung open and David McAllister walked in. David was larger than life in every way, his booming voice, physical size and exuberant confidence making it impossible to believe he'd ever been able to work as a field agent.

He wrapped her in a huge hug, almost certainly in violation of dozens of HR directives, but he was the boss and a firm believer in the principle of "do what I say, not what I do". He'd also been

Nadia's mentor since her first day and they were both fully aware that he'd come to fill the father-shaped void in her life.

'Welcome back, Nadia. Sorry it's all a bit hectic. You must be exhausted.'

'Great to see you, Sir. It's good to be home.'

He patted her on the shoulder. 'I noticed the security report on Sue's desk. Sorry to see that. Tell me about it later. Yes?'

Nadia nodded and David turned to the two men standing behind him. 'You know Phil,' he said. 'And this is Ed Bailey who's over from Six. He'll be working with you on this.'

Phil Castle was MI5's Senior Operations Director and not one of Nadia's favourite people. Leaving aside the occasion when he'd come on to her drunkenly at a Christmas party, there was something about him which sent shivers down her spine. Most people called him Voldemort – a strong hint that others felt the same way.

She would give her new partner the benefit of the doubt – he looked harmless enough – although the services didn't tend to mix that well. International operations often involved a lot of "champagne work" – hobnobbing with senior diplomats and politicians – and the snobbery and self-importance tended to rub off. On first look, Ed didn't seem like that type – half-shaven, crumpled jeans, even more crumpled linen shirt and dark rings under his eyes. Decent looking after a shower and a night's sleep, but no pretty boy.

His smile was genuine and his handshake dry and firm. 'Pleased to meet you Nadia,' he said. 'Sorry about the appearance. I'm straight off the plane. Hopefully I'll be able to help.'

11:06

Jim

Jim was still hunched forward but his breathing was steady and the tightness around his chest was almost gone. Before straitening up, he absent-mindedly registered the immaculate shine of his perfectly polished shoes with a sneaky, self-satisfied smile. That wasn't something just anyone could get right.

The booming hall was almost empty. Not even a few tasty young mothers to brighten things up and to help Jim pass the time in lazy lechery. There had been a group of schoolgirls in about an hour earlier and a few of them had definitely been tweaking their school uniforms for the field trip to London – shortened skirts pulled up high and blouses a couple of sizes too small. That had helped half an hour go by.

Jim smiled at the memory before giving himself a mental slap on the wrist. He needed to watch himself. Kaylee, his granddaughter, was almost fourteen; it was time he stopped eying up girls of that age. The young mums were fair game, but he needed to draw the line somewhere. To be fair, it was only looking, but even so.

He would need to sharpen up his act and get a bit of discipline back into his life. Jim patted his sagging belly which reminded him it wasn't just his ogling habits that needed taking in hand. He might be a proud granddad, but he wasn't old enough to give up the ghost yet.

He leant back in his chair and looked around the huge hall with lazy eyes. The permanent resident had impressed him for ten minutes or so, but the boredom dragged him down soon enough and another week of the usual same-old, same-old yawned in front of him.

They rotated locations every fortnight which was supposed to stimulate interest and keep them engaged and alert. Did the museum management really believe their own bullshit? It worked for maybe ten minutes but, after that, every posting was just a different old stone room full of crumbling bones and stuffed animals.

Monday mornings were the high point of the week, but only because the rest of the week was so unbelievably dull. He wondered again how he'd ended up there? He was better than this. The most depressing part was that, if Julie's dad hadn't called in a big favour with someone he played darts with, Jim would probably have still been out there, queuing with all those sad bastards down at the Job Centre and being turned down for jobs again and again. It was illegal to discriminate based on age, but did they really believe anyone took any notice?

Who could blame him for a bit of soft-porn daydreaming? As long as he kept the age of consent in mind; he wasn't going to have anyone calling him a nonce – even thinking about those disgusting pervs made his blood boil.

There had been one time in Belfast, back in the day. Jim had been on guard duty at the main gate – it was pissing down as usual – when a woman came storming up, dragging a young girl in school uniform behind her. The woman was wearing a grey raincoat and one of those transparent plastic headscarves, but that hadn't hidden the fury in her eyes or the disdainful sneer which twisted her mouth.

The girl had definitely wanted to be somewhere else, hanging head and crimson blotches on her cheeks telling the story of more than just embarrassment. She was pretty enough, but only a kid.

'Do you know how old she is?' the woman had dragged the girl forwards and shouted at him, her accent and anger melding and making it almost impossible for him to pick out the words.

'I'm sorry, madam. I don't know what you're talking about,' he'd replied, genuinely none-the-wiser.

'She's fourteen. She's only bloody fourteen, and she's a good girl. Or at least she was until one of your lot started pawing at her.'

'I still don't understand. Do you want to make a complaint?' By then Jim had understood perfectly well. They'd been five months without a break and the lads were bored and restless.

But this was out of order. The girl was clearly underage, and they had their standards. They needed to set some sort of example to these murdering terrorist bastards.

'Too bloody right, I want to complain,' she'd said, getting right in his face. 'One of your boys grabbed my Jenny here and pinned her up against a wall down by the canal. He started groping her even though she told him not to. She's a good girl, my Jenny. God knows what might have happened if three of her brother's mates hadn't shown up.'

They'd all been jumpy for weeks by that stage and Jim had taken a step backwards, half lifting his weapon. 'I'm going to need to ask you to move away from the gate, Madam.'

It hadn't been any sort of set-up. She was an angry mother, nothing more, but he could tell she was ready to lash out, gun or no gun. 'I'm sorry,' he'd continued, speaking as slowly and calmly as he could while pulling the rifle up and around inch by inch. 'It's regulations. If you move back from the gate, I'll call someone to come and take a formal complaint.'

'All right. Keep your hair on,' she'd said after a few seconds, pulling herself away but holding him locked in her furious gaze.

Jim remembered thinking she was tasty enough herself once some of the scowl was wiped off her face, and moving back from the confrontation was enough to calm her down a bit. She looked like she had a good body under the raincoat and she'd reminded him of his Julie.

And not much older than Julie if he'd had to guess. When Mrs Outraged-of-the-Falls-Road had got herself up the duff she'd probably been about the same age as her daughter was now. Not surprising that she didn't want her Jenny caught in the same hopeless mess just for a damp knee-trembler with a faceless squaddie.

Jim had picked up the gatehouse phone and called it in, but he could still remember how tense he'd been. Watching Jenny and her mum, but also flicking his eyes up and down the street, checking the boarded-up windows and the rooftops for any movement. At the time, he'd been less than a week away from the end of his tour and it was going to be his last. He'd had enough. He was only thirty-seven and had already been treated twice for stomach ulcers.

Only a few more days. It would have been so bloody typical for something to have happened right at the end. It had been all he'd been able to think about for weeks.

'Someone will be out in a couple of minutes,' he said, turning to the daughter. 'So what did this guy look like, Jenny? Are you sure he was one of us?'

'Of course she's bloody sure,' said the mother. 'Any moron can spot one of your lot at half a mile. You don't exactly blend in.'

Jim ignored her and carried on talking to Jenny. 'Was he tall or short, blonde or dark? Did he tell you his name?'

Jenny looked up at him and he could see the adult woman behind those child's eyes, waiting to break surface. 'He was tall,' she said. 'Dark hair. He said his name was Pete.'

That narrowed it down to a field of one and, in any case, Jim would've put money that Pete Mitchell was lurking behind the curtains somewhere. Not that he believed Jenny's mother's protestations for a second. Jenny wasn't a "good girl" however much her mum insisted. She'd have been up for a bit of fun, but Pete had taken it too far. That type always did.

They'd stood there in silence for ten uncomfortable minutes before the duty officer had sauntered over. Captain Watson was a complete waste of space and one of the reasons why Jim was ready to hand in his ticket.

'What have we got here, Sergeant?' he said, ignoring the two women.

'Mother here says one of our lads assaulted her daughter, Sir.' said Jim, saluting crisply.

'Does she indeed? Well, I suppose we'd better take her statement hadn't we? Keep your eyes peeled, Pritchard. She looks like a shifty cow.'

As the captain had ushered the two women into a small covered shelter next to the guard post, Jim had felt slightly sorry for them.

Not only a waste of space, Captain Watson was also a lazy, arrogant bastard who would most likely use the report to wipe his arse. There would be no official investigation. To him, they were just a couple of Provo sluts with their knickers round their ankles.

That didn't mean there wouldn't be justice. Everyone knew it wasn't right to mess with young girls like that Jenny. She probably had been flirting in the first place, but that was no excuse. There was a code, Pete Mitchell had broken it and he had a visit the same evening. By the time they'd finished with him, Jim was fairly sure Pete knew the difference between right and wrong where underage girls were concerned.

Jim's attention drifted back to the present time, and he watched as a young man in a fetching purple fleece came sauntering across the hall – a big cocky grin plastered over his face. He'd been sharing shifts with Will for almost a month now and they got on well enough. He would have loved to have had a boy of his own, but it hadn't worked out that way.

Will was always chirpy and, for a posh student, was surprisingly normal. He was a good-looking lad and had that lanky, physical confidence which comes with having always been good at sports. Apparently he'd even won some sort of important rowing race at Henley Regatta while he was still at school.

'Morning Jimbo,' said Will, leaning against the wall next to Jim and pretending to watch the hall.

'All right, Will,' he replied. 'You forgotten that we're not supposed to talk on shift?'

'Oh, come on,' Will said. 'Let's face it. There aren't exactly hundreds of hammer-wielding vandals running about.'

Part of the relative excitement of a Monday was getting the key fact sheet for their new room and Jim now knew it was two hundred and thirty-five feet long and eighty-three feet wide. He swung his head slowly from left to right. At ten past eleven, the population was precisely three, and that included the two of them. The only other resident was an old boy wearing a trilby who'd been sitting and reading for the previous ten minutes. He looked tired and sad but that wasn't Jim's problem.

'Yeah. Good point, well made,' Jim said. 'And Hatchet-face won't be round again for another half hour.'

Will let out a spluttering guffaw loud enough to make the old man look up from his book. 'Hatchet-face! Most excellent. Does she know you call her that?'

'Of course she bloody doesn't know, you plonker. And she's not going to. This may be a crap job, but some of us need the work.'

'Fair enough, mate. But Hatchet-face is ace. I love it.'

Jim had known a fair few young lads like Will in the army. They used to call them Ruperts. Most of the second lieutenants he'd worked with had been just like Will at the start. They weren't all idiots like Captain Watson; most just needed their soft edges roughening up a little, which didn't take long if you knew how.

'To be fair, she ain't much of a smiler, is she?' He enjoyed the way that Will seemed to look up to him. 'Anyway, have you come over to brag about your love life again?' Will seemed to be with a different girl every night and Jim enjoyed his daily updates.

'Would I?' said Will, lifting his hands up in mock outrage. 'Although it's pretty damn good, as you ask. You know that bet I've got on with my flatmate? I'm already two ahead for the month.'

'Bloody Nora,' said Jim. 'I'm not asking what the total is. We had free love when I was a lad, but it wasn't like that. You still had to put in the groundwork.'

'Not any more. You figure out who wants the same as you and that's about it. It's still usually the guy making the running, but not always.'

'And you're not just talking about slags?'

'Of course not,' Will looked almost offended. 'I only go for nice girls.'

'Jeezus H. Christ. It's a different world, and that's a bloody fact.'

'Maybe not so different,' Will said. 'I'm sure you were a bit of a dog back in the day.'

Jim thought back to his days of dating Julie which had been much more traditional. Over the years, he'd had a few one-night-stands here and there, but only a few and, thinking of the girls and the situations, they were best forgotten. Especially the ones where his wallet had ended up lighter by a week's pay.

'Nah. Not so much,' he said. 'Sometimes when I was on tour but only when I was too pissed to remember much. We used to have relationships. You not interested in that?'

'Of course I am,' said Will. 'I'll get spliced, have sprogs, the works, but I'm only twenty-two. I've got loads of time.'

'Well, the best of British to you, son. It sounds cushtie enough, but I'm past all that. These days, I'm knackered after a couple of beers and the X-Factor.'

Hassan

Hassan was much too early. He didn't need to be there until just before twelve and it wasn't far. That left him with three quarters of an hour to kill.

He'd never quite managed to develop a taste for coffee; at home it had always been milky-sweet and flavoured with cardamom and cinnamon which he couldn't stand and, on the rare occasions when he'd been forced to go to a coffee shop, he could never get his mind around the idea of forking out two or three quid on a cup of hot milk with a chocolate fern swirled into it.

It was a good day to make an exception as he needed somewhere to sit and wait. Excitement and impatience weren't good reasons to turn up earlier than planned so he crossed the road – threading his way between the stationary cars – and walked into the cafe on the other side. It looked a bit posh, but so did all the shops and restaurants and he suspected everywhere would be the same.

Maybe not.

Hassan realised his mistake as soon as he was inside. This must be the place where all the models and ex-models in London came to hang out together. He was the only man in the room and, on top of that, he was the only person who could remotely be described as ordinary. He stood out like a rotten apple.

It wasn't a matter of race or colour – the women came from everywhere under the sun – but, whether the cheeks, legs, arms and bare shoulders were porcelain, coffee-cream or dark chocolate there wasn't a single blemish or imperfection to be found. And as for the way they were dressed … He could feel every smouldering eye turned on him and his clumsy feet threatened to betray him more than once. No point in making a scene and walking out. All he needed to do was to buy a coffee and sit down quietly in the corner.

'What can I get you?'

'I – I – I'll have a black coffee please,' he said eventually. The girl behind the counter was just as beautiful as the customers and she smiled at him.

'Bradford boy, eh?' she said, her accent slipping seamlessly into familiar territory.

'Yeah,' he replied. 'That obvious is it?'

She raised one eyebrow and grinned again.

He laughed. 'Stupid question I guess?'

' 'tis to a Bradford girl. Where ya from?'

'Manningham. You?'

'Toller. Just on Heaton Road. You down to see rellies?'

'Yeah. Just for a couple of days. And I've always wanted to see the Natural History Museum.'

'Oh.' She didn't seem to share his enthusiasm. 'Well, whatever floats your boat. Look, it's waitress service here, so grab a seat somewhere and I'll bring your coffee over.'

The place was jam-packed, but he managed to find a small table in the far corner. As he squeezed his way through the pushchairs and bags of shopping, he wondered – not for the first time – how his life had led him to be there. It wasn't how things had been expected to turn out, that was for sure.

After tucking his holdall under the chair – he'd read somewhere that London was rammed full of pickpockets and bag-snatchers – he sat upright, stiff as a Lego man, hands on the table in front of him, while he waited for his coffee. God, he wanted a piss so badly. Why did he need to have such a small bladder?

It was hardly Hassan's fault that he wasn't good at sports. His brothers, Rafi and Omar were bigger and stronger even though he was the eldest and they had that mysterious eye-hand-foot-head co-ordination which he lacked. Add in asthma and weak eyes and, whatever his dad might have wanted, he was destined for geekdom.

Luckily, the world of geeks celebrates other skills and Hassan was smart, a gene which must have slipped silently along the maternal line. Maybe not the smartest in his school but certainly up there with the best. He learnt quickly and remembered everything. When everyone around him was hunched forward, sucking the ends of their pens, neanderthal brows furrowed with the effort of remembering and regurgitating some pointless fact, Hassan had already finished the test and was passing the time sketching complicated graphics from memory.

He would have swapped his brains and artistic sensitivity for other abilities in a heartbeat. To be bigger, stronger, less spotty and four-eyed, anything to help him fit in and be the boy everyone expected him to be. It wasn't as though he hadn't tried; he would never forget the long hours spent at the cricket nets, trembling in his oversized pads and gloves and watching the dark shape of his father pounding out of the sun towards the crease. The ball was on him before he saw it, and the heavy bat moved too slowly every time.

For the first few years his Dad had responded to his feeble efforts with shouts of encouragement – 'good swing', 'almost got that one', 'remember to lead with your elbow' – and he had dutifully taken the tips onboard. As the years went by and his brothers grew, the language and mood changed and little-by-little, his father's disappointment became dominant – 'put a bit of bloody effort into it', 'what's wrong with you?', 'why can't you be more like your brothers?'. Hassan never stopped trying but, by the time he was thirteen, his father had stopped taking him along to the nets.

No, he hadn't only been bullied by random racist goras. He was also a regular target for the big, strong and stupid from his own community. It seemed as though he had an invisible sign hanging above his head inviting people to pick him out especially. To pick on him especially.

Unsurprisingly, his father was the worst bully of them all but, perversely, that didn't stop a part of Hassan craving his approval.

Everything had changed on the day the letter arrived.

'Open it, Haso!' his mother had been standing in front of him, her hands clasped to her chest and her whole body tensed. 'Open it.'

'Shouldn't I wait until later? When Dad's back.'

'No. No. I've been looking at the bloody thing all day. It's been sitting on the table glaring at me for hours. I'm not waiting any longer. Anyway, your father told you not to bother applying, so why wait for him?'

It was the first time Hassan had heard his mother swear, and he was shocked enough to set aside any worries about what his dad might say. 'OK,' he mumbled, as he tore open the envelope. He could still remember unfolding the single sheet of paper and looking at it, eyes struggling to focus as he read it once, twice, three times.

'Well? Well?' His mother was beside herself with excitement.

Hassan had handed her the letter silently, unable to trust his mouth with words. She'd looked at it for a few seconds before dropping it to the floor and enveloping him in an overwhelming maternal hug. She'd pulled her head back and kissed him on the forehead before squeezing him to her breast and whispering into his ear.

He could feel her warm tears trickling down his neck as she spoke. 'You did it. My clever little boy. You did it. I knew you would.'

His father's predictable flash of anger had been short-lived. Once he'd heard the results, all the ingrained negativity towards his eldest son seemed to vanish like a magician in a purple puff of smoke. Abracadabra! Alacazam! The world changed.

'Oxford. Bloody Oxford. My son's going to Oxford.' He clapped Hassan on the shoulder so hard that he knocked him sideways into the wall. 'I knew you'd do it,' he went on. 'I told you he would, didn't I, Naira?'

Hassan's mother smiled and nodded, her eyes lowered, and Hassan could see it was another lie. His father had always said that university was a waste of time. He'd not gone himself and it hadn't done him any harm, after all. An objective observer might have said that it depended on how highly you rated the role of Assistant

Manager in an uncle's small furniture shop, but it was unlikely that anyone would be bringing that point up any time soon. And if they did, it was almost certain that such critical words would have fallen on stony ground in any case. Luckily, Hassan was so overcome with his own euphoria that he didn't care about his father's crassness. He was only being his usual self.

Thinking back, he couldn't remember if his dad had actually bothered to congratulate him before he rushed out of the door to begin the weeks and months of bragging to friends and neighbours – the first moments in a vicarious victory campaign of puffed-up self-congratulation which hadn't involved Hassan at all.

'Come on boy. Time to celebrate.' The bottle of Chivas Regal had sat between them on the table in the best room, two cut-crystal glasses flanking it like solid, chunky bodyguards.

As Hassan sat opposite his father in one of the soft-cushioned, wing-backed armchairs, he looked at his glazed eyes and loose-jawed smile and suspected that there may have already been some "celebrating" going on during the afternoon's victory tour. He sat without speaking as his father poured the whisky.

'Two fingers for you ...,' his father said, lifting the tumbler up to the light as he measured out the golden liquid. '... And two for me.' His fingers spread apart as he poured his own measure, and he chuckled at his own cleverness. He handed the smaller glass to Hassan and raised his own. 'Cheers,' he said. 'Well done.'

'Thanks, Dad,' said Hassan as he touched his lips tentatively to the cold crystal. The heavy smoke of old peat bogs filled his nostrils, and he fought back the reflexive desire to cough and splutter as he took his first sip. Not as bad as he feared, the smell was worse than the bite, and he liked the way the whisky burned as it slipped down into his stomach. 'Nice whisky.' He did his best to affect a manly attitude as he put the half-empty glass down on the table.

'Not on the table!' his father had shouted, sending Hassan cowering back into the depths of the chair, before picking up the glass and sliding a coaster underneath. 'Your mother will bloody kill me.' He'd laughed and leant forward. 'Now, how much is all of this going to cost?'

As Hassan sat in that over-priced cafe in South Kensington, busting for a piss, he pictured his father's arrogant leering face thrusting towards him and felt a twinge of guilt. Not guilt for letting his father down – although he most certainly had – but rather for the total absence of filial love which he felt when remembering him.

Shuna

'Tell us about the holiday, Mum,' said Zoe as she scooped warm, chocolate-heavy gloops of melted marshmallow from her cup. Miraculously, she seemed to be stuck in perfect-daughter mode and Shuna smiled as she realised that Spike must be quite special.

'Yes, Mum. Please.' Anna was bouncing up and down in her chair with excitement and, with the cafe even more jam-packed than usual, Shuna had visions of macchiatos and lattes sent flying across all the neighbouring tables.

'OK. But first you need to calm down and sit still,' she said. 'Nothing's booked yet and I'm not sure we can afford it. We'll pop into the travel agents in a minute and see what they've put together.'

The look on her girls' faces told its own story. Shuna knew well enough that they had little or no experience of 'it's a bit expensive' or 'not sure if we can afford it' being followed by 'sorry, we can't'. If, or rather when, they left home to go to university, they would be in for a shock.

'You always say that,' said Zoe. 'Tell us anyway.'

'OK,' said Shuna and her heart skipped double time as she looked across the table at the fresh, innocent eyes shining with excitement. 'Well, first of all, you need to remember that this trip is mostly for your dad. It's his fiftieth birthday surprise and we need to give him the best holiday we possibly can. Coping with me for the past six months must have been a nightmare and now I'm better I want to show him an amazing time.'

The girls nodded in unison.

Shuna suddenly felt tearful. 'And it's for both of you, too,' she said. 'I don't know how I could have made it through everything without you to help cheer me up.'

Both Zoe and Anna looked down at the table without replying. They were too young to know how to respond and Shuna couldn't imagine that they felt they'd done such a great job of cheering her up in any case. Maybe they would all be able to have that conversation after a few years?

She moved back to safer ground. 'And you know your Dad's always wanted you guys to see Africa?'

'Yeah,' said Zoe. 'I think he's a bit weird about it. The way I see it, there's no difference from you saying it's important for us to see Holland, because you're from South Africa.'

'I'm not sure I agree, but I'll leave him to explain ... again. Anyway we have taken you to Holland. Twice.'

'But Dad's family's from Jamaica and we've been there a hundred times,' said Zoe. 'That's the same thing, but Africa's different.'

'A slight exaggeration maybe?' said Shuna, trying not to laugh at her daughter's persistence. 'We've been to Kingston five times and you know full well why your Dad wants to take you to Africa. It's about heritage and roots. Enough already!'

'Whatever,' said Zoe. 'Just tell us about the holiday.'

'I will, but calm down. I'll get there. We've still got ten minutes and you need a little context.'

Zoe drew a zip closed across her lips with thumb and forefinger and laid her hands on the table, one on top of the other.

'I would love to have taken you all to South Africa,' Shuna said, marvelling again at her new perfect changeling daughter, 'but I can't do that without going home and ... I'm not ready to do that yet.' She regretted mentioning South Africa before the thought had reached her mouth, but it was too late. The events of the last few months had left her fragile and vulnerable and it took very little to switch her from laughter to tears. She often didn't know what set her off although, as far as her beloved Stellenbosch went, the reasons were clear.

Shuna took a sip of her hot chocolate, not daring to try to speak while she battled with the surge of anger and grief. She then took three deep breaths, snorting out the fury. It was time for her to get a grip on her emotions and behave like an adult. Like a proper mother.

'It's OK, Mum,' said Zoe. 'We can find out more when we get to the travel agents. And stop saying how much the holiday's for us and Dad. It's for all of us.'

'Of course it is,' Shuna said. 'And we're going to have an amazing time.' She looked at her watch. 'Anyway, we have to boogie. Anyone need the loo?'

'You took your time,' said Shuna.

'Sorry. It wasn't my fault.' Zoe rolled her eyes up and backwards over her right shoulder.

'What?' said Shuna. 'Are you having a chocolate fit?'

'Mum. Don't be so lame,' said Zoe repeating the gesture. 'Look behind me, but don't stare. D'you see that guy over there? The one who looks like he should be somewhere else?'

Shuna looked across the room and nodded her head.

'Well, I've been watching him since we came in. He's been trying to get to the loo for twenty minutes, but every time he gets up, someone beats him to it. So, every time he goes back to his table, sits down to wait and then the same thing happens again. It was quite funny for a while but then, when I walked up right in front of him, I actually thought he might wet himself. So I let him go first.'

'That was very kind and thoughtful,' said Shuna. 'Wonders will never cease.'

Anna laughed, but Zoe appeared less impressed. 'You could give me a break sometimes, you know,' she said stomping towards the door. 'Come on. I thought we were in a hurry to get to the museum.'

Dan

The trials and tribulations of his Swedish heroine would never lift these books to stand alongside the Russians who'd been Dan's lifelong companions, but there was no shortage of twists and turns. He was actually finding he needed to leaf back and forth to double-check plot points all the time. He might be tired and old, but it wasn't only that; the books were damn complicated. Sophisticated even?

The other frustration was that, because it was a trilogy, and because he was sitting on a bench in a London museum, he couldn't go back to his bookshelves to check on people and plot twists from the first two volumes.

Dan slid the bookmark into place and laid the book down beside him, noting absent mindedly the deep patina of the wooden bench. He could imagine the rich, chocolate Heart-of-Darkness mahogany receiving its daily polishings for the past century and a half – with the exception perhaps of a handful of war years – and glowing with pleasure every time.

Perhaps Dostoevsky had sat on this very bench when he came to London for the Great Exhibition? Wouldn't that be something?

He took off his glasses and placed them on the Swedish girl's naked and tattooed back. He was tired and his stomach hurt with a twisting, unforgiving ache which did nothing to help his headache. He'd taken some Vicodin a while ago. How long? Was he due some more?

Rachel wouldn't be along until twelve. The prospect of sitting alone on the hard bench, with or without Fyodor's ghost, wasn't thrilling, but he couldn't muster up the energy to move.

He knew perfectly well he wasn't due any more painkillers, but he needed something to distract him from the pain and the book wasn't enough.

He felt a presence next to him and his wish was magically realised.

'Enjoying that?'

The girl was not more than twenty, long dark hair framing a pretty face and honest eyes. Spanish, if he had to guess, although the accent was a bit of a giveaway and he might have to concede he was cheating a little.

'Yes,' he said. 'More than I expected, actually.'

'I've just finished the first one. Can't wait to know what's going to happen.'

'Well ...' he flinched as he saw the look of mock terror on her face.

'... don't worry,' he said. 'I'm not going to tell you. I only wanted to say you won't be disappointed.'

She took her hands from her ears and laughed. 'It's OK. I didn't think you would, but just in case …'

Her open, smiling face and lisping accent took Dan back to another person, time and place … a lifetime ago. A time of sunshine and simple pleasures.

'I'm Dan,' he said, reaching out his hand. 'Dan Bukowski.'

'Ramona. Pleased to meet you, Dan.'

'Spanish?'

'Yes. But I've been in London for two years now.'

'Doing what?'

'I did a research master's at Imperial last year and then my tutor offered me a job assisting him. I love London so …'

'You must be good. What are you working on?'

'My MRes was in cancer biology and my team's trialling a treatment for late stage leptomeningeal carcinomatosis. It's a type of brain cancer.'

'Oh,' said Dan, looking down as the pain reminded him it wasn't going anywhere.

'Are you OK?' she said, reaching forward to squeeze his shoulder.

The morning sunlight streamed through the windows and bathed the unlikely pair in its weak, eight-minute-old rays. Dan felt the spasm ease. Not much, but enough.

'I'm fine,' he said. 'Probably British ale disagreeing with me.'

'Eeergh. I can't stand it. Warm and brown. It's revolting.'

Dan laughed. What was it about Spanish women? They had such expressive lips and mouths and weren't afraid to make themselves ugly when showing disgust. It didn't matter whether they were joking or deadly serious, they could contort their faces into a horrible sneer and then slip seamlessly back to sultry beauty. Much more honest than mirror-conscious Brits or North Americans.

'What part of the States are you from?' said Ramona.

'I'm Canadian, actually. From Toronto.'

'Ahhh. Much better,' she said. 'Everyone loves Canadians. I went to the States to see family last year. To Texas. I felt like a second-class citizen half of the time.' She leant back and straightened her jacket. 'Do I look so much like an illegal immigrant?'

Dan looked at her raven-black hair, brown eyes and olive skin and thought back to his time in Austin; he raised his eyebrows and smiled. 'Well, from the perspective of an oil-rich good 'ol boy in cowboy boots … in a certain light …'

'Huh,' she said, pouting extravagantly. 'Maybe Canadians aren't so great after all.'

'I'm sorry,' he said. 'Not everyone appreciates my sense of humour.'

'It's OK. I knew you were joking.'

'I didn't say I was joking,' he said, forcing himself to repress a childish giggle. Talking with her made him feel young again, and he was happy to wallow in the moment for a while longer.

Ramona just smiled and arched her eyebrows. 'You sound like you know Texas?'

'I used to. Once upon a time.'

'Which part?'

'I studied at UT. The University of Texas. In Austin.' Dan hadn't talked about that time for so long that the words seemed to be coming from someone else's lips. 'Then I stayed on for a few years afterwards to work as an associate professor. A bit like you really.'

'That sounds great. Austin was the only place I went where most people knew that Spain was a real country.'

'It was fabulous for a few years,' he said, turning away. 'It was a wonderful time, such a time as is only possible when we are young …'

'Sounds like heaven,' said Ramona. 'I'm surprised you wanted to move back to somewhere cold like Toronto.'

'It was never the plan,' said Dan, his eyes fixed on the huge skull hanging in the air across the hall. 'But that's the way life goes, isn't it? We don't always get a say in what happens.'

'That's for sure,' she said. 'But …'

Dan couldn't face digging deeper into memories which had been buried for so long. 'Would you mind talking about something else?' He managed to remain gentle and polite even as he interrupted her. 'Why do you keep looking at that young museum guard?'

Ramona giggled like a naughty schoolgirl.

'His name's Will,' she said. 'I met him on Saturday and we're going out for a drink tonight. What do you think?'

Dan looked over at the young man, who was now chinwagging with the grumpy guard he'd seen earlier. The old one seemed less sour than before, but they made a strange pair in their matching purple fleece tops. Almost like an old music hall double act. They weren't doing a lot of guarding as far as he could see.

'He seems nice enough,' said Dan, not sure what his opinion had to do with anything.

'I just popped in here to check everything was OK for tonight, but he's been talking to the other guard since I arrived.' Will looked over and Ramona waved.

Dan watched as Will waved back before leaning forward and saying something to his companion. They both laughed, Will oozing the cockiness of youth as he stood up and turned to go. A little too full of himself, thought Dan as he watched him saunter over to the other side of the hall. Ramona needed to be careful of that one.

'I'm going over to say hello. I'll be back in a minute. Don't go anywhere.'

'I'll be here,' said Dan, wondering to himself where else he might go, anyway.

Ramona's questions had dug a little too deeply into his papery skin and, as he settled back onto the hard bench, the worst memories came flooding back … Everything happening at once … The sound of sirens … People shouting, screaming and running … But none of them knowing which way to run.

Nadia

'OK. If Nadia has it right, we've got very little time. Quick, concise, stick to the facts.' David looked over at Nadia. 'Let's start with Birmingham.'

Nadia stood up. 'Thanks, David.' She looked around the table. The three men were all leaning forward, alert and expectant. She would probably disappoint them. 'As you know,' she said, 'for the past six months I've been working undercover at the Birmingham Central Mosque. When Snowflake went overseas, a lot of flags were tripped and I was sent in to find out what I could. A job as a cleaner was the best that could be done at short notice, but at least it left me with good access to documents and files.'

'What was the mosque like?' said Ed. 'It's never been on the radar as far as I know.' He looked exhausted, but his eyes were bright and he seemed full of energy, pianist's fingers twitching and tapping on the white table.

'No reason why you should know anything about it,' said Nadia. 'It's very moderate. Imam Khan's been there since the nineties and he's got a great reputation in the city for reaching across communities. From what I observed, he deserves that reputation.' She took a sip of water. 'As you might imagine, the female cleaning staff are mostly invisible in a place like that, but the imam knew everyone by name and made a point of greeting all of us politely and thanking us for our work. Watching him in action was the only real highlight in an otherwise shitty assignment.'

The assignment had been shitty – boring and demeaning – but there had been benefits. Until Birmingham, Nadia hadn't been near a mosque since her parents died and she'd been surprised by the way the experience had made her feel. Being around so many devout Moslems had helped to remind Nadia of her mother and, in particular, the modest unobtrusive way she would always find a place to pray without fuss or fanfare. For some reason she'd found herself able to picture her mother's face and gentle smile better than she had in years.

'So there was no sign that Snowflake was being radicalised, and that he was a potential threat?' asked Phil, jerking Nadia back into the real world.

'Absolutely none,' said Nadia. 'That being said, the place is huge – maybe five thousand worshippers on an average Friday – and it would have been easy to miss something. Unfortunately Snowflake's personal belongings were all cleared out before I got there, but his digital history is clean. All I picked up was an association with a group of young guys in Birmingham – including the imam's son – who would meet up once a week and rant about discrimination and injustice; even there, I couldn't find anything to suggest they were doing anything more than talking. You've all seen Snowflake's profile – there are no indicators to suggest he might be a person of interest and, even after everything that's happened since, I'm struggling to see him as a potential recruit.'

'Unless there's something else. Something you missed,' said Phil.

'Indeed,' said Nadia. 'We can't exclude that. I'm just telling you what I think.'

Typical of Phil to suggest she might have missed something. Prick.

'Let's move on,' said David, before Phil had a chance to respond. 'What about the scholarship to the madrassa in Peshawar? Anything of note?'

'We accessed all related digital records,' said Nadia, 'and I was able to get eyes on Imam Khan's notes as well as the mosque's council minutes. It's all in the file. I can't see anything unusual. Mullah Akthar ul-Haq, who ran the madrassa, was an old friend of the imam's and there's no evidence to suggest the Peshawar scholarship was anything other than a genuine project. Snowflake was expected to work as a teacher at the Madrassa while studying himself and the mosque had plans for him to enter local politics on his return to Birmingham.'

'But Mullah Akthar died over two months ago, didn't he?' said Ed.

'Yes,' said Nadia. 'Although I don't see what that changes.'

She looked around the room, seeing the disappointment on each face. It wasn't much to show for six months work.

'I know it's not a lot, but I genuinely believe there wasn't much there. It's only in the last couple of weeks that I've found out anything … I'm now convinced that an attack is imminent, but we still don't enough to tell us what, where or when.'

'What happened two weeks ago?' said Ed. 'Sorry. I'm a bit behind.'

'That was when Snowflake landed back in the UK three months earlier than expected,' said Nadia. 'Or to be more accurate, things changed when we lost him. David will know more details but, as I understand it, we had eyes on him for four days, as well as trackers in his shoes and bags, and then he disappeared. Is that right, David?'

'Just so,' said David. 'Either he's had some high level training or someone must have helped him. Whatever the explanation, we lost him and I decided to pull Nadia out. She knows more about his background than anyone.'

'But there are still some big gaps,' said Nadia. 'Since I came out from undercover, I've been following down all the background leads I have, trying to find him. A bunch of dead ends with one exception. I asked the counter terrorism unit in Birmingham to arrest Imam Khan's son, Sadiq, and one of his other friends. It didn't take much to get them talking. Sadiq told us Snowflake called him three days ago out of the blue. The guy didn't know much – apparently Snowflake mostly wanted to chat, ask about friends and the imam, general life stuff. However, he did say that he was planning a visit to London in a few days which is why we're here now.'

'Nothing else?' said Ed.

'Nothing concrete,' said Nadia. 'Although, right at the end of the call, after he'd said he needed to go, Snowflake asked Sadiq to pray for him.'

The room fell silent and Nadia could feel the tension spreading out like a poisonous cloud.

'Shit,' said David. 'Whatever you think about this guy, Nadia, we have to assume that the threat is real and imminent. I need to speak to Susan. Wait here. I won't be long.'

He turned and left the room.

'Who's Susan?' said Ed.

'Susan Hammersley, head of JTAC - the Joint Terrorism Advisory Committee,' said Phil. 'The current UK threat level is already Severe. David must be recommending a move to Critical.' He looked at Nadia. 'There'll be plenty of flak if it's a false alarm.'

'You think he's over-reacting?' said Nadia.

'Actually, no,' said Phil. 'I'm disappointed at how little we have, but we can't ignore this.'

'I think my intel will reinforce that decision,' said Ed. 'Something's going down.' He leant forward and opened the folder in front of him.

'We'll wait for David,' snapped Phil.

Ed scowled as he closed the folder and leant back in his chair, Phil had made another friend.

Nadia thought back to the police interview at Birmingham's Colmore Circus. Had she missed anything? She'd been behind the glass in case one of Snowflake's friends recognised her from the mosque, but she'd played back the recordings dozens of times afterwards and there wasn't anything more. The young men weren't hiding anything, she was sure of that. Whatever their political views – many of which she half-sympathised with – a group of well-educated, polite intellectuals were unlikely to be high risk.

They'd been afraid – the counter terrorism officers had made sure of that – although they seemed to be mostly worried that someone would tell their families or the imam that they'd been arrested. She was good at her job and she wasn't wrong about them. The image which stuck in her mind, however, was the face of the second witness when he mentioned that Snowflake had asked him to pray for him. There was no doubt that he'd been surprised and that those words had left a strong impression.

During her training and subsequent career, Nadia had built a reputation for an almost-supernatural ability to piece together limited information and to find the connections that were invisible to her colleagues. She'd become very used to male colleagues whinging about women's intuition and how it was an unfair advantage. She was familiar with explaining to them that it was simply shortcomings in their intellectual talents which made the difference.

Nadia had spent six months studying Snowflake and trying to assess him. She thought she knew him even though they'd never met; the man she thought she knew wasn't a high risk radicalisation target, but the few bits of hard evidence they had pointed elsewhere. What had she missed?

11:12

Jim

'You're not too old,' said Will, stepping back and looking Jim up and down. 'Not in bad shape for your age either. Plenty of girls like a bit of experience.' He grinned. 'You should come out with us one night.'

Jim felt a half-remembered twinge in his stomach as he imagined himself leaning against the bar of some seedy West End nightclub, sipping a Mojito and sharing his tales of adventure and bravery with a gorgeous dewy-eyed blonde. Maybe Will was right, and he'd given up too soon? He was still in his early sixties – there was plenty of life in the old dog yet.

The problem was that the blonde at the bar always ended up having the same face. However hard he tried to imagine someone different, it was always her. The bloody woman had somehow even managed to invade his fantasies, and he hated the way that made him feel – angry, of course, but also sad, pathetic and weak.

He looked at Will – big, perfect teeth flashing confidence, all square-shouldered and oozing vitality. He wasn't taking the piss, but he was talking bollocks. Jim could barely motivate himself to get up and go to work these days. He wasn't too old, but he was too tired and he couldn't be bothered any more.

He held out his left hand, palm up and fingers splayed. The gold band wrapping his third finger was hardly shining, but it managed a dull glow.

Will's goofy smile got bigger if anything. 'All that says is that there won't be complications. I've got mates who put on rings when they go out cause they reckon it helps.'

'I'm married. I've got two grandkids.'

'Come on Jim. Are you telling me you wouldn't? … If it was on a plate?'

Jim toyed with the idea of getting annoyed. There were limits to how far Will could be allowed to go before he would need to be straightened out. But the cheeky young bastard was right. Jim would have been unfaithful without batting an eyelid. Marital loyalty had always been a one-way street in his world.

Will had no idea that he might be overstepping a boundary and ploughed on.

'Have a look at those two on the bench over there,' he said. 'The old bloke and the girl who's just come in. He's seventy-five if he's a day and she's about twenty and very tasty. If he can, then why shouldn't you?'

'Leave it out. They're never a couple,' said Jim. 'She's not his daughter though, I'll give you that.' He cocked his head to one side like a pigeon and squinted. 'Unless he married a dago, and he doesn't look the type.'

'Jim!' Will's voice had pitched up an octave and his eyes were stretched wide.

'What?'

'You can't say stuff like that.'

'Like what?'

Will's voice dropped to a whisper. 'You can't call people dagos any more. You just can't.' The girl had seen that they were looking at her. She half lifted her hand and smiled.

Will waved back at her, his shocked face gone in an instant. '… And besides, Ramona would be extremely pissed off with you if she heard what you said.'

'You what?' Jim was struggling to keep up. 'Ramona? You know that girl?'

'Course I do,' said Will, giggling. 'She said she'd pop by this morning. I'm seeing her tonight. Had you going for a second there though, didn't I?'

There was a moment when the old Jim surfaced and he felt his body tense. A second or two longer and he'd have wiped the smile of that smug face, job or no job. Not today, though. He looked over to the girl and back to Will.

'Has anyone ever told you you're a twat?' he said. 'Now piss off back to your station before you get us both fired.'

Jim's smile faded uncomfortably as Will sauntered back across the hall. He was a decent enough kid, but he went too far sometimes. A bit more respect was in order.

The girl was pretty though. Head arching back in uninhibited laughter at something the old git was saying, her smooth, dark throat exposed and white teeth flashing. Jim licked his lips and smiled.

Before his Dad died, they always used to go to Javea on the Costa Brava. The first two weeks of August, every year without fail. The area was full of sun-starved Brits, ready to make the leap from pasty pale to livid lobster without passing "Go". Javea was a little Margate with sunshine and cheap wine but, for a young East End boy, it was packed full of exotic promise.

The English were everywhere, but they weren't alone; there were plenty of locals and tourists from Madrid as well, all tanned golden brown like well-basted turkeys. The Spaniards would spend the whole day roasting in the sun, stretched out in neat rows along the beach like dominos, only moving when they turned over, cooled off in the sea or pranced about playing that stupid bat and ball game in their Speedos.

When he and his mates used the term "dago", it was usually in the context of lustful envy, an arms-length worship of the unobtainable. Sultry Spanish girls, white bikinis pinned onto firm, young flesh, taunting them with their sibilant esses. The best his gang could manage was a quick snog with some slapper from Solihull and a skinful of the local lager that they'd serve to anyone, even thirteen-year-olds.

Sun, sea, alcohol and sexual frustration. It was a classic holiday combination and no-one was surprised when it led to violence from time to time. The local girls may have been unobtainable, but the boys were easy bait. They strutted about with puffed-out chests like trainee matadors but most of them didn't have a clue how to look after themselves and usually ended up getting a good kicking.

Jim and his mates always kept an eye out for the knives though. That was something different and a couple of them had been badly cut up one summer. Knives weren't fair, but what could you expect from a bloody dago?

They would always stay in this great flat in the middle of town with a balcony looking over the sea. Even as a kid, he'd known it was out of their league, but it was owned by one of the guys who came into the pub, and certain friends could borrow it for free.

It was only later that Jim learnt that the flat's owner wasn't just one of the guys – Dave Vickers also owned their pub and a lot of other businesses in that part of Southwark. Once his dad was properly buried, and the funeral was out of the way, it was no surprise that Dave wanted someone else – someone who wasn't Jim's mother – behind the bar of the Beehive.

She was looked after well enough – given a small flat and some cleaning work – but it wasn't the same and money was tight until Jim was able to get a proper job. He could have worked for Dave – the offer was on the table – but he didn't want to get involved. There was serious money and a glamorous lifestyle for a few but he'd seen what it was like to live life looking over your shoulder.

No. The army had suited Jim just fine. It was a proper man's job, and it got him out of the East End which was what he'd wanted. He sent money back to his mum, but otherwise he was free.

It wasn't only about escaping from home and not becoming his dad, though. As Jim thought back over those twenty years, he realised how much he'd belonged in the army. Even from the first, shitty day of basic training and induction he'd fitted the life, or rather the life had fitted him. He'd known it, and everyone around him had known it, too.

Hassan

No-one had actually expected Hassan to get a place at Oxford. Not Mr James, the teacher who'd pushed him to apply; not his pig of a father; not his loyal, but realistic, mother; not either of his sneering brothers; not any of the other three applicants at his school; not any of the mates he'd stupidly told; not, and least of all, Hassan himself.

Oxford wasn't the place for someone like him and so, as there'd been no possibility of getting in, it hadn't seemed worth looking at the costs in too much detail. He had a rough idea of how expensive it would be, and it was definitely much more than they could afford.

Hassan remembered how he'd looked at his father over the rim of his whisky tumbler and felt the warm glow in his stomach cooling.

'I don't know exactly, Dad,' he said. 'I never really thought I'd get in.' He took another sip as though it might help. 'It's going to be a lot though. A hell of a lot.'

'What are we talking here?' said his father, sweeping his glass slowly in an expansive man-of-the-world arc. 'Three, four thousand a year? And you can get a loan, right?'

So, whisky could freeze at room temperature. He wasn't surprised his father didn't have a clue what it cost to go to Oxford, but he hadn't expected him to be that far wrong.

Hassan may not have had the exact details, but he knew it would cost much, much more and was certain his father would go apeshit when he found out. Despite what he felt about the self-centred old git, Hassan had enjoyed being the golden boy for a few brief hours. He took another sip of his whisky, hoping to stay in the moment a while longer.

'Well?' His dad's tone was that of a headmaster or sergeant major. He didn't like to be kept waiting and was hunching forward in his chair. 'Come on boy! You must have some sort of idea?'

'Yeah, I sort of know the big numbers,' said Hassan. 'I can get a loan, but it's going to cost way more than you said. It's nine grand a year just for the fees now.' His father looked blankly at him and Hassan pressed on, keen to get it over with. 'Then you've got accommodation, food, text books and everything else. The Oxford website said all of that would be another ten thousand at least.'

'Bloody hell.' Hassan's father refilled his glass and leant back into his chair. The room was silent except for the clicking and whirring of mental cogs and wheels and Hassan shrunk into himself, waiting for the storm to break over him.

'Bloody hell,' repeated his father, each syllable filled the small room with outrage, but not with anger. 'What do we pay our bloody taxes for?'

'I'm sorry,' said Hassan in a soft voice.

'Well, it's not your bloody fault is it?' said his father, the proud, paternalistic smile reappearing like sunshine from behind a cloud. 'You don't make the rules.'

Something was going on, but Hassan couldn't figure out what it was. 'No, Dad. That's for sure,' he said, still waiting for the thunder and lightning.

It had never struck. His father had kept on smiling. 'Well I've told everyone you're going now,' he'd said. 'So we'll need to find a way. Find out what's what and let me know tomorrow.' Then he'd reached forward and clapped Hassan on the shoulder. 'Now drink up. We can't just sit in here all evening.'

Having eventually received the proud paternal pat on the back; there was no doubt that he was now the golden child. It felt good, but Hassan's own feelings and memories weren't about to evaporate in a puff of magic smoke.

Much to their shock and surprise, his brothers became the new targets. 'Why don't you study a bit harder, you boneheads? Look at what my Hassan has done. The first student from St. Michaels to get a place at Oxford. Ever. Do you hear that? Ever! If you two spent a bit less time playing cricket and chasing after girls, you might make something of your lives.' At that point, whichever one was nearest would get a cuff around the ear and a meaningful look. 'Like your brother has.'

There was no doubt that his father had a special talent; how easy it must have been to live life that way, ignoring inconvenient truths, washing away memories that didn't suit you, doing whatever you wanted and, most of all, always being right.

Hassan tried his best to walk back to his table without brushing against any bare skin, although the cafe seemed to be getting more packed by the minute. He sat back in his chair and checked that his bag was still there. If that girl hadn't been kind enough to let him go to the toilet before her, Hassan was convinced he would have wet himself. He was out of place in London. The rules were different and the last thing he wanted was to make a scene by pushing in front of someone. But there wasn't enough room to wait outside the toilet and, every time he'd gone back to his table, another woman had magically materialised just as the door was opening.

But the girl had been sweet and disaster averted. She'd given him a lovely look as she gestured for him to go ahead of her. Only a kid still – fifteen at most – but nearly a woman and, like so many girls of her age, her clothes, her posture, her every movement were conscious, practiced statements of that fact. She reminded Hassan of his little sister, but his sister would never advertise her charms in public like that. His father might be happy to show double standards where his own whisky drinking was concerned, but he wasn't about to let his daughter shame the family.

He watched the girl as she came out of the toilet and felt a sharp stab of anguish at the base of his throat as other lives, other futures flashed through his mind. If only he hadn't been so stupid, so weak, everything could have been different.

The girl walked past his table and smiled at him again. It wasn't a flirtatious, coquettish smile; it was as though she understood his pain and inner struggle and felt sympathy for him. Of course he was being an idiot, but for some reason that brief moment of human contact was important.

She wasn't Asian – there was too much milk in the coffee of her skin – and she wasn't from anywhere in the Middle East as far as he could see. He watched her all the way back to her table. The girl she sat next to was a smaller copy – she must have been her sister – but the older woman with her back to him had long blonde hair hanging loose over her shoulders. If that was her mother, then the girl must be a mix of something. A beautiful mix.

All of a sudden, the blonde woman turned and looked straight at him, protective eyes searching and accusing. He dropped his head and stared into his empty coffee cup, shoulders tensed as he waited for her to come over and say something. What was wrong with him? Why couldn't he simply maintain a low profile and keep himself to himself like he'd meant to?

Hassan forced himself to count to a thousand before he dared to lift his head and sneak a glance over to their table. The waitress from Bradford was standing there, putting empty cups onto a tray.

The woman and the two girls were gone.

Hassan looked at his watch. Not even twenty past even though it seemed like he'd been sitting there for ever. He still had time to kill, but he couldn't stay in the cafe any longer and it was time to get changed. He'd finished his coffee and, if anything, the place was getting busier.

As he stood up, his knees caught the table leg and the coffee cup clattered onto its side, rolling towards the edge. He caught it just in time, but he could tell that everyone was staring at him as he put it carefully back on the saucer. He was such a clumsy prat.

He pulled on his jacket and squeezed through the press of women blocking the doorway, feeling the brush of breast and buttocks like his skin was on fire. As he stepped out into the street and the fresh air, his breath rushed out in a massive sigh of relief. Which way, left or right? He saw a bus stop further up the street and started walking towards it. There would be a map there.

He hadn't made it more than ten yards when he felt a hand on his shoulder. He spun round and stepped back, fists clenched.

'Whoah. Take it easy, Bradford Boy!' It was the waitress from the cafe. 'You're not in the King's Arms at kicking out time.'

'Sorry. You just made me jump.'

'Well, you're bloody twitchy if you ask me. You OK?'

'Yeah. I'm fine. It's not exactly like home here though. Is it?'

'Right enough,' the girl said. 'Most folk round here've got more brass than brains but, to be fair, no-one's going to walk up and twat you in the street on a Monday morning.'

'I guess not,' Hassan replied. 'I'm probably just a bit hyped up.'

'About what?'

'About going to the museum,' said Hassan, looking at his shoes.

The girl raised one eyebrow. 'How old are you?' she said.

'Twenty-six. Why?'

'Don't you think you're old enough by now to be excited by other things? Rather than a bunch of old bones.'

'It's complicated,' said Hassan.

'Ah. Complicated is it?' the girl said, showing her perfect teeth in a broad smile. 'Well, if it's so complicated, why don't you tell me all about it over a drink or two?'

'A drink? What?' The day was getting stranger by the minute.

'I get off shift at three. Meet me outside.' The girl looked him in the eye and Hassan stood, shuffling his feet and wondering if it was some sort of joke.

'OK. Three o'clock,' he said at last. 'Outside the cafe.'

'Great. It'll be good to catch up with someone from Bradistan,' she said. 'I'm Sally, by the way.'

'Hassan,' he said, holding out his hand.

'Nice to meet you Hassan,' she said, her fingertips cool against his moist palm. 'I'll see you later.'

He was turning to go when she laughed. 'God, I'm a bloody idiot some times.'

'What?'

'I totally forgot why I came out after you,' said Sally, slapping her hand on her forehead like a bad soap actress. 'You forgot your bag.'

Hassan saw that his blue holdall was on the ground by her feet. How could he have forgotten it? It was as though his brain wasn't functioning. Half the neurones seemed to have taken the day off.

'Thanks,' he said, picking it up. 'Thanks very much. I'd forget my head if it wasn't screwed on.'

'It's bloody heavy for an overnight bag,' Sally said. 'You planning on staying a while?'

'Probably not. Just got some pressies for my nephews.'

'Oh. Shame,' said Sally. 'Anyway. I'll see you later.'

'At three,' said Hassan. 'And thanks for the bag. I'd be stuffed if I lost it.'

He turned and walked away, feeling his heart racing. He needed to find somewhere quiet to pray. Everything was moving too fast, and it felt like the ropes and chains which tethered him to the real world were snapping one by one. Ten minutes of quiet prayer, even if it was just on a bit of grass somewhere, would help to tie him back down.

The bus stop was quiet and the street map amazingly undamaged by paint, pen or Stanley knife. He wasn't far from Hyde Park, and there were toilets there too. As he turned into Queen's Gate he could feel the boiling tension inside him easing to a gentle simmer. One step at a time.

Shuna

The streets were strangely quiet; it was as though the gaggles of tourists with yellow umbrellas and selfie sticks had decided to take the morning off. If only London were always so peaceful.

Shuna looked at the two girls striding ahead of her, holding hands and deep in animated chatter. For a moment, they looked like small children again, but they weren't. It wouldn't be long before they left the nest without a backwards glance. Less than five years perhaps, and those years would pass in a flash.

What would she do then? Sit around in their lovely flat, waiting for Simon to come home? Maybe pop out for coffee with friends; take in an exhibition; go to yoga, the manicurist or whatever; always make sure that there was something delicious on the table for dinner. Growing up, that had been her mother's life, and she'd always sworn it wouldn't be hers. She would be different and never allow herself to be caught up in such hide-bound routines and single-minded bigotries.

It was easy to say, but the danger was always that it was much, much easier to avoid the issue and enjoy the padded comfort of a privileged life.

Thoughts of padded comfort made her shiver. The last two years had been a terrifying reminder of how fragile happiness can be. Like the smooth, hard surface of a blown eggshell, seemingly solid as marble, but ready to crack open at the flick of a fingernail.

This holiday was important for them all. Shuna needed the time and space to prove to Zoe, Anna and Simon that she was ready and able to take back her role in the family – as mother, wife, lover, friend and equal partner. It was time.

She'd recently dug out a diary written a couple of years earlier, during their last wonderful holiday in Sydney. It was full of plans and ideas for the next phase of her life, each plan backed up by neat columns of pros and cons. Reading it had been quite a shock. She'd thought she was fully recovered – back to herself again – but the diary might as well have been written by a different person.

That was OK, though. She was moving in the right direction and, even though she'd lost nearly two years, there was still time. She'd start to work on those plans again, start to focus on the future again. Going back to university, taking on a part-time job, writing a best-selling novel. Something. Anything.

Over the coming years, the girls might not think they needed her so much, but they still would. They would want the freedom to find their own way, discover who they were and to make their own mistakes. Her job would be to let them believe they had that freedom and choice, while standing back and watching to make sure their mistakes weren't too serious.

Zoe was a beautiful girl, and the boys were already starting to swarm around her like locusts. Who was this boy Spike? As far as Shuna knew, Zoe's friends were all decent enough, but there was often someone on the edge of these groups – a little older, a bit more exciting, more dangerous. Was Spike that boy?

She couldn't stop thinking about the young Asian man at Muriel's. He had been so out of place in his cheap windcheater and generic jeans. When she'd looked over at him, he'd definitely been staring at Zoe, and with the most peculiar expression on his face. It was the kind of expression which Renaissance artists would always paint on the faces of the disciples when they were kneeling and looking up at Jesus. What was that all about?

And then, when he'd seen her looking, he'd ducked his head as though caught in the middle of something. She'd watched him for a long while but he'd kept his head down and stared into his coffee cup. There was definitely something not quite right about him, but he was probably harmless enough.

'Mum!' shouted Anna. 'Where are you going? It's just there.'

'I sometimes wonder if you listen to a word I say,' said Shuna. 'I only told you five minutes ago ...'

'... we're going to the travel agents first.' said Zoe. 'See. I listen.'

'And we'll come back to the museum in about half an hour,' said Shuna.

'Oh yeah,' said Anna. 'I remember now.'

Zoe looked down at her sister, shook her head and pressed her lips together in a world-weary frown. 'Kids! What can you do?' she said to Shuna, which earned her a hard punch on the arm.

'Stop it the pair of you,' said Shuna, before Zoe had a chance to retaliate. 'If you're going to bicker, I'll make you wait outside.' She stood still until the ceasefire had held for long enough before setting off once again. 'It's just up here. By the park.'

Evolution Travel made a point of being exclusive and bespoke. The prices tended to match the promise, but Shuna and Simon had been using the company for over ten years and had never had a bad experience. If anyone could make this birthday trip seamless, it would be Jonny Burbridge.

Seamless or not, she could still feel hidden fears and resentments trying to resurface like foul-smelling bubbles in a witch's cauldron. She hadn't expected to be so nervous – it had been more than ten years, after all.

Shuna took a deep breath. It wasn't like they were even going home. At the closest, they would be almost five thousand kilometres from the Western Cape.

But Africa was Africa ... And Africa was in Shuna's blood.

She missed home like a missing limb. She could look around her and see that Africa was far away, but she could still feel it. Always. She only needed to close her eyes for a minute and she would be back.

Apart from the children, every important milestone in her life had taken place in Africa; her first horse, Nomsa; her first hunting trip; her first kiss; her first everything. And, fifteen years ago, Simon had proposed to her on the sands at Knysna. Fifteen years. Almost to the day.

Her parents were already separated by then. That had been on the cards from well before Shuna had left for London and, although they'd not yet divorced, the separation had been amazingly conflict-free.

One of Shuna's closest friends was a family lawyer and had once told her there was only one way for a divorce to be amicable – one party had to be ready to give in on absolutely everything. It only took one glowing ember of face-saving resistance: a favourite painting; half a dozen vinyl albums or an extra half-hour of visiting rights, to kindle a fire of righteous conflict which would leave little but burnt twigs and lawyer's fees in its wake.

Shuna's father was the one who refused to fight. He hadn't married an heiress for her land or money and didn't need much to be happy. He was overjoyed when it was suggested that he move to the small Knysna summer house which, perched on the Eastern Head with steps dropping down to the lagoon, was a writer's paradise.

Her mother had kept the ranch and vineyards, of course. They had been in her family for almost six generations, since the days of the first voortrekkers. The Queen of Stellenbosch would no doubt be buried there, in the small, white-walled graveyard, together with her forebears.

It was amazing that her parents had stayed together so long; on the face of it, they'd never had anything in common and it was perhaps more unusual that they'd got together in the first place. Maybe her mother had done it to spite her own parents; there was nothing out of the ordinary in that.

Her mum had been young – only just nineteen, her dad was a good looking man and, when his first novel was shortlisted for a major prize, he quickly became a darling of the cocktail circuit. Not so hard to see how the story might have unfolded.

Shuna could only remember happy times until she was about twelve or thirteen. Her world was one of sun and laughter and the house was always full of interesting people and noisy wine-rich debate.

But, the gaps between her mother and her father started to yawn ever wider even as their beloved homeland started the long process of healing its own divisions. They both loved their country, but in quite different ways. The debates slowly morphed into dogma-fuelled arguments and the guests stopped coming.

By the time Shuna was fifteen, she had understood that she no longer liked her mother. It was more than a simple disagreement about important principles, she actively disliked everything her mother had become – and probably always had been.

In spite of that, she'd still loved her – strange how the mother-daughter bond can survive so much bitterness – and probably would have continued to do so if it hadn't been for that last trip fifteen years earlier. There was a horrible predictability to what had happened, but that didn't make it any more forgivable.

It felt good to be going back to Africa, even if it wasn't to the Western Cape. Shuna could feel herself standing taller as she saw the travel agent's up ahead. The African sun would cleanse her and the soil would ground her once again.

Dan

Strange how, once the cork was pulled, and the genie let out of the bottle, it took one hell of an effort to persuade it to go back in.

Dan had struggled for many years to lock those Austin memories away and to get on with life. Rachel had helped, of course. She was one of those women with an infinite capacity for patience and understanding and she'd known that the end of the tunnel wasn't so far away even when he was flailing in the dark certainty of nothingness. Nothing apart from the fact that the world would never be truly right again.

He would always remember Rachel's bright, burning faith in him and, as he watched the young Spanish girl walking over to her boyfriend with a light, excited step, he wondered if he'd been a good enough husband to Rachel over the years. She deserved that and more, but he doubted he'd managed to give her as much as she'd given him.

The fact that children hadn't chosen to bless them wasn't his fault

– he knew that – but, in their absence, maybe he could have done more.

As the old memories continued to snake their way through his thoughts, he was reminded that the thing which Rachel would have really wanted from him wasn't in his power to give. He cared deeply for her and was grateful for her unconditional love, but he didn't really love her. Not in the way she loved him. The capacity for love had been burned out of him before they even met, and nothing could change that.

Not only did the genie not want to go back in the bottle, for the first time in all those years, Dan was no longer sure how hard he wanted to push. What did it matter now? Everything that had happened was a part of his life and, at the bottom of all things, a part of who he was.

His beloved Dostoevsky questioned how it was possible for a man to live a life and to have no story to tell. Well, for Dan, Austin was a part of his story, Rosa was a part of his story and, without a doubt, Whitman was a part of his story.

He wondered if he'd been a coward to hide it all away. He and Rachel had been together for most of his life – through good times and bad – but he'd never told her about Austin. Maybe she'd worked it out for herself, but he doubted it. He wouldn't run away any more. At the very least, he owed her that.

It was a lifetime ago. Almost fifty years had disappeared since he'd left. When the University of Toronto had offered him a tenure, he'd jumped at it. With things turning out as they had, there was nothing left for him in Texas but a never-ending spiral of blame and guilt.

Dan could remember that morning in vivid detail. The August sun was already sweltering and he and Rosa were running late. She was beautiful in the yellow sun dress he'd bought her, the smooth curve of her belly just beginning to stretch the material. Everything about her was glowing with life and youth as she took a final gulp of her coffee and picked up her bag.

They both worked in the same building which was only twenty-five minutes on foot, and they had time to make plans while they walked. Rosa had a late tutorial so Dan had agreed to pick up groceries on his way home and start supper. It had started like any normal, blissful day.

Much as he'd tried to repress the memories of what had happened next, he'd never been able to stop himself replaying the day's events over and over, looking at them from different angles trying to find answers or explanations. The thoughts usually slipped in uninvited during those unguarded moments between sleeping and waking – should someone have spotted the signals ahead of time? Could they have reacted faster? At least warned people to stay away?

Nadia
David swept back into the room, breathing heavily.

'Sorry,' he said. 'That couldn't wait.'

'Critical?' said Phil.

David nodded, his jaw clenched and the wrinkles showing dark around his eyes.

Nadia knew the cost of moving the threat level to critical was huge. All non-essential leave would be cancelled and relevant departments in the police and security services would be granted blanket overtime authorisation. If it turned out to be a false alarm there would be consequences … but if it wasn't a false alarm …? Prestige and money be damned – she wouldn't want David's job.

'Ed,' said David, now back in his chair. 'What have you got for us?'

Ed used his phone to cast an image onto the TV. The huge screen was filled with the face of a heavily bearded man, piercing green eyes shining deep in his leathery face. A long scar ran over his right temple and across the bridge of his nose. His hair and beard were black, but liberally sprinkled with silver.

'You'll all have heard of Unicorn,' he said. 'Also known as Ibrahim Abdel Hak and Mohammed Assam. Until recently, we thought he was Afghani because of his Mujahideen background. In fact, we're now fairly sure his real name is Fathi Auon. We believe he's early 50s, born in Sidon in Lebanon, but we don't know much about his childhood. He's been a high priority person of interest for almost twenty years, linked to the Afghan Mujahideen, the Afghan Taliban and, most recently the TTP, the Tehrik-i-Taliban Pakistan.

Nadia looked at the face on the screen and felt the emerald eyes staring straight at her; the cruel, sardonic sneer was meant only for her. She shivered. Her mother's family were all from Sidon and this man was only two years older than her mother would have been. Had they met as children? It wasn't impossible.

She'd not been back there since she was a small child, but she could still remember her grandmother's smile and the taste of the tomatoes which grew against the wall at the back of the house. Every day of that last visit, her grandmother would give Nadia a small jug of precious water and they would visit the tomato plants. She would stand back and watch as Nadia carefully divided the water, a few drops at a time, between each plant. It was the first time in Nadia's life that she had felt useful, the first time she'd experienced that special sensation of completing a task which needed to be done.

Thinking back with adult eyes, she could see how desolate the town had been – sand and concrete dust everywhere, rusty steel bars poking at random angles from collapsed walls and wild dogs slinking in and out of abandoned buildings. A far cry from the streets of her Paris home.

And still, in the midst of all that, and the fear which lurked behind every corner, her grandmother had smiled, and the tomatoes had glowed red against the dirty white concrete.

For all Nadia knew, the hard brutal man staring down from the screen had once been a small boy, standing on that same street, watching her own mother watering tomatoes from a small jug. She shivered again.

Ed continued. 'I've been working with an asset in Peshawar for the past three years. He informed me two weeks ago that Unicorn turned up at the Deobandi madrasa a month or so before Mullah Akthar suddenly passed away. He was working as a teacher, either hiding out or possibly recruiting. We don't know.'

'You think there might be a link between him and the mullah's death?' said Phil. 'If so, why?'

'We haven't found a direct connection,' said Ed, 'but it appears that everything changed after Mullah Akthar's death. The school moved from being moderate and progressive to becoming something quite different. And Unicorn is likely to have been one of the drivers of that change.'

'You think he might have got to Snowflake?' said Nadia, chill fingers of doubt creeping into her thoughts like an icy mist. Maybe she was wrong about him after all.

'Again, we don't know for sure,' replied Ed. 'My source told me he thought they were sharing a room, so it seems likely.' He looked around the table. 'This is a very dangerous man; he's always been one step ahead of us and his operations have a habit of succeeding as planned. As soon as we confirmed his location in Peshawar, we contacted the Americans and a joint operation was approved last week.'

'To neutralise him?' said Phil.

'No,' replied Ed. 'We don't do that. The plan was to take him alive.'

'What happened?' said Nadia.

Ed tapped his phone and the wall display went black. 'He vanished. He left Peshawar the day after the operation was approved. It was as though he knew we were coming for him. We have him leaving Karachi airport two days ago on a flight to Dubai and that's it. As far as we can tell, he never arrived in Dubai. We've lost him again.'

David was the first to break the silence. 'Even though we have very little to go on, I think we have to assume that Snowflake and Unicorn are connected.'

Nadia could see that Phil and Ed agreed and, in spite of her internal conflicts, she knew that it was a logical assumption.

'And ...' David's words hung heavily in the still room. ' ... We have to work on the basis that an attack is planned for London. An imminent attack.'

Nadia could tell the three men were struggling with the same frustration and tension as she was. There was enough evidence to conclude that something was about to happen, but they had nothing to hold on to. Nothing to help them decide what to do next. The fight-or-flight adrenalin had no outlet.

It wasn't the first time she'd felt that way – in fact it was fast becoming the norm. Technology allowed them to collect more information, more quickly, than ever before; the problem was that there was so much of it and, after years of austerity and the political implosion caused by the Brexit vote there were more and more people voicing anger and outrage. Only a tiny fraction of those people would ever seriously consider a terrorist action, but trying to focus limited resources in the right place always came with a massive risk of missing something.

In fact, beyond arresting everyone with tattoos, a shaven head or a black beard, there was often little that could be done apart from waiting until an incident was close to happening – holding back until someone broke cover or a pattern suddenly emerged. That increased the risk of failing to be there in time and they were all struggling with the pressure of living with that Sword of Damocles permanently hanging overhead.

David continued. 'I'm expecting an update from GCHQ any minute. They've dropped all other projects to run known aliases for Unicorn and Snowflake through the database and query all London CCTV footage for the last three days.'

'What if one or both of them has shaven their beards?' said Nadia.

'We changed standard face-recognition protocols while you were away,' said Phil. 'It's standard practice now to match for ten different disguise permutations, including glasses, facial hair and skin colouring.'

'Aha. That makes sense. Thanks, Phil,' she said, struggling not to be annoyed by his smug, patronising manner. Neither David nor Ed seemed to have noticed.

There was a knock on the door and Sue walked in, carrying a slim file. 'Sorry to disturb, but these are just in. You'll want to see them.' She handed the file to David and left.

He took just a few seconds to flick through the papers before passing the file to Phil.

'OK,' he said. 'We have something. An individual with an 85% match to Snowflake was picked up at Kings Cross half an hour ago. No beard, carrying a blue holdall. Copies of the files and images should be with you by now.'

Nadia pulled out her phone and scrolled through the pictures. Snowflake was looking around the station with wide eyes like a small boy just arrived in the big city. Difficult to imagine him as a threat.

'I've asked the Met to send CT officers to Kings Cross,' said David. 'As you can see, there's also a lower quality match from fifteen minutes ago at South Kensington tube station.' He looked at Nadia. 'Nadia?'

'Sir?'

'You and Ed go there and see what you can find. There's a car waiting for you. Post any updates to the thread. I'll ping you if anything changes.'

Nadia stood up, feeling a surge of energy and relief as the pumping adrenalin found an outlet. 'On it,' she said, turning towards Ed. 'Ready?'

He was already opening the door. 'Let's go,' he said.

David grabbed her arm as she walked past. 'I want you armed,' he said. 'And keep an eye out for Unicorn. He's somewhere behind this. I know it.'

11:18

Jim

Jim looked at his watch. Almost twenty past. His supervisor, Janet, would be making her rounds soon and he wasn't in the mood for any of her sarky comments. He did what he could to straighten his fleece and made sure his thermos and cup were tucked neatly behind his chair – if twenty years in the Army taught you anything, it was the critical importance of a regular flow of "hot wets".

A purple fleece. What sort of bloody uniform was that? Did they want the museum guards to be respected or laughed at?

He'd enjoyed watching Will's bit of Spanish fluff get up from the bench and walk over to the other side of the hall where the young idiot was back in his spot, smug contentment plastered all over his stupid face. Ramona was wearing tight jeans, and she knew how to walk. Two bunnies in a bag. That's how he and his mates would have described that walk once upon a time.

The conversation with Will had sent Jim's mind spiralling into forgotten places, scraping up thoughts and feelings which were buried for good reason. He'd lost all interest in sex after what happened at the tribunal and, to be honest, he didn't miss it much. Life was much simpler when you weren't being led about by your dick.

Funny how easily those thoughts could pop up to the surface again. He'd never stopped subconsciously comparing women and ranking them in mental lists but, for some years, that hadn't translated into physical desire. Until now.

Will was smart enough to know that Hatchet Face would be along soon and kept his conversation with Ramona short; she was already walking back towards the bench and the old geezer. The girl really was gorgeous and images of lost opportunities flicked though Jim's mind, each frame reminding him that he was getting old. Anything exciting which he hadn't done or seen already wasn't going to get done now.

He'd always thought he was cleverer than most and that his life had been rich and full. All this crap everyone banged on about – seize the day, enjoy the moment, be mindful – that was for losers. He'd always done that, anyway. That was who he was. Wasn't it?

Jim had recently discovered the masochistic pleasure of allowing his thoughts to wallow in muddy puddles of defeatism and was tempted, not for the first time, to simply give up. What would happen if he took that stupid fleece and told Ms Janet Wilson to stick it where the sun don't shine? What would happen if he just wandered back home, grabbed a beer, switched on the TV and waited for life to decide what was next?

He took one more look at Ramona as she leant over to talk to the old man on the bench. She was so bloody young. So happy and excited about her date. She was alive.

Jim turned away and pretended to look carefully and professionally around the hall. He could feel saliva balling in the back of his throat and his whole body starting to crumple. Was he about to cry? What was wrong with him?

He forced himself to attention and drove back those treacherous sensations. He still had some self-discipline. A casual observer would have seen the strong man, the former soldier, with his confident, commanding posture, but Jim's eyes glistened in the bright lights and the biting sensation of loss and regret lingered for a long while.

In spite of his end-of-tour paranoia, Jim had got out of Northern Ireland without being shot or blown up. He'd done his twenty years and the long-service pension had been in the bag. That had felt good.

It had felt good, but for the first couple of years afterwards, he'd missed the army more than he'd expected. At the very start, it was great being home with his family. His girls were nine and eleven and Jim was there every day when they came home from school, even if he was going out to work later. Julie seemed to enjoy having him home, he was learning the Knowledge, and the master plan was moving forward. If everything stayed on schedule, he'd been on track to have his taxi licence within two years.

After less than a month, the first cracks had started to show. There were so many things to think about in civvy life. He had choices and options where before there had been either simple, clear orders or the alternative – which was waiting around for orders to be given. Whichever one it was, you'd always be with your mates and you'd mostly have a laugh somewhere along the line.

The worst part of being out was the responsibility. As an experienced sergeant, he'd had a lot of responsibility before, but it was different. In the army, you always had someone to blame if things didn't work out. You were just following orders, after all. Do what you're told and, when it doesn't go according to plan, blame someone else. It made life so much easier, even when doing what you were told involved standing in the cold rain for four hours waiting for some angry Provo to open up at you with an AK-47.

It wasn't the same back in the real world. It was up to him whether or not he got on his Honda scooter and drove around London with a clipboard. No-one was going to call him in for a bollocking. If he forgot to pay the electric bill, and the power was cut off, he couldn't laugh and blame the useless logistics people. If he began to realise that his wife was a nag and having kids wasn't all it was cracked up to be, he couldn't put in for a transfer.

As he sat in the museum and waited for morning inspection, Jim remembered how he'd felt back then – as though he was on a boat on rough seas, cut loose and with no engine or tiller. All he'd been able to do was to hold on and hope for the best.

Jim had always had a short fuse and was used to telling people what was what. In the months which followed his short honeymoon period, he was like a bear with a sore head whenever he was home and Julie and the girls learned to keep a low profile if they didn't want their heads bitten off … or worse.

He didn't care if his family were afraid of him. There was nothing wrong with a bit of respect and it helped to keep them in line. He was proud to be a man with natural authority, able to fulfil the traditional obligations of family head.

It had taken a while, but he'd got back in touch with a few of the boys from the Costa Blanca days and they'd started to get together every Friday for a few beers. None of them apart from him had moved far from home and after twenty years, like a bad penny, he was back as well, just two streets down from the Beehive and across the road from his mum. So much for great dreams.

They usually met in the Beehive which was still owned by Dave Vickers, and a few beers would normally move on to a few more, followed by whisky chasers and a late night lock-in. The Friday night "quick drink after work" would generally wipe out most of Saturday.

One of the guys, Bonehead Bonham, had always been a hanger-on. He wasn't the sharpest tool in the box, but that wasn't where the name came from. Jim had never managed to find out the true story, he only knew it had something to do with a girl in Spain. Something that had happened the summer after Jim joined the army. It pissed him off that no-one would tell him – even twenty years on – but the more pissed off he was, the funnier it was for the others to keep him in the dark.

The thing about Bonehead was that he had no social skills. None. He would always say the wrong thing at the wrong time and, if they ever got into a spot of bother, it was a sure bet that Bonehead would be somewhere behind it.

One Friday night, about six months after Jim came home, they'd had a few more than usual – it was hot and sticky and they were all thirsty. Jim was telling them army stories. They were mostly true, with a little embellishment to spice things up and make Jim look good.

'… So that was why we never made it back home until Boxing Day,' Jim said, bringing the story to an end. 'But, if you'd seen Janie and Conchita, I'd give you ten to one you'd have done the same.'

He winked and everyone around the table snorted their approval.

'Must've been tough for Julie and the girls though?' said Bonehead.

Where had that come from? 'Yeah, well,' said Jim, spreading his arms wide like Tony Soprano. 'Wadd'ya gonna do?'

Everyone laughed and Jim finished his pint in one gulp. Telling stories was thirsty work.

'Is that why she took up with that bloke, then?' said Bonehead.

'What?' Jim had instantly sobered up 'What the fuck are you talking about?'

'He's just talking bollocks,' said Phil, Jim's oldest mate. 'Aren't you, Bonehead? Piss-talk bollocks.'

Jim remembered that Bonehead's eyes had been flicking from side to side as he tried to understand what was going on.

'Shut it, Phil,' Jim had said. 'I wasn't fucking asking you, was I?' He'd then taken hold of Bonehead's chin, twisting his face around and staring into his eyes. 'Go on then,' he'd snarled. 'If you've got something to say, fucking say it.'

Jim would love to have been able to wipe out all memories of the year and a half that followed and it wasn't really until he got his black cab license that life began to get back on track.

Being a Knowledge boy and riding the runs through central London was hard work and you didn't have any status. You were a nobody and over half of the boys never lasted the distance.

It was only once you passed the final exam and got your license that you became worth something; Jim desperately needed to patch together his ego and self-esteem, which was a big part of what drove him forward day after day.

It had taken him more than two years and he'd sometimes thought his head was going to explode, but the day of his twelfth and final *appearance*, navigating yet another random route with a Black Cab examiner, was the best day of his life.

He'd stood on the pavement outside the Drury Lane Theatre looking at the examiner who was still making notes on his clipboard. Hordes of strangers were pushing past them as though the two men weren't there and, despite the traffic, Jim could hear the sound of the pen scratching his future into the paper. After an age, the examiner had looked up at him with a cheeky grin and held out his hand.

'Well done, my son,' he said. 'You did it. You're one of us now.'
Uncle Don had retired years earlier but, when Jim went to visit him together with his spanking new license, there had been no need for words. It was the end of a long journey which had started when Jim was a six-year-old and at last he was out there keeping the Pritchard traditions alive. He could see how proud Don was and knew that, just like Jim, he was wishing Jim's father could have been there.

Things hadn't improved much at home but it didn't seem to matter so much. Every day, Jim would get in his shining cab, tuck his thermos carefully into its holder and set off for another fourteen hour shift. He knew exactly what he was doing, everyone loved a London Cabbie and all of them looked out for each other.

It was almost like being back in the Army.

Hassan
The only cars moving along the tree-lined street were taxis. London's famous black cabs were prowling up and down, hunting for gullible tourists probably. Hassan wasn't one of them; he couldn't quite imagine what it would be like to stretch out an arm and jump in the back of a cab whenever you wanted. Money might not make people happy, but it could definitely make life easier.

There were a few other cars in between, but it was the parked cars which caught his eye. They were all top-end, expensive models, RangeRovers, BMWs, Mercedes … three DB9s in the space of a hundred metres.

Hassan had always liked cars. He liked their sleekness and the almost miraculous precision of their engineering. So many tiny perfect parts fitting together exactly as they were supposed to. It was easy to admire them, even to lust after them, but they were also glaring symbols of waste, pollution and inequality. How much money was sitting on this single street? And who needed a RangeRover in central London?

He was impatient to find a spot to pray and the green of Hyde

Park up ahead was a welcome sight. He glanced at his watch, hoisted his bag onto his other shoulder and stepped forward.

As he got closer to Hyde Park, he was reminded of home, of the day after he'd found out about Oxford.

He'd managed to avoid his dad; he told his mother to say he was in a special study group for top students, but the reality was that he spent the entire time walking around Peel Park, pacing aggressively up and down, desperately trying to decide what to do.

Hassan hadn't needed long to find out exactly how much a four-year biochemistry degree was going to cost him. It was all there on the web in black and white and with lots of zeros.

What had surprised him was that he could borrow almost all of it, although the thought of having a debt like that had him sweating bucketloads whenever he imagined it. The maximum loan would add up to more than their house was worth and the chances of ever paying it back were vanishingly small.

There was no-one to talk to who would understand. With each angry step, he felt more lonely than ever.

He'd got his place at Oxford through luck, a clerical error, or some sort of misplaced positive discrimination. They didn't want someone like him there. He'd read the books and seen the films. It wasn't exactly racism but, if you had brown skin you needed at least to balance it with a proper public school accent or to be some president's son. Most of all, you needed money and the lazy, drawling confidence that came with it.

It wasn't only the books and the films. He'd seen it with his own eyes when he went for his interviews. Of course they were all smiles and praise for his grades, but it was obvious what they really thought of him and the lunch with his fellow applicants had been the icing on the cake. It was rugby league versus rugby union and Hassan wasn't even interested in rugby league.

They didn't want some working class Muslim boy with a shop assistant for a father and a broad Yorkshire accent. He wouldn't last a week.

Hassan had always been lonely at home, but it was a familiar loneliness and he did have a few friends, even if they were all misfits like him.

Why exchange that for the slow, drip-drip-dripping of inevitable failure? The sneering disdain of all of those rich, entitled bastards and the agony of realising, lecture-by-lecture that he didn't really understand his subject, the final proof that, in their world, he wasn't quite good enough.

Not only failure, but a failure that came packaged with a life-crippling debt and the humiliation and shame of having let everybody down. He would have nowhere to go but, at the same time, nowhere else to go.

Oxford University wasn't for the likes of Hassan and he would tell his father that. There would be shouting and maybe a slap or two, but it would pass. He would find himself a job somewhere local and life would go back to normal.

'What?'

'I've decided not to go.'

'What do you mean *decided not to go*?' Hassan's father's face was dark at the best of times, but the storm clouds building behind his cheeks and forehead had been pulsing coal black under the fluorescent lighting. His mother was backed into the corner by the fridge, building a wall of silence and insignificance around herself.

'I'm sorry, Dad,' said Hassan, feeling his reserves of determination instantly melt away. 'I spent all day yesterday thinking about it and I don't think I should go to Oxford. It's too much money.'

'So you're just going to tell your father how things are? Is that it?'

'No … Yes … I just think it's for the best.' Hassan watched as his father stood and stepped around the table, his chair balancing on two legs for two or three long seconds before clattering to the floor. He stood still as the big man moved towards him, not out of bravery, but hypnotised as if by a cobra.

His father stopped when his face was only inches away and Hassan felt the fingers prodding into his chest, punctuating every word his father spoke. 'Well … we'll … see … about … that.'

They stood like statues while the real world continued as normal. Babies were born, people died. None of these things mattered in their private bubble. Hassan waited for the first slap to land.

But it never came. He'd completely misjudged the situation yet again.

His father's face miraculously transformed as though nothing had happened. The dark clouds disappeared and a big smile appeared on his face. He put his arm around Hassan's shoulders and turned him towards the living room door. 'It's good to see you're becoming a man at last,' he said in his rich, booming voice. 'Now let's go and have a man-to-man talk about this whole Oxford business.'

He led Hassan through the door and closed it behind them.

Hyde Park was huge.

Hassan walked along the curving path and through the looming shrubs, green leaves dark as a stagnant pond, and emerged into the countryside. London was gone and he could see nothing but soaring trees and grass in all directions. There were more people and dogs than would be found in the average wood – and most weren't exactly dressed for a pub walk – but even those human reminders were swallowed up by the size of the place.

It wasn't as though he was a country boy, but London was so big and the weight of millions of strangers had been pressing down, squeezing his chest and lungs, since the morning. Being in this open space was a release and he found himself able to breathe again.

Hassan looked at his watch. He still had half an hour.

He unrolled his prayer mat under a massive oak, smiling as he reflected that his eighteen-year-old self would have found that more shocking than anything else that had happened in his life.

He was a scientist. He'd been a scientist since before he even knew what science was and that knowledge and mindset was completely incompatible with religion.

It had been easier for the great minds of the past to reconcile belief in God with rational thought; they were just beginning to discover the secrets of the world and of the universe. But so many mysteries had been uncovered since then. The answers and explanations were exposed and open for everyone to see.

It wasn't only evolution and quantum physics; every branch of scientific study continued to dig into areas of existence which were once the exclusive preserves of whichever God you happened to believe in. Religious philosophy had been pushed further and further back on its heels. There was no longer a place for a theological debate which could logically justify either God or organised religion.

All that was left was faith. Faith was the trump card which the beleaguered imams, rabbis, priests and vicars pulled out when nothing else was left to them. If you had faith, everything was clear and there was no need for pointless discussions about the sex of the angels, or the origin of everything. It was simple. You only had to believe.

It was a cheap argument and Hassan had never been tempted to try too hard. He'd gone through the motions like most of his friends – in Islam apostasy came with a big price tag – but praying was no different from cleaning his teeth or attending assembly at school. Just another routine thing which you simply didn't bother to question.

Until, one winter morning, faith had turned up on the doorstep unexpected and uninvited. Hassan chose to romanticise the memories – reality had been more gritty – but that was how it felt when he looked back.

First of all, his world had imploded and he'd fallen into a deep, black hole, barely able to see the small circle of light far above, which was shrinking day by day as he sank deeper and deeper down. He had started to believe that he would never find his way out and, in his rare moments of lucidity, he'd decided that it was probably for the best.

And then, miraculously, God had saved him; the shrinking circle of light started to grow and shine brighter and his small life was lifted back to the surface and given meaning again. It wasn't rational, and it didn't need explaining. It simply *was*.

So many years of paying lip service to his faith had left Hassan with a huge deficit. Even though he offered extra prayers as often as possible, he would never be able to make up for those years in the wasteland.

He smiled as he looked around at the trees and the shapes of people scurrying by, busying themselves in their daily lives. We could only do what it was in us to do. There was nothing more.

Hassan washed his hands in bottled water, knelt down on the mat and emptied his mind.

Shuna

'Ah, Shuna. Come in.' Jonny Burbridge stood and kissed Shuna on both cheeks. 'It was lovely to see you last week. Thanks again for the invitation.'

'Not a problem,' said Shuna. 'We had fun, didn't we?' She sat down heavily in one of the soft chairs in front of the desk. 'You should have seen the number of bottles that went into the recycling though. Absolutely disgusting.'

'I blame Giles,' said Jonny. 'He seems to breathe wine.' He walked over to Zoe and Anna. 'Hello girls. Welcome to Evolution Travel. You get bigger and more beautiful every time I see you.'

'Hello, Mr Burbridge,' the girls mumbled in unison, both looking down at their shoes.

Jonny took a pile of brochures from his desk and put them on the small, round coffee table in the corner. 'Have a look through these while I chat to your mum,' he said. 'These are some of the places you might be going to.'

The two girls sat down on the carpet by the coffee table and started leafing through the brochures. Jonny walked back to his chair and Shuna was reminded of the close bond between her two daughters. A wave of happiness and pride ran through her as she looked at them squashed together, their heads touching and their quiet murmuring occasionally interrupted by soft squeals of excitement. Would her life have been different if she hadn't been an only child?

'How's it all looking?' she said to Jonny, smoothing her skirt down.

'Pretty good,' he replied. 'I've got provisional bookings for flights, accommodation and transfers. All I need now is to confirm that you're happy with the overall plan and then we can look at a few details.'

He handed Shuna a dark-blue folder and leant back in his chair while she leafed through the thick sheets of creamy paper. She was grateful that he gave her enough time to read though the overview a couple of times without feeling the need to distract her with additional information or small talk. That was another thing you paid extra for.

She'd made notes in her diary and, once she was sure everything matched, she put the folder back on the table.

'That looks perfect,' she said. 'Just as we discussed.'

'I'm pleased,' said Jonny. 'It's looking like a fabulous trip. I'm deeply jealous.'

'And the extras and options?' Shuna continued, lifting up the folder with one hand. 'Is everything in here?'

'Yes. I've put in a range of diving packages, a balloon trip over the Serengeti and a slavery tour in Zanzibar. I know it's not totally relevant, but I thought Simon would be interested, anyway.'

'I'm sure he will be,' said Shuna. 'But I'm planning on making the whole thing as a surprise, so I'll have to decide for him.'

'Don't worry about that. We can change most things on short notice while you're out there, anyway.'

'Excellent,' said Shuna, standing and picking up her bag. 'You do look after us, Jonny.'

'All part of the service,' said Jonny, standing and moving round the desk.

'... And reflected in the bill.' Shuna laughed as she leant forward to kiss him goodbye. 'Can you confirm all the flights and accommodation please?' she said. 'I'll get back to you about the bits and pieces next week.'

'Perfect,' he said. 'Phone or email. Whatever works.'

'Come on girls,' said Shuna. 'Time to go.'

As she shepherded her small flock out onto the street, her mind was filled with memories of South Africa: that unique light filtering through wooden slats, the sound of the Southern ocean pounding the rocks at Cape Point; the multi-coloured scent of a thousand different fynbos herbs crushed under foot or hoof; her father's crooked smile wrinkling his eggshell eyes, and the touch of his gentle fingers resting on her cheek.

She and Simon had already been together for a year and a half before she'd plucked up the courage to take him home. The decision about who to visit first hadn't been difficult. Simon had read all of her father's novels years before he'd met Shuna and she knew the two of them would hit it off.

Her mother would be a different story. She'd done her best to warn Simon, but he was such an incorrigible optimist that he refused to listen. By the time they left, he'd almost managed to convince her she was just being paranoid.

Those days in Knysna were frozen in her thoughts like a recurring dream. It had been wonderful to be home and the hope that Simon's optimism would triumph was contagious. Everything had changed in South Africa. It was a new world.

Would it have been the same if she'd known then it would be the last time she'd see her father? Surely not?

It was late March. The worst of the tourist rush was over and the weather was showing its best face. Each morning, the sea mist filled the lagoon with unearthly, ground-hugging clouds – almost like an overfilled dry ice machine at a school disco – which then rolled out with the tide and vanished without trace.

Perfect, sharp African sunshine every day and even the notorious "Cape Doctor" wind stayed in hiding.

One cherished moment stood out in her dreams and made her smile every time.

The water was slipping discretely out through the Heads, leaving acres of yellow sand in its wake, drying pale in the morning sun. Shuna stood on the terrace, leaning against the wooden balcony as she watched the seagulls dip and dive for clams and crabs.

Simon had grabbed her hand and pulled her down the stone steps to the beach. 'Come on,' he said, unusually fired up for eight o'clock in the morning. On a normal work day, he would be out of the house by six-thirty, but he had an uncanny ability to flip his body clock the moment he was on holiday. For the past few days, he hadn't reached the breakfast table until after nine and Shuna remembered wondering what had got into him that morning.

'I spoke to your father this morning,' said Simon, as they reached the water's edge.

'So did I,' said Shuna. 'What did you guys talk about?'

'I had something that I wanted to ask him ...' Simon's voice trailed off and he looked out to sea as though searching for a lost boat. Shuna had already been up for hours but her brain was clearly lagging behind and it was only after several seconds that she started to piece things together.

Before the butterflies had reached her stomach and well before she'd convinced her mouth not to smile prematurely, Simon had turned and dropped to one knee on the damp sand.

'Well?' Shuna looked at Zoe and Anna as they stepped out into the sunshine.

'It sounds amazing,' said Zoe. 'I can't believe we're really going to Africa at last. After years of you going on and on about how incredible it is.'

'... They had photos of the balloon trips,' said Anna, hopping from one foot to the other. 'There are like millions of huge wildebeest stomping across the desert, but they can't hear you because the balloon makes no noise, and you can drop down until you're almost touching them and they still don't know you're there.' She stopped talking to draw breath.

'Will Dad like it?' said Shuna. 'It's his birthday treat, after all.' She was still thinking about that magical moment in Knysna when Simon had proposed. With everything that had happened after Sydney, they'd lost a lot of that magic. Hopefully this trip would be the catalyst which brought it back.

'Of course he will,' said Zoe. 'What's not to like?' She grabbed Shuna's arm and looked up at her. '... And Mum ...?'

'Yes,' said Shuna.

'Will I be allowed to have cocktails? Real ones, not virgin ones like Anna.'

'We'll see,' said Shuna. 'I'm not making that decision without discussing it with your father. But maybe.'

'Thanks, Mum.' Zoe appeared to have taken that as a 'yes'. 'I won't have too many though.'

'I said "maybe",' said Shuna, shaking her head. 'Anyway, we need to get a move on. I don't want to rush through the exhibition and Dad's only got an hour for lunch.'

'I think it's going to be even better than Sydney,' said Anna as they started walking. 'And that was the best ever.'

Shuna stopped and opened her bag. 'Hang on a sec,' she said, taking out the blue folder and scribbling in the margin. 'Talking of the Australia trip reminds me. I need to remember to get Jonny to arrange an airport pick-up this time.'

She couldn't help noticing the way her girls looked at each other when she mentioned the airport transfer. That was when it had all started, after all.

Dan

'Hi, Dan.'

'Oh. Hello, Ramona. You're back already.' The image of that far-off August morning was still floating at the back of Dan's eyes as he looked up and saw Ramona's smiling face. 'That didn't take long.'

'Will's working, and his boss will be round soon, so he can't chat. I just wanted to check that I was still seeing him tonight,' said Ramona. She looked down at the floor. 'And I am.'

'Good for you,' said Dan. 'But you should take care with that young man. I'm guessing he's a little too big for his boots.'

'You're very sweet,' said Ramona. 'But I'm twenty-five and quite capable of looking after myself.'

'Of course you are.' Dan realised that he was making a fool of himself. 'I'm sorry. It's got nothing to do with me, anyway.'

'You're still very kind,' she said. 'I appreciate it.'

Ramona stood up and leant over to give Dan a soft kiss on the cheek. 'I have to run,' she said. 'It was lovely to meet you, Dan. I hope you enjoy the rest of the book.'

'You too. Good luck.'

Ramona didn't look much like Rosa but there was something in the way she moved. He watched her until she was out of sight and then settled his skinny butt back onto the unforgiving mahogany.

Once again, he was alone with his thoughts.

Dan didn't think he would be able to cope with waiting another half-hour for Rachel. He would call her in ten minutes or so and ask her to come straight away. They could go for lunch a little earlier than planned and then he would try to sleep for a few hours before the theatre.

Over lunch, he would talk to Rachel. It was time. He needed to tell her.

He swallowed a couple more Vicodin – it couldn't matter so much if he took a few more than he was supposed to – and reached for his book.

After the welcome interlude with Ramona, Dan had no problem focusing on the text, but it was then his mind's turn to betray him; he couldn't concentrate for long enough to keep up with the pace of the quick-fire revelations and to tie each new piece of information together with the others.

That was the problem with this kind of book. It was well written – or at least well translated – and the whole thing was carefully constructed, but modern readers seemed to demand an ever-increasing number of twists and turns. There was a point where it became absurd.

There was no doubt that the book would be an exciting read if he were able to completely immerse himself in the roller-coaster plot, and there were some very clever and imaginative surprises. But the moment he lost concentration and stepped back, the sheer volume of contrived coincidences stood out in sharp relief and it all seemed a little silly.

Dan couldn't fully immerse himself in anything any more; the pain never left his side and a growing need to reflect on, and review, his life was filling his thoughts. It was like a nagging wife who wouldn't leave him be.

Thank God, Rachel had never been a nag. He had watched a few couples he knew sink into the roles of "nag" and "nagee" and it was an ugly path to follow. In the early years, a gloss of humour would cloak most exchanges and the repartee could appear charming and affectionate. As the years wore on, however, each guilty party grew inexorably into the roles which came to define, not only their relationship as a couple but, in Dan's experience, who they actually were as individuals.

He could say what he wanted about contrived coincidences, but, if it hadn't been for a simple twist of fate, he would never have met Rosa in the first place. He'd always believed in the hand of Man, not the hand of Destiny, but the events of that distant April morning left Dan with many more questions than answers.

Much as he'd tried, and despite everything that happened, Dan could never bring himself to wish the day had turned out differently and that they'd never met. If the stars hadn't chosen that particular moment to line up so perfectly, he would have been spared a lifetime of pain, but …

And there was always that 'but'.

He had lived a full life afterwards. He hoped a good life, whatever that was … *but* … would he exchange a single hour of his time with Rosa for a year of that other life?

He doubted it.

He'd been working on his doctorate for three years. *The Devil Inside: Dostoevsky and Modern Terrorism* was almost finished, and he already knew it would be much more than a PhD thesis for him.

Dan had found his purpose and seventy-five thousand words was barely enough to scratch the surface of the project which would grow to become the backbone of his life. Many people thought of terrorism as a new, post-war phenomenon, but fiction writers like Dostoevsky had been exploring the ideas and motivations behind terrorism before the end of the nineteenth century. It had been a terrorist act which sparked the beginning of the Great War, after all.

In those days terrorism may have appeared different, but the fundamental moral dilemma remained the same as that explored by

Dostoevsky; could great evil ever be justified in the name of a worthy cause? Or was it simply evil?

Two world wars hadn't improved matters and, as colonial empires started to implode, the tensions across arbitrary national borders were everywhere. His thesis – which had later become a well-respected book – had predicted the global increase in terrorism and guerrilla warfare with unfortunate accuracy.

By the time his paper was nearing completion, he already had a provisional job offer from his professor. If all went to plan, he would take up a fellowship in his department and start work in the coming September.

The darling buds of May were already blossoming and Dan was well aware that academia was strewn with the white-boned carcasses of PhD theses which had been "almost there" for decades. He had no intention of joining their ranks.

Strict discipline was the answer and, as the child of a banker and a schoolteacher, Dan understood structure. He'd established a tight routine – in the library by eight-thirty, a maximum of four fifteen-minute coffee breaks and half an hour for lunch. He didn't allow himself to leave the library until seven at the earliest and was usually in bed by nine.

At twenty-five, with a few exceptions, Dan was immune to the undergraduate seductions of impromptu all-night parties followed by days spent pretending to study under the dappled shade of the huge Monterey oaks. He wasn't too old to let his hair down but could resist until he'd handed in his thesis.

That morning was like any other; his briefcase was packed, and he was halfway out of the door when the phone rang.

Nadia

The car – a seemingly innocuous black Audi saloon – was waiting for them on Thorney Street. There was nothing innocuous about what was under the bonnet, however, and Nadia was slammed back in her seat the moment they were inside.

'Should have you in South Ken in twelve minutes,' said the security guard in the passenger seat. 'I'll need you to sign this,

80

please.' He handed Nadia a clipboard holding a blue form.

Nadia scanned the document briefly before signing the form, handing it back and taking the offered leather shoulder holster. Although intelligence officers almost never carried guns, Nadia had still been expected to train regularly and there were always times when calling in SCO19 wasn't an option. She took out the Glock 19, checked it carefully and strapped the holster under her jacket. She wasn't expecting to need it.

Nadia didn't see herself as aggressive, but she couldn't ignore the buzz she got from holding a pistol – the weight, the balance, the cold metal, the engineered precision, they all combined to feel natural and right in her hand. It was no wonder that her name stood unchallenged at the top of the Service's firing range hall of fame.

She didn't really understand what was behind it. It wasn't the power – OK, maybe it was partly the power – but there was something like a craftsman's pleasure, the comfort of handling a familiar tool. It was ironic that, having discovered this talent, she almost never had a reason to use it. Unfortunately, the only time she'd needed to fire a weapon in anger, things hadn't ended well.

She and Ed hadn't spoken as they'd rushed out to the car and Nadia turned to look at him. His face was a pallid grey-white and he was staring straight ahead as though bolted in position.

'You OK?' she said, reaching over to touch his arm.

A slight nod was all the response she got. Ed's eyes remained locked on the headrest in front of him.

'You don't look OK,' she said.

'I'm bloody terrified,' he said, turning to Nadia and showing the whites of his eyes. 'No-one said anything about guns and car chases.'

'What? I thought you MI6 guys were all ex-SAS macho men?'

'Some of them are,' he said. 'Not me. I started at GCHQ. I'm an analyst. They only transferred me to Six when they needed a senior techie in Karachi. That was three years ago.'

'... And you've not been through basic training? Never been out in the field?'

'Christ, no,' he said, tugging on his sandy-blond hair. 'I'm hardly going to go unnoticed in Peshawar, am I?'

He turned back to face the headrest as the driver flicked on his blue light and jumped two red lights on the Embankment. Ed had clearly got the wrong end of the stick somehow – it wasn't as though they were about to get into a gunfight. They were only there to figure out what was happening and to pick up Snowflake's trail if there was anything to pick up. The pistol was a standard precaution. Any consequent follow-up would be for SCO19, not them.

Although it didn't always work out as planned.

'You don't need to worry,' she said to Ed. 'Nothing's going to happen. She patted the pistol on her chest. This is going to stay right here.'

The engine screamed as the car threaded its way through an impossible gap between a bus and a cyclist – Nadia could see that her comforting assurances were falling on deaf ears.

'It's all right,' he said, from between clenched teeth. 'I'm not actually that much of a wimp. I just hate driving fast. I'll be better once we stop.'

Nadia didn't feel especially reassured. Why had David given her this guy?

'Ed,' she said. 'I don't want to be rude, but what exactly are you doing here? I mean, you're not trained for this and we've no time to waste.'

Was that a small smile? She couldn't be sure.

'It's OK,' he said. 'I get it. Things would have been clearer if there'd been ten minutes for proper introductions.' He took a deep breath. 'I'm not just an IT nerd. My first degree was in psychology. I'm a profiler and I've been assigned to Unicorn for a long time - ever since he was linked to the Karachi embassy bombings. If anyone can double guess what he's going to do, it should be me.'

'Aha,' said Nadia. 'Now I get it. And you're convinced he's behind this?'

'Ninety per cent,' said Ed. 'It smells like him. Sorry if that sounds a bit unscientific; it's actually based on eight years of living with him in my mind, day-in and day-out.'

'Nothing wrong with gut feel,' said Nadia. 'It's often all we have.'

Ed nodded. 'And I know your gut feel is telling you that Snowflake isn't capable of anything like this,' he said. 'But don't underestimate Unicorn. He's got a kind of evangelical charisma, I don't know how else to describe it. One way or another, his acolytes will do anything for him. It's like they become hypnotised or brainwashed.'

Nadia nodded, although she still wasn't convinced.

At least there was a valid reason why David had saddled her with a desk jockey and Ed seemed to be calming down. For a while, she'd been certain he was going to throw up.

He turned towards her. 'Changing the subject,' he said, pointing at the bulge in her jacket. 'You ever had to use that?'

'Just once,' said Nadia. 'And I'm happy to keep it that way.'

'What happened?'

'You don't want to hear about that,' said Nadia, turning to look out of the window. It was a time she tried to forget although she knew no-one else had. Her career had taken a boost and, at the same time, a distance had formed between her and her colleagues. It was as though everyone had taken a quarter of a step backwards and Nadia's personal space had become slightly bigger overnight.

'Go on,' said Ed. 'Tell me.'

'OK,' she said. 'If you're here for a few days, you'll probably hear about it, anyway.' She shifted in her seat. 'It was two years ago. My partner, Mark, and I were staking out a pub in Streatham. There was a room at the back where National Action used to meet – as nasty a bunch of right-wing fascists as you're ever likely to come across.

'Anyway, the room was miked up and a good friend of mine had been undercover in the group for over a year. Things had suddenly jumped up a few gears when our inside guy told us they were planning an attack on a synagogue within two weeks. The main man, Stu Ronson, had been a roughneck on oil rigs in the North Sea and had managed to source explosives from one of his old contacts. Serious stuff - shaped charges, RDX, hugely powerful.'

'Bloody hell,' said Ed. 'Surely that sort of thing is always logged and secured?'

'Apparently not well enough,' said Nadia. 'Anyway, we weren't expecting anything out of the ordinary that night. There were only three of them in the room and the explosives weren't due for two days. They were drinking and playing Madness at full volume; it was difficult to hear what was being said until the sound of arguing and smashing furniture drowned out the music.

'We called for SCO19 back-up as soon as we picked up Stu shouting "you fucking traitor", and then moved in when we heard our agent screaming, "I would never do that to you." That was one of our abort phrases; there was no time to wait for the cavalry so we kicked in the door and piled into the room.

'The third guy saw our guns and immediately lifted his hands, but Stu was standing in front of our agent and, before we could do anything, he'd spun round behind him and was pressing an evil-looking commando knife into his neck. I tried to calm things down, telling him that more armed police were on their way and he had no way out. But he muttered something about having nothing left to lose and that's when I saw something change in his eyes.'

'How do you mean?' said Ed.

'It was as though he gave up all hope and all that was left was his bitterness and resentment. I was convinced he was going to cut our man's throat.'

'So what did you do?'

'I took the only shot I had, Stu was thrown backwards before he could use the knife, and then SCO19 arrived. It was all a bit of a blur after that.'

'Sounds incredible. You saved the day.'

'Maybe,' said Nadia. 'And maybe he wasn't planning on doing anything stupid. The bit I haven't mentioned is that the shot I took was through our guy's shoulder. I aimed for the soft tissue, but unfortunately, the bullet clipped a nerve and he'll probably never make a full recovery.'

'But he's alive because of you,' said Ed.

'I guess,' said Nadia. She looked at Ed. 'What sort of person deliberately shoots a friend in cold blood, though? Everyone pretends it's good-humoured banter, but I know they're all a bit scared of me now.'

11:24

Jim

Janet Wilson, Security Team Supervisor (AKA Hatchet Face), was doing her rounds.

She was a sharp-nosed witch of a woman who looked like she should have been in charge of a 1960s hospital ward, possibly in some dodgy black-and-white film comedy. Although probably not much over thirty, she was already pumped full of her own importance and worshipped policies and regulations. Jim enjoyed imagining her slinking home from the museum to a lonely flat, feeding the cats and then settling in to read Fifty Shades of Grey for the tenth time.

He watched her talking to Will across the hall. Ramona had already left and Will would almost certainly be turning on the boyish charm; Janet would probably be lapping it up. It wouldn't work for Jim, not that he'd ever tried. They both knew that he hated the job and Hatchet Face seemed to have made it her life's mission to find new reasons to make him hate it even more.

He hadn't given up on the idea of telling her exactly what she could do with her stupid coaching and development targets; it wasn't the worst idea in the world and even the thought of doing it made him stand up straighter.

Even better, it would be sweet to give her a slap at the same time. Wipe that smug grin off her pompous little face, pick up his flask and walk out with his head held high. She'd probably sue him though, and he couldn't face going through all of that again.

Jim had been brought up with a cast iron set of unwritten rules:

you never hit a woman; you never swore in front of a woman and you never cried. That was what made a man.

Beyond that, of course, there were the ten commandments and the laws of the land but, as far as they went, there tended to be a lot more flexibility. It was like that pirate bloke said in the Disney films his girls loved; they were more like 'guidelines'.

But, circumstances changed. Even cast-iron rules got broken and, once broken, the shattered pieces could never be put back together.

Jim hadn't gone home from the pub after he learnt about Julie's betrayal.

After Bonehead had told him what little he knew, the temptation to storm out and across the road to confront her was almost overwhelming.

But, a small voice inside him held him back, and he chose the only alternative – to test the boundaries of science and medicine and find out just how much whisky a man could drink without dying.

His mates must have looked out for him, as he'd woken up face down on Phil's living room floor, having apparently fallen off the sofa at some point during the night. As he lifted his head, the memories of stale Hamlets and whisky-flavoured bile were still oozing from the rancid carpet fibres which were stuck to his tongue.

He couldn't remember getting home or anything else that had happened as the night degenerated, but Bonehead's words were seared into his memory in black, charred letters six feet high. Even as he bent over the stained toilet bowl, hacking and retching, the images of Julie with Grant Andrews wouldn't leave him in peace.

He knew Grant, of course. Grant worked for Dave Vickers and could often be seen round and about in his white BMW, black aviators pushed back over his pathetic comb-over. He was a nasty, vicious little man and word was that Dave used him whenever he had a need to send a message that couldn't be misunderstood.

Jim swilled his mouth out with tepid tap water and staggered into the kitchen where Phil was hunched over the sink, trying to fill the kettle. Jim was pleased to see that Phil looked as bad as Jim felt.

'Where's the tea?' he said.

Phil reached down and pulled a box out of a drawer. 'Got no milk though,' he said. 'Not been so good with the shopping since Sal left. Might be some powdered.' He scrabbled about in the grimy cupboard next to the water heater and grunted with apparent surprise as he pulled out a half-full jar of CoffeeMate. 'Who'd have thought it?' he said, plonking it down on the unit. 'Who says I ain't got it together?'

The two men stood leaning against the kitchen units sipping their tea. It was still early and the weak January sunlight, combined with the overhead fluorescent tubes, did nothing to add colour or life to Phil's grey, pasty face. Jim suspected that they looked like a pair of corpses propped upright as part of some sick undertaker's joke.

'Grant Andrews,' said Jim. 'Grant Fucking Andrews?'

Phil looked down at his cup and shrugged his shoulders.

'And you knew?' said Jim.

'Of course I fucking knew,' said Phil. 'Everyone knew.'

'And you didn't think it might be an idea to tell me?'

'No. I didn't think that would be a fucking clever idea,' said Phil. 'What fucking use would that have been? You were in Ulster and some of us still had to live round here.'

'So is it over, then?'

'As far as I know, it's been over for a year.' Phil looked up at Jim. 'I'm sorry mate, but would you have told me? If it hadn't been for fucking Bonehead ...'

Jim couldn't help smiling. 'How many times have we said that?' said Jim, his laugh turning into a choking cough. 'If it hadn't been for fucking Bonehead ... Why's he still around?'

'Beats me,' said Phil.

They stood in silence while Jim struggled to control the images which wouldn't stop flashing in front of him. 'Grant Fucking Andrews,' he said again. Streaks and blotches of crimson were spreading across his waxy cheeks and he could feel the rage building.

'You can't do anything, Jim,' said Phil. 'Grant's on the inside. You can't touch him.'

'Do I look like someone who gives a fuck?' said Jim as he picked up his jacket and turned towards the door.

Julie must have seen him coming out of Phil's and was waiting for him in the narrow hall. She didn't have a rolling pin in her hand but her hands were firmly planted on her hips and she was clearly planning on giving him a proper earful.

As Jim walked into the house and closed the door behind him, Julie stood facing him, mouth half open, angry words half spoken, frozen in mid flow. She'd seen the look in his eyes.

Jim was pleased to see that he still had the presence to put her in her place without a word, but it didn't do much to help his struggle for self-control. He ached all over and the pain from the nail gun working overtime on his right temple was curdling the stale tea in his stomach. The only thing holding him upright was the burning flame of betrayal and that was threatening to overwhelm him.

'What is it, Jim?' said Julie, stepping towards him. 'You look terrible.'

'How could you?' Jim shrank back, pressing himself against the door and lifting a hand in warning. He was surprised to hear his own voice, calm and controlled and quite unlike him.

Julie wasn't reading the signals and came closer, arms stretching towards him. 'How could I what? I don't know what you're talking about.'

It wasn't Jim's hand that slapped her. Twice. Hard.

As she spun sideways and fell, smacking her head into the door jamb, Jim remembered thinking that she deserved that and more.

'Slag!' he said. 'Did you think I wouldn't find out?'

Her eyes changed colour, two black circles filled with fear. She knew what he was talking about, she knew she'd crossed the line and this was the day that had always been coming.

It wasn't the time for Jim to take things further though. Apart from the fact that he could barely stand upright, it would be best to let her stew for a while. He looked at her lying there; she'd pushed herself back to the foot of the stairs and was curled up in a ball, bright blood flowing from her nose and pooling crimson on her white blouse.

Julie's hands were lifted in a weak, half-hearted attempt to protect herself and the look in her eyes said 'please don't hit me again.' Jim liked that. This wasn't over, but it was a good start.

He pushed past her roughly and started up the stairs. 'I'm going to bed,' he said. 'Clean yourself up.' He turned when he got to the top of the stairs. '… And don't fucking go anywhere.'

He wasn't proud that he'd hit Julie and it had only ever happened on four, maybe five, occasions afterwards; he'd never taken it too far, but the worrying thing was that he'd enjoyed the feeling every time. It was like a cocaine rush, filling him with strength, wellbeing and invulnerability.

Slapping Janet, the supervisor, wouldn't come with any complicated guilt strings. She had just finished with Will and was walking across the hall towards him with her no-nonsense gait. Each step was identical, her sensible heels clacking against the tiles in perfect clockwork rhythm.

'Good morning, Jim. How are we this morning?' She looked him up and down with a sneer as though so much about Jim was sub-standard that she didn't know where to start. It was like the first day of army basic training – bad enough when you're eighteen, but now? He was sixty-two for Christ's sake.

'Good morning Janet. I'm all right thanks.'

'Everything in order here?' She surveyed the hall with her supervisor's eyes, blessed with superpowers which a mere security guard couldn't imagine.

'Seems to be. Never seen it so quiet though.' Jim only had to endure this for a couple of minutes and then she'd be on her way.

'What about him?' she said, nodding her head towards Dan.

'I've been keeping an eye on him and don't think there's anything to worry about. Five minutes ago he was chatting to a young girl and looked perky enough then.' Jim peered at Dan who had put his book down on the bench and was leaning forward, hands gripping his knees. 'He doesn't look so great just now,' Jim said. 'I'll give you that … But he's no spring chicken is he?'

'Indeed no,' said Hatchet Face, drawing herself up to her full five foot two. 'Have you any idea what would happen if someone died on our shift. We'd be up to our necks in bureaucracy for hours.' She smoothed her skirt and straightened her black jacket – supervisors didn't have to wear the stupid fleeces. 'I don't know about you, but I have plans this evening and need to leave on time.'

She gave Jim a look which made it clear that he'd let the side down again, sighed and turned towards Dan. 'Seeing as I'm here, I might as well go and check on him myself,' she said, before launching back into her metronome march.

Hassan

Hassan had felt strong fingers digging into his upper arm as his father steered him towards one of the matching coffee-brown armchairs and eased him down without speaking. The chairs were still covered in protective plastic which squeaked in protest as he sank into the soft cushions.

Nothing was going as planned. He'd made up his mind about Oxford and had been ready for a fight. He knew his dad and had no delusions about his expectations of obedience. 'My way or the highway' was a favourite in the Qureishi household, usually delivered with a horrific cowboy accent and a satisfied chuckle.

But, there had been no fight and his father had even given the impression that he was proud of his son for making up his own mind. The events of the previous days had turned Hassan's world on its head and he felt reality slipping away. There had to be a catch.

And, of course, there was.

'Dad. Look. I'm really sorry to mess you around but …'

'Hush boy. You've said your piece.' The whisky appeared on the table along with two glasses and Hassan heard the golden liquid gurgling happily out of the bottle. 'It's time for me to explain how things are going to be.'

Hassan took the glass from his father and nodded. This was more like reality.

'OK,' his dad continued. 'I've spoken to a few people and we can raise the money ourselves. There's no need to get the government involved. After all, who knows when they're going to change the rules?'

'But Dad…' Hassan was on the edge of his seat.

'Let me finish. Didn't I teach you any manners? What will they think of you at Oxford?' His father sat back and sipped his whisky until Hassan slunk once more into the embrace of his chair. 'So. As I was saying. We can raise the money. Not for a flash lifestyle, but enough. Your Uncle Sami has offered to cover your costs.'

'Uncle Sami!' said Hassan. 'But he's a drug dealer.'

'Drug dealer? No. No. No. Don't listen to all those nasty rumours,' said his father, smiling. 'He's a successful businessman that's all. He's so proud of you. The first in our family to get a place at Oxford. Did you know that Benazir Bhutto went … and her father also?'

'Yes, dad. I knew that,' said Hassan. 'But …'

'But, "Thank you Baba" is all I need to hear from you right now.' The world hadn't really turned upside down and Hassan realised that this was the usual one-way conversation. He needed time to think.

His father continued without pausing for breath. 'And all he's asked from you is to work for him when you finish. Just for three years and he'll pay you a good salary as well. How decent is that?'

After a lifetime of experience, Hassan knew when he was beaten. The euphoria of his success had dribbled away and things were back to normal; he was his usual pathetic, spineless self, being pushed around by everyone.

His plan had been a good one; give up the place at Oxford, stay at home, get a job and lead a normal life. But he should have known from the start that, once his father had set off to bray about his genius son, there would be no going back. That door was closed.

If he'd had the guts, he could have simply upped sticks and left to start a new life. Take control for once. Maybe even go abroad? To Canada or the US?

But he'd need to do that without family and, with his brown skin, having no family would mark him with the stigma of the black sheep every step of the way. He would have no friends, no family, no job and no money.

Maybe he was pathetic, but he didn't have that sort of courage and, in any case, life as an exiled pariah sounded much worse than simply going to Oxford – drug dealing uncle or not. All he needed to do was to keep his head down, get a good degree and then he would see.

The six months before Hassan went up to Oxford had flashed by. Giving up and accepting the inevitable had been a much more comfortable place to be. The world was back on its axis, spinning away as usual.

He'd sat down with his Uncle Sami soon after his father had laid down the law and they'd agreed that Hassan would work for him until that October and during each of his summer breaks. He actually was a businessman (as well as being a notorious drug dealer) and had a medium-sized company which imported specialist fruit and vegetables from India and Pakistan. As Hassan was the genius in the family, he was put in the office and became responsible for sorting out the mess of paperwork – from order forms to VAT returns – that no-one else wanted to touch.

He had no idea what he was doing to begin with, but was a quick learner and soon got the hang of it – although he never shook off the belief that there would be a knock on the door one morning and Uncle Sami would be standing there, waving the keys to a battered brown-and-orange campervan which would be standing in the driveway.

'Pack yourself a bag, boy. It's time to earn your keep.'

In his dream, Hassan would be surprised. 'What are you talking about, Chacha? What's the old van for?'

'Not just an old campervan,' Uncle Sami would say, wrapping a burly arm around Hassan's shoulders and giving him the tour. 'I see a bright young chemist, a mobile laboratory and lots of shiny blue crystals.' By then, his uncle's bulging eyes would actually be glinting aquamarine in his dark face. 'Crystal meth, boy. Lovely, pure crystal meth.'

The campervan hadn't appeared and Hassan found himself, almost by accident, sitting in a huge lecture theatre, half way through the first year of his biochemistry degree at Oxford University. He was smiling. He seemed to be smiling a lot of the time.

It had turned out that he was easily smart enough for Oxford, although he was probably a little too brown, a tad too Yorkshire and he definitely didn't have enough money. But even that wasn't a disaster; there were plenty of people just like him and, with the best will in the world, most biochemists weren't exactly fashionistas, anyway.

The first weeks had been lonely and confusing for all of them. Most first-year students wandered through quads and along cobbled streets with an identical transfixed-rabbit look while they tried to get to grips with strange and complex timings and locations. Adding in a baffling set of social options, fuelled by the heady first flush of freedom, was almost guaranteed to drive criminally poor decision-making on every level.

Excessive alcohol and ill-advised one-night-stands were simply the inevitable cherries on the cake (unless you subscribed to the school of thought that believed student sex couldn't be categorised as ill-advised by definition). In Hassan's case, the cherry wasn't metaphorical, the alcohol was fortunately not too excessive, and he definitely didn't think the sex was ill-advised.

Her name was Mona, and she was the most beautiful and amazing thing that Hassan had ever seen. He had no idea at the time how much finding Mona would transform his life.

If he'd never met Mona, there was no chance that he would have been praying under a tree in London's Hyde Park. Without Mona, he would have been working for his Uncle Sami, waiting for the imaginary campervan to appear. Without Mona, he wouldn't have come to know God and he wouldn't have understood that God had a purpose for him. Without Mona, everything would have been much simpler.

But, somewhere back in time, a young student sat in an Oxford lecture hall and smiled. His world would never be the same again.

The people were still scurrying along and Hyde Park's trees loomed tall above him but, until Hassan rose after his final Salaam, he wouldn't have noticed if they'd all vanished for ten minutes.

He rolled up his mat, tucked it carefully into his bag and set off towards the toilets. They were next to the park entrance and, being linked to a cafe and tennis club, would definitely be open.

He felt closer to Allah than ever after his prayers, light-headed and floating, almost like he had cotton wool stuffed in his ears. Everyone around him was moving more slowly than usual. A crowd of Japanese school kids ran into the park as he cut across the main path, but he found himself weaving effortlessly through the jostling, chattering youngsters as though they were standing still.

Hassan had never liked public toilets; even if they were well looked after, the smell of stale piss was ever present, catching at the back of the throat like chlorine or nitric acid and dragging back teenage memories which were best forgotten. The toilets he'd chosen were not strictly public, but they still reeked.

The farthest cubicle was for disabled users and was luckily unoccupied. No, not luck. As Hassan locked the door behind him, he understood that he was no longer alone. From now on, God would be by his side. He needed him now more than ever.

Momentarily filled with certainty, confidence and calm, he hung up his jacket, opened his holdall and took out the plastic-wrapped bundle which didn't feel so heavy after all. There was even a baby changing table in the corner; he could unroll the package without touching the floor tiles which, however well scrubbed, must hold the memories and homeopathic traces of each drop of urine (or worse) which had ever contaminated them.

Stretched out in front of him, the white cotton vest looked pure and harmless, but that didn't prevent his instant of peace and tranquillity vanishing as quickly as it had appeared; Hassan's pulse started racing as fast as a tapping finger and he felt cold beads of sweat popping out, one by one, on his forehead.

The rollercoaster had reached the top of its climb. There was no point in looking to his parents for ways out any more. He was locked into his seat. There was only one way forward. This was happening. No more talk. This was happening.

Shuna

As she put the holiday folder back in her bag, Shuna looked at Zoe and Anna who were already walking ahead of her back down Exhibition Road. They were muttering in each other's ears. Stupid children. She overheard the words 'bloody taxi driver', but she already knew what they were talking about. They understood perfectly well why she needed to remember to book a car back from Heathrow.

Try as she might, Shuna couldn't see the joke. It should have become old history by now, the whole story passed into dinner party legend; each telling and retelling building up the characters and dialogue into a cod-Dickensian tragedy with the story tellers competing for the best (or worst) cockney accents.

Objectively, even the final scene hadn't been such an enormous deal – nothing had actually happened – but Shuna struggled to find perspective. The anger and fear were consigned to memory most of the time, but the grubby feelings of guilt and shame persisted and she still refused to take a black cab.

Most people saw black cabs as one of the few remaining pillars of civilised society; the moment you entered a cab, you were stepping into a sanctuary and were protected from the mid-day mayhem of the West End or the sinister shadows of a misty London night.

Not Shuna. Until just a few weeks earlier, whenever she saw that orange cyclops eye hovering above its stubby black nose, she would stop breathing and her muscles would tense reflexively in an overwhelming urge to run.

It wasn't as bad any more – taxis were back to being a part of the landscape –but the story still wasn't actually funny.

It had never been funny.

The "bloody taxi driver" had first entered their lives a few years earlier. They'd just landed at Heathrow after an amazing three weeks in Australia. Simon was a great holiday organiser and the Sydney trip had been the best ever. They'd swapped their South Kensington flat for a stunning house in Double Bay – six en-suite bedrooms with balconies looking out over Sydney Harbour, a huge infinity pool and beautiful, modern designer furniture everywhere. Shuna had been in seventh heaven and the kids had spent the entire time pretending they were film stars.

They'd flown club class and on the way home had stopped over for a day in Singapore, but it was still a fifteen hour flight and she remembered how dazed she'd felt as they flowed out of the airport into the alien chill of a black London evening. A wet, sleety rain was softening the streetlights, and she shivered. As she turned to Anna, Zoe and Simon, she saw their happy holiday bubbles also popping one by one.

'Good to be home, eh?' she'd said, doing her best to produce a rueful smile.

'Yeah. Great,' chorused the girls, suddenly looking small and helpless. No more Sophia Loren sunglasses for them for a while.

'But it was an amazing holiday, wasn't it?' said Simon, his big, cheesy smile lighting up the dank walkway. 'Come on. Let's grab a cab.'

The biggest problem with house swaps was matching dates and flight times and they weren't due to get their flat back until eleven o'clock on the following morning. It wasn't the end of the world to spend a night at an airport hotel but, after all the travelling, Shuna was impatient to get back home and her heart sank at the thought of checking in to some faceless, bland hotel room. Unfortunately, there wasn't a better option; if they'd flown a day later, it would have cost two thousand pounds more.

The taxi queue was mercifully short and Simon gave the black cab driver the name of their hotel.

'Never heard of it,' said the cabbie, looking down at his feet. 'You'll have to give me the postcode.'

'It's an airport hotel,' said Simon. 'I think it's fairly new, but you must know where it is.'

'Naah,' said the cabbie, still looking down. 'Give me the postcode and I'll look it up.'

Shuna could remember thinking that, if cabbies were going to be that rude, black cabs would definitely lose the fight with Uber. And, on top of the rudeness and aggression, he didn't even know where the hotel was? Wasn't that what "The Knowledge" was all about? She was tired, and the guy was already pissing her off. He had that East London swagger which reminded her of one of those UKIP supporters who'd been all over the TV since Brexit.

Simon, as always, was biting his tongue and trying to be pragmatic. He'd learnt patience the hard way. He searched for the hotel on his phone and told the cabbie the postcode. 'Google says it'll take thirteen minutes,' he added.

The driver stopped looking at his own phone, put it back in his pocket and stepped towards Simon, shoulders hunching and fists clenched. 'Are you bloody telling me how long it's going to take now? I don't give a toss what Google says. We don't use Google, and it'll take as long as it takes.'

Shuna was amazed at Simon's self control and could see that he was still trying to find a practical resolution to get them from the cold, rainy pavement to their comfortable beds. But she'd had enough.

'What's wrong with you?' she shouted. 'First you don't know where an airport hotel is even though we're at the bloody airport, and then you're giving my husband a hard time because he told you where it was and how far away. If you'd known where it was in the first place, we'd have been there by now.'

He turned to Shuna with a snarl. 'Look lady. I've been doing this job for twenty years. I work bloody hard and I don't need to take this sort of grief from anyone. If you don't want a cab, that's your problem. I'll take whoever's next.' He turned and walked back over to his cab, followed by a young couple who clearly wanted no part of the argument. They just wanted to get home.

Shuna wasn't finished, but Simon put his hand on her shoulder to hold her back. 'Leave it,' he said. 'We'll get another one.'

There was a man in a Day-Glo jacket managing the taxi queue and he turned to Simon. 'The thing is, sir,' he said. 'If one cab's refused to take you, then the others will refuse too. It's how it is. I'm sorry.'

By this time Shuna was ready to explode. 'What! This is ridiculous,' she said. 'First that guy starts a fight with us for no reason and then we can't get another cab. I've got two young kids. I've been on a plane for fifteen hours. I don't believe this.'

'I'm sorry Madam,' said Day-Glo man. 'It's just the way it works.'

Shuna had been on the point of tears when she felt a tap on her shoulder. A youngish man in a white polo shirt was standing there, smiling. 'Don't worry,' he said. 'I'll take you.'

They'd had to wait for three other taxis which were ahead in the queue, but were loaded up and on their way soon enough.

'Thank you,' said Simon. 'I don't believe that guy.'

'No problem,' said the driver. 'He gets up everybody's nose. He does it all the time. If someone only wants to go a short distance, he starts a fight, uses that as an excuse to refuse the fare, and moves on to the next punter.'

'You're saying that was all an act?' said Shuna. 'Bloody hell.'

'It's sort of understandable,' said the cabbie. 'Most days, we have to wait for three or four hours at Heathrow before we get to the pick-up zone.'

'So you've waited four hours and then you offered to take us even though it's a small fare?' said Simon. 'That's unbelievably kind of you.'

'It's not that bad. They give us an hour's grace, so as long as I'm back within the sixty minutes, I won't have to wait again. That's why that other bloke's so out of order. He's got no real excuse.'

'I'm surprised that some of you don't take him aside and straighten him out,' said Simon. 'As you say, he's not doing the rest of you any favours.'

'Some guys have come close, but he's a hard bugger. Ex-army. No-one wants to mess with him … and besides, we stick together as a rule.' The taxi stopped for a red light and the driver turned to Simon with a half-smile. 'He's had a few complaints made to the public carriage office, but nothing's come of it. No-one wants to take away a man's livelihood.'

'Of course not,' said Shuna. 'But he shouldn't be allowed to keep behaving like that. If you hadn't been there, we might've waited ages. I wish I'd been smart enough to note down his number.'

The girls had been quiet throughout the entire incident, wide-eyes flicking between the various actors, unsure what would happen next. As Shuna voiced her frustration, Zoe pulled on the sleeve of her coat.

'We have got it, Mum,' she said, holding out her phone. 'I took a photo when you were all arguing. It's got his number on it.'

Dan

Dan had toyed with the idea of not answering the phone that day, but it would have bugged him all morning and he wouldn't have been able to concentrate.

'Dan?'

'Hey Mom. What's up?'

'Nothing much. Just thought I'd call my boy and see how he's doing.'

If Dan had put aside a dollar each time his mother had called him in the six years he'd been in Texas, he'd barely have enough saved for a blow-out breakfast at McDonald's; when she eventually did get around to calling, it was never about "nothing much". There was always a drama to share.

'That's nice,' he said. 'I'm great, thank you. Look Mom, I'm halfway out the door. Can I call you later?'

'I guess. But ...'

'... That's great. About seven.' Dan felt slightly bad as he hung up the phone, but the guilt had evaporated by the time he'd locked the door behind him. She'd have told him if anything was seriously wrong and he was probably going to miss his bus in any case.

He missed the bus.

There is something deeply sorrowful in the sight of a bus or train shrinking into the distance; it leaves you abandoned in its wake, solitary and breathless.

Dan was not one for cursing – again a consequence of his background – but he remembered making a special exception that day. The next bus wasn't for half an hour which was about the same time it would take him to walk in. One way or the other, by the time he got settled, he would have lost a precious hour of his day.

Nothing he could do about it, but typical of his mother. She'd always had uncanny timing.

As Dan thought back to his mother and that phone call, he felt the same confused mix of feelings that he always did. The same ones that had fed his colourful curses over fifty years earlier.

It was lucky she hadn't called often as his first reaction was always anger. She'd always been self-centred in a way that couldn't be ignored, which somehow announced itself even before the phone had stopped ringing.

There was no point in feeling that way any more. His mother had been dead for fifteen years. It was long past time to forgive and forget. What was done couldn't be undone, and she'd probably made the right choices. Would it have been better if she'd rejected her chance of happiness and stayed in a loveless marriage? And why? Out of convention or misplaced loyalty?

For himself, he could forgive ... but for his father ...

The Hintze hall was busier than earlier. It was steadily filling with brightly coloured tourists, some in twos or threes; other, much bigger groups were sporting matching T-shirts and following pennants and umbrellas as mindlessly as Hamelin's children.

The older of the two guards was talking to a smartly dressed woman and, if anything, he looked more sour-faced than before. Ramona hadn't come back.

As far as the phone call went, and thinking about what had happened as a result of him missing his bus half a century earlier, he could only be grateful.

The walk into Austin had been pleasant enough and, after fifteen minutes, Dan convinced himself that the exercise and time to think would actually help him get more work done, even with the late start.

As he approached the main square, he remembered the other

reason he'd had for starting earlier in the day; the student demonstrations had been going on for weeks now and the noise – which could hardly be heard from the library – carried easily for several blocks.

They didn't usually start much before 10:00 and Dan suspected that most of the demonstrators came from the all night partying and studying under the trees demographic. By arriving late, he was obliged to push his way though the crowds and couldn't help seeing the banners and hearing the chants.

For a Toronto boy, the whole circus was absurd. It was obvious why they were fighting for equal rights and he couldn't understand how the government could still be defending the status quo. Austin wasn't too bad but, take a short drive out of town and it was like stepping back a hundred years. It baffled him but, until his Green Card came through, he was going to keep his head down.

A girl pushed out from the crowd in front of him and thrust a leaflet into his hands. 'You need to take a side,' she said. 'Are you with us, or are you with them?' The contemptuous flamenco flick of her head towards the ranks of white policemen was filled with pride and youthful passion and he caught barely a glimpse of her flashing brown eyes before she moved on to her next target.

It was enough. Dan clutched the leaflet between his clammy fingers like a holy relic as he watched her disappear into the crowd.

His world would never be the same again.

'Are you all right, sir?'

Dan was far away in a different time and the woman's voice was outside him. A dream voice floating in space.

He felt a hand on his shoulder and the voice intruded again. 'Excuse me. Is everything all right?'

He pulled back reflexively and opened his eyes; the smartly dressed woman was leaning over him.

'Oh. I'm sorry,' he said. 'I must have nodded off.'

The woman continued to stare as she leant towards him. Concerned eyes, but no warmth.

'I'm fine, thank you,' he continued. 'I'm just waiting for my wife.

She'll be along in a few minutes. She's shopping in Harrods and I wanted to give her some space. Do you work here?'

'Yes,' she said. 'I'm the security team supervisor.'

'Huh. Sounds pretty impressive.'

The woman almost smiled, but appeared to think better of it. What was it with the English?

'Yes. Well,' she said. 'As long as you're OK. Not in need of medical attention?'

'No. I'm full of beans,' he said. 'No need to worry about me.'

'Good,' she said and turned around.

As she walked away, Dan amused himself by wondering whether the poker was stuck up the back of her jacket or somewhere more permanent.

'Rachel?'

'Yes, hon. How are you doing?'

'I'm not feeling so great, actually. Are you nearly done?'

'Pretty much. Would you like me to swing by a little sooner?'

'If it's not a problem, that would be great.'

'Sure. I'll quickly pay for these things and I'll be with you in ten minutes. Are you OK?'

'Yeah. I'm just tired. Sorry to be a pain.'

'You're never a pain. I'll see you in a jiffy.'

Nadia

'I think you're being too hard on yourself,' said Ed. 'It strikes me that you took the right decision based on what was in front of you. What else could you do?'

Nadia shrugged. She'd always found blaming herself to be the easiest option. Not always, perhaps, but for a very long time.

'Anyway,' he said. 'I'm impressed. It must have been terrifying. What about the right-wing guy, Stu? Did you kill him?'

'No,' said Nadia. 'He was sentenced to ten years last October. He's appealing the conviction of course … and still threatening a civil action against me for unnecessary force. Sometimes I wish I had killed him.'

Nadia looked at her phone. With the increased threat level, new info was flowing in continuously, most of it already out of date. There were, however, a slew of likely CCTV matches around South Kensington. They were going to the right place.

'You worked as a cleaner in the mosque?' said Ed as they finally turned away from the river.

Nadia nodded. 'Yup,' she said. 'Fucking awful job. Had to stay fully covered, and they ran the heating overtime. I'll tell you, salwar kameez can be comfortable enough, but not if you're on your knees scrubbing floors. It was grim.'

Ed laughed. 'No, Nadia. Tell me what you really think.'

Nadia realised she'd been ranting like a mad woman and smiled. 'Sorry. It's been a crazy time and I haven't had a chance to adjust. No reason to take it out on you, though.'

'Not a problem,' he said. 'So … are you a Moslem, then?'

'No,' said Nadia. 'Although my mum was. My dad was French and, despite the fact that neither of them were particularly religious, they decided to bring me up learning about both.' She reached up and squeezed the small crucifix under her blouse. Her father had given it to her when she was ten and she could still picture his smiling eyes as he'd hung it around her neck. 'Just in case,' he'd said. '… Just in case.'

'They wanted to give you the chance to make your own mind up when you were older?' said Ed.

'Exactly,' she said. 'And I did. I decided there was way too much misery in the world for either of those Gods to deserve my belief and trust. I try not think about religion to tell you the truth. It only makes me angry.'

'This is the part when I tell you that I'm a passionate born-again Evangelist,' said Ed.

'Oh, shit,' said Nadia, feeling the blood rush to her cheeks. 'I'm sorry. God … I didn't mean …'

'Hey,' said Ed, sharply. 'Hello? Only joking … You really are uptight, aren't you?'

He grinned like a schoolboy and Nadia realised for the first time that he was actually a very good looking man.

As they took a squealing left turn up Franklin Row, Nadia realised she'd shared more personal details with this virtual stranger than she had with any of her other colleagues. And she'd only known him for twenty minutes. Enough was enough. She had no wish to share her parents' tragic story with anyone. She'd learnt to keep that well and truly buried. And as for her own relationship status, she hadn't even begun to process the previous night's debacle. The clock was ticking and allowing herself to imagine a life without Jamie would have to wait.

'Enough about me,' she said, checking their position on Google Maps. 'We've still got a couple of minutes. Tell me how a nice boy like you got caught up in all this?'

'The usual way, I guess,' said Ed. 'I studied psychology because I've always been fascinated by what makes us tick. It didn't take me long to realise that the bills weren't going to get paid by working as a counsellor and that I'd need to find a real job. I've always found programming easy – I used to be a bit of a hacker when I was a kid – and managed to get accepted for a Computer Science masters at Imperial.'

'Imperial?' said Nadia. 'Impressive. So you know South Ken well, then?'

'Yeah. I guess,' said Ed. 'Although if you saw the workload of my course, you'd be surprised I ever got out of the labs.'

'And GCHQ picked you up from there?'

'That's right. The idea had never crossed my mind, but a few years in Cheltenham on a good salary had its appeal.'

'… and they didn't have a problem with you being some sort of anarchist hacker?'

'Funnily enough, no,' said Ed, laughing. 'Although to be fair, the closest thing to anarchy we ever managed was hacking the Conservative Party website and putting a picture of a floating duck island on the front page.'

Nadia looked at him with wide eyes. 'That was you?' she said.

Ed nodded. 'Afraid so.'

'That was probably what got you the job,' said Nadia.

The security guard turned around to face them, no sign on his face that he'd been listening in. 'We'll be there in two minutes,' he said. 'Where do you want to be dropped?'

'Hang on,' said Nadia. 'I'll just check the updates.'

'There's a cafe called Muriel's — on Cromwell Place,' she said as she scrolled to the end. 'Can you drop us there, please? You'll need to wait, I'm afraid.'

'No worries. That's what we're here for,' said the guard.

11:30

Jim

Jim looked at his watch.

Hatchet face had finished with the old codger – surprise, surprise, he wasn't dead – and had stalked off to bother some of the other guards.

He hung the purple fleece carefully over the back of his folding chair and walked over to Will who was looking surprisingly alert. Maybe the boyish charm hadn't worked so well after all and the arrogant bugger had also had his ear bent by the boss lady.

'I'm off on my break,' he said, lifting his right hand to get Will's attention. 'You're on your own.'

'OK,' said Will, flashing his perfect teeth – no shortage of dentist's bills there. 'I think I'll cope.'

The truth was that neither of them would have been too fussed if the next batch of school kids had decided to use the dinosaur skeleton as a climbing frame. It wasn't only that they had the boss from hell, the job itself was almost impossible to care about.

Jim walked down the wide aisle to the North of the hall, his step quickening almost to a run. He only had fifteen minutes and didn't want to waste any of them. The girl at the ticket desk nodded and smiled as he walked by. This was where he'd spent every minute of every break since the exhibition had started a week earlier.

The Wildlife Photographer of the Year was the world's most prestigious photography exhibition and every one of the hundred or so prizewinners on display was jaw-droppingly beautiful. Jim would have given his right arm to have taken just one shot which was half as good as any on display.

He'd decided to focus on a single image each time he went and today's selection was from India. A parakeet family was trying to evict a large monitor lizard which had decided to squat in their tree-branch apartment. The photo showed one parakeet leaning back in the air, outstretched wings flapping green and yellow in a David versus Goliath tug-of-war as it pulled on the lizard's tail. The lizard was a massive grey-brown dullard in comparison, hanging upside down, dug in to the branch with every claw, long tail flexing in a perfect 'S' as it struggled to dislodge the crimson beak clamped onto its tip.

There was always a story behind these pictures – they were almost never simply lucky snaps; it took days and weeks of hard work to be in the right place at the right time. In this case, the evicted family had spent two days persecuting the lizard – biting, tugging, scratching and clawing – until it finally accepted defeat and slunk off in search of alternative accommodation. The photographer had sat high in a neighbouring tree keeping them company throughout.

Jim had loved wildlife photography with a secret passion for almost forty years; it wasn't possible to talk about it with anyone he knew. He'd half-tried a couple of times, but the piss-taking was comprehensive and immediate. Even Julie – especially Julie – would have thought there was something wrong with him.

Like almost everything good in Jim's life, it had started in the Army. He'd been posted for six months to Belize in the late seventies. Belize was the ultimate cushy number and sadly he'd only had the one tour. As a first posting after being promoted to Sergeant, it was ideal and, for a couple of months, there had only been about twenty of them, setting things up ahead of a big jungle warfare exercise with the Americans.

His Second Lieutenant, Alastair, was a classic Rupert, fresh out of Sandhurst, all teeth and confidence – a bit like Will. He and Jim were the same age, but Jim already had five years service under his belt and knew enough to fill in the gaps in his boss's knowledge and experience.

Under the unwritten rules dividing the NCOs from the officers, friendly banter was fine, but real friendship was frowned upon. It interfered with the proper functioning of the machine, especially if things got lively.

Belize was different. Rules – written or unwritten – hadn't seemed to matter under the tropical sun and base protocol was exceptionally relaxed. Alastair had a lot to learn and Jim helped him to get through his early months in command without making too much of a prat of himself. The two young men's backgrounds couldn't have been more different but, despite that, they became good mates.

It was Alastair who introduced Jim to photography. Still years before digital cameras, proper photography wasn't an option for most people. What with dark rooms, chemicals, coated paper, film, lenses and the cameras themselves, you needed time and a lot of money … And, for a professional squaddie from the East End, it wasn't exactly a manly pursuit.

One particular afternoon, the troop had just finished recce-ing an island in the middle of a lake which was set to be the target command centre for the exercise. Jim was taking a breather, sat leant against a tree, swigging warm, brown water from his canteen. The water wasn't actually brown, but it tasted that way. The rest of the troop had gone to fetch the raft and Alastair was messing about with his bloody camera as always.

'Do you want to try?' he said to Jim, holding out the camera.

'Nah. Not really for me, boss,' said Jim. 'We didn't do artistic at my school.'

'So, how do you know it's not for you then? Go on. Give it a go.'

Jim had been secretly watching Alastair for weeks, fascinated by the way he set up the camera for each individual situation, clicking different lenses in and out without thinking about it. And then the photos he came up with – birds, monkeys, flowers, insects – it was like he saw things differently. Jim was actually aching to have a try.

'What the fuck! There's bugger all else to do.'

Alastair gave him a five minute course in exposure and focus and handed over the camera.

'Have a look around,' he said. 'Find something interesting and take pictures of it.'

It had been almost a week later when they were having their morning catch-up meeting. Alastair pushed an envelope across the desk.

'Sorry it took so long,' he said. 'I needed to finish the film.'

They were Jim's photos, but nothing like he'd expected. There were a few rubbish ones, of course, but five or six of them looked like the real thing. The best one was of a macaw, zoomed in so that the head and massive beak filled the frame and the yellow eye stared straight at him like it was popping out of the paper. It was amazing.

'Bloody hell,' said Jim. 'Who'd have thought it?'

'Get it now?' said Alastair. 'You've got an eye, Jim.'

And that was it; he was hooked. Jim became more and more engaged with the ways you could twist and bend light and shadow and spent as much time as he could taking photographs with Alastair. Unsurprisingly, their long walks in the jungle and the hours in the darkroom together fuelled plenty of rumours.

Luckily, Jim got on well with the rest of the troop which, combined with a reputation for being hard as nails, made sure that no-one was stupid enough to accuse him of being limp-wristed. And, in any case, Belize was like a holiday from real life; they'd all done things on nights out which would be best forgotten when they got home.

As he looked at the parakeet doing Tarzan impressions on the poor lizard's tail, Jim pictured himself as the photographer, strapped onto an overhanging branch, sitting still for hour after hour, only occasionally firing off a string of shots before settling back to wait for the petulant, uncooperative actors to find their marks.

Once upon a time, he'd toyed with the idea of giving it all up and training to be a professional photographer, but his taxi master plan was well underway by that stage and he couldn't just leave that behind.

Besides, everyone would laugh at him; the people from the

photography world would find him curious for a while maybe, but they wouldn't let him in; everyone in his world would either take the piss or scream at him. Or probably both. And, at the end of all that, he'd end up scratching a living taking portraits of grumpy kids or bloody wedding photos.

The conclusion had always been the same – stick to the plan, be who you were brought up to be, and keep the rest of it to yourself.

But the master plan had gone pear shaped and the memories and regrets were still worrying away at the edges of his mind as he made his way out of the exhibition.

What had it all been for, after all? Where had his great plan led him? His grandchildren were little angels, but neither of his daughters were speaking to him. That cut him to the bone, although he knew why and couldn't really blame them. The strange thing was that, despite everything that had happened, he and Julie had reached a point where they muddled along all right together. But apart from that, what was there? A fold up chair and a purple fleece? It wasn't much of a life.

The photography exhibition was an underground maze, dimly lit aisles and dark cloth everywhere, except for the bright, back-lit images on every wall. The high point was the overall prize winner, blown up to poster size and set alone in a small alcove.

He knew what it was – a picture of an orangutan climbing a vine, but he made a point of not looking; he was saving that for last. The blonde-haired woman standing in front of it snatched at the edge of his vision like a burr or a teasel on the sleeve of a jumper, but he walked on past. He was going to be late.

He wasn't shocked to discover that the dinosaur hall hadn't changed much while he was away. Will was still at his post and he waved as Jim paced hurriedly back to his chair and picked up his fleece.

The half-caught image of the blonde woman in front of the picture wasn't going away. He'd only caught a brief glimpse in profile, but there was something about her.

No. It couldn't be. That would be impossible.

Hassan

Mona was Egyptian. She was smart, funny, and she actually looked like Elizabeth Taylor playing Cleopatra.

She was also very posh. Despite having never lived outside Egypt, Mona spoke English perfectly with the same lazy, dismissive drawl used by all the wealthy Arabs, Indians and Pakistanis who floated around Oxford in their designer clothing and rowing blazers. She also spoke French, German and, of course, Arabic. Hassan suspected she was equally relaxed in each of them.

It was a funny thing. Because Mona was so far out of his league, their differences didn't seem to matter. They could get along perfectly well without discussing the realities of their backgrounds and their families. Oxford was their world; a hermetically sealed microcosm where they were just two young biochemists; in their little bubble, the fact that Mona's handbag was probably worth more than his dad's car didn't have to be a problem.

University was supposed to be the place where you made friendships for life; where you learnt how to think, to argue and to grow; where your true self emerged, slowly at first, but then all in a rush, like blue-green bacteria colonising a Petri dish. University was supposed to set you up with a network for life and, if you were at Oxford or Cambridge, it was supposed to set you up for life at the top of the tree.

It wasn't like that for Hassan. Not at all.

He met Mona on his third day at Oxford. The biochemists had their first practical session in the lab and, as with every classroom he'd ever been in, Hassan had found the quietest corner of the brightly lit room, insulated from his peers by an empty workstation. The lab was nothing like they'd had at school, more like the pictures he'd seen of top research laboratories than the grimy wooden-benches, tired equipment and stark tube lighting he was used to.

The lecturer had talked them through the instructions and the room faded into silence as each white-coated student nervously measured liquids and triple-checked their notes. Whatever their backgrounds – public school or Bradford comprehensive – Oxford was a different world and the wrinkled brows, squinting eyes and trembling hands were evidence that they all knew it.

Over half an hour into the three-hour lab session, a new girl swept into the room, long black hair pulled back into a pony tail and buttoning her lab coat as she entered. Hassan watched the lecturer pointedly look at his watch and waited for the roasting which was surely coming.

It never did. The girl leant towards the lecturer and smiled, probably mumbling words of apology. Whatever she said, it worked like magic; the lecturer mirrored her smile, tucked his about-to-be-wagging finger behind his back, and pointed towards Hassan's corner.

It isn't easy to make a straight white lab coat sexy. Not easy, but the girl walking towards him managed it without trying and without seeming to be even slightly aware of the impact she was having – even though every eye in the room was locked onto this outrageously late, outrageously confident, outrageously beautiful apparition.

Hassan watched as she approached, realising much too late that he was staring too hard. He snapped his sagging jaw closed, looked down at the bench in front of him and mumbled into the lapel of his coat.

'Hi there,' he said. 'Y'alright?'

The long manicured fingers thrust out in front of his eyes obliged him to look up. He raised his head and took the proffered hand, trying not to stare at the lovely girl.

'Hi. I'm Mona,' she said, arching one eyebrow.

After a few seconds Hassan wondered if he'd been holding her soft warm hand for too long and released her. The girl, Mona, continued to look at him, now with both eyebrows raised and an amused smile lifting the corners of her mouth.

'... And you are?' she said, eventually.

'Oh ... Sorry ... Yes ... I'm Hassan.' Why was he such a clumsy idiot?

'Pleased to meet you, Hassan.' She tucked her expensive-looking leather shoulder bag under the bench and sat down. 'It looks like we're going to be lab partners. I hope you're very smart.'

It was fortunate Hassan turned out to be smart even by Oxford standards as he quickly learned that the relationship with his new lab partner was going to be far from equal and balanced.

As far as he could tell, Mona was bright and naturally academic, but her life was complicated in ways that Hassan's simply wasn't. She had to balance her studies with a full calendar of social engagements; hairdresser's appointments, shopping trips to London, family parties, cocktail-induced lie-ins. There simply weren't enough hours in the day and she needed someone – someone like Hassan – to help her to fill in the gaps.

He didn't mind at all. He was happy to write more than his share of their lab notes, prepare lecture summaries for her on the days she wasn't available ... even tell lies for her on occasion. He'd fallen in love when their fingers touched and he heard her rich, sultry voice speaking her name for the first time. From that moment on he'd been hers, body and soul.

That was all in a different life. Memories weren't harmful as such, although dragging up what might have been, achieved less than nothing.

The white cotton vest stretched out on the changing table in front of him like a flag of surrender as Hassan stripped to the waist and washed himself in the small basin. He wasn't usually a smelly man, but it had been a stressful morning and he struggled to banish the pungent stink of nervousness.

He was dreaming, but awake, slowly moving through a practised sequence of actions, his fingers steady and precise, aware of every movement, each muscle and tendon in perfect control. The human body was a marvellous creation. Unimaginably complex and beautiful, but fragile as a blown eggshell.

He had brought a clean, dry T-shirt which he put on once he'd dried off as well as he could manage. As he reached for the vest, he was jolted out of his trance by a loud banging on the door.

'You going to be in there all day?' said the voice. 'I really need the loo.'

'Give me a couple of minutes,' he said. '... Sorry.'

'OK. Just don't be long.'

Any remnants of peace and self-awareness evaporated in the shock of the interruption and Hassan's hands were shaking as he grabbed the vest and threw it on roughly, only just remembering to take care to strap it smoothly around him.

His hoodie was three sizes too large and fitted loosely over the top. He looked in the mirror, turning from side to side and craning his neck. It looked fine. He breathed in and out slowly. Five times.

It was time for the terrifying bit; he took the two wires from the vest and fed them from the inside through the hole in his hoodie pocket. He then took the detonator battery unit from its box, noting the US army safety warnings stamped on every side. How could the Americans have been so stupid as to leave that sort of technology lying around?

It was a sealed unit about the size of a cigarette packet which also functioned as the trigger and he remembered to flick the switch back and forth a few times to make sure it was disabled before clicking the safety cover back into place. Even then, he stopped breathing as he pushed the two wires into their sockets. The LED glowed red, staring at him like a one-eyed devil, but there was no terrible, humiliating, accidental explosion.

Hassan double-checked that the connections were firm before slipping the whole thing back into his pocket and straightening his jacket. Facing him in the grubby mirror was an ordinary young Asian man, a little overweight, badly dressed and scowling like he'd just lost a month's salary on the horses. Not someone who'd stand out in a crowd.

There was more banging on the door.

'Just coming,' he shouted.

'Thank God,' said the panicky voice on the other side.

Hassan stuffed the rest of his clothing into his bag, quickly made sure he hadn't forgotten anything, and opened the door.

The waiting man pushed past him with a muttered 'thanks' and slammed the door shut. He was in one of those sporty wheelchairs like they used at the Paralympics and couldn't have been more than mid-twenties. He had what looked like a military haircut and Hassan wondered if he was an ex-soldier, maybe injured in Afghanistan. It would fit.

A part of Hassan felt sorry for the men sent out there; he understood that the big decisions were taken elsewhere and the individual soldiers were just pawns. But they still had choices. It was still them who pulled the triggers, who fired the mortars, who called in the air strikes. What did they expect? Gratitude? What right did they have to go meddling in another people's lives, thousands of miles from home and in a different world?

Hassan was from Bradford and life there was what he understood. The world had seen enough interfering, especially from those countries where the damp, sweaty underarms of colonial guilt were still moist. It was time for governments to focus on looking after their own houses and leave others alone. That was a fight worth dying for.

As he walked out of the cafe and towards the main park gates, Hassan tried to imagine fighting to defend Bradford, but the idea was too absurd and he gave up. He stopped at the cafe entrance and looked around carefully before flipping open the lid of a big green wheelie bin and dropping his holdall inside.

Shuna

'So, Zoe,' said Shuna. 'Tell me about Spike then. How old is he? Where does he go to school?'

They were standing in the blissfully short security queue at the Natural History Museum and Zoe had nowhere to hide.

'Do we have to do this, Mum?' said Zoe. 'He's just a boy I know.'

'Yes, we do,' said Shuna. 'You're not even fourteen yet. We going to need to do this for a while longer, I'm afraid.'

'OK. Whatever.' Zoe knew she was going to lose this battle, but they'd be through security in a couple of minutes and then she'd have some space to wriggle free of interrogations. 'Look, he's

115

sixteen, OK? It's no big deal. He goes to the Lycee.'

'Sixteen,' said Shuna. 'That's pushing it, isn't it? What's he doing hanging around with your lot?'

'He's Marie's brother. I met him at her party. Happy now?'

'Not really. I'm not comfortable with this at all. He's a lot older than you.'

'It's fine, Mum. Really. There'll be loads of us. We're just going to meet at half three, play some softball and hang out. You have to trust me a little.'

'Three thirty? I thought you said four.'

'It's changed, OK?' said Zoe walking past the security guard. 'Honestly, you can be a real fascist sometimes.'

Anna had been quietly watching her mother and sister sparring but it had become predictable and boring. She was impatient to see the wildlife photography exhibition, which was why they had come.

'Come on,' she said, tugging at Shuna's sleeve. 'We've only got half an hour before we're meeting Dad.'

Shuna breathed a deep sigh and allowed herself to be dragged along. 'I'm coming,' she said. 'Don't worry. We've got plenty of time.'

It was only a group of friends meeting in Hyde Park. In the middle of the afternoon. What could be more innocent?

They had seen the exhibition of the previous year's winners and Shuna and Anna had been looking forward to coming for months. Zoe had enjoyed it last time, but her interests had moved on and she was clearly only killing time before her date.

The pictures would be amazing, that was certain. Anna loved the underwater shots, but for Shuna, it was about a glimpse of home. Jungles and open plains, soaring trees surrounding emerald lakes, nature red in tooth and claw, the colours and light of Africa. She had never met a South African who didn't feel the same way. It was simply the way it was.

After Simon's marriage proposal – joyfully accepted – they'd had two more glorious champagne-filled days with her father in Knysna before setting off for Stellenbosch.

For reasons known only to herself, Shuna's mother had insisted that they return their hire car to the airport; she would send a driver to pick them up and bring them to the estate. As the three of them sat on the balcony after a final dinner, Simon was looking at the drive times on his phone.

'We should do it in five hours,' he said. 'But it's crazy that we're dropping the car off first. We'd be quicker going straight there and it would be much less hassle. Why don't we tell your mum that's what we're doing?'

Shuna's father shrugged his shoulders and smiled and Shuna felt her fears and forebodings rolling back in like the sea mist. The coming days were going to be tough.

South Africa had been hard for Simon, even in Knysna. For most of the time, he was the only black person in the room who wasn't staff and, even when there were a few middle-class black couples in the same restaurant, none of them were mixed.

He'd accepted the situation with his usual grace and good humour, but Shuna could see that it was getting to him. Two weeks was definitely long enough.

'Darling,' said Shuna. 'God knows why Mummy has decided that's what she wants, but it's not worth arguing with her. My guess is that, if the prodigal daughter is going to turn up at Kleinbosch with a fiancee of the wrong colour, at least she won't be arriving in a crappy rental car.'

'Oh Christ,' said Simon. 'This is going to be hell, isn't it?'

Shuna and her father both sat silently, looking at him, until Shuna's father snorted with laughter and raised his glass in a mock toast.

'Still, look on the bright side. She doesn't know you're engaged yet. I'd love to be there when you tell her that.'

It was a five hour drive back to the airport. Shuna drove the first half as far as Swellendam, where they stopped for a pizza and to stretch their legs. Neither of them had much to say. After lunch,

Simon drove and Shuna slipped into a fitful, restless sleep.

She didn't wake until they were almost at the airport.

'Hiya,' she said. 'You still awake?'

'It goes on for ever,' he replied.

'What?' Shuna was still half asleep.

'This bloody pit of a shanty town. We've been driving through it for miles. It makes Kingston look civilised.'

'Mmmnh. Crossroads,' said Shuna. 'One of apartheid's proudest legacies. The whole East side of Cape Town is pretty much the same, I'm afraid.'

Simon didn't reply and Shuna could feel the tension shimmering in the afternoon heat.

Shuna wasn't surprised to see the same old Mercedes waiting for them, paintwork and trim in perfect, shining condition as though it had left the factory that morning rather than decades earlier.

'Nice to see you, Miss Shuna,' said the driver from under the shadow of his extravagantly peaked cap. 'Welcome home.'

Shuna took half a step backwards. 'Joseph? Joseph, is that you?'

'Yes, Miss.' The driver looked up at her, flashing a broad, wrinkled smile. 'So, who else would it be?'

'It's so wonderful to see you.' Shuna reached for Simon's hand and pulled him close. 'This is Simon.' She turned to Simon. 'Joseph has been at Kleinbosch since before I was born. He always took care of me when I was small.'

'Very pleased to meet you, Joseph,' said Simon, reaching out his hand.

'And you too, Mr Simon,' said Joseph, shaking Simon's hand firmly. 'We're all very excited to have you here.'

As the Mercedes glided past the huge, stone gateposts, the driveway stretched through immaculate vineyards and up the gentle slope of the hill. Perfect white roses dotted the end of each row, but there were no buildings in sight.

'Is this all part of the estate?' said Simon, struggling not to be impressed.

'I said it was big,' said Shuna, smiling.

'Yes, but not this big,' said Simon.

'Two thousand, four hundred and thirty-six hectares,' said Joseph, as the car reached the top of the hill and the house, gardens and lake unfolded below.

Shuna would always remember that moment. After ten years away she'd forgotten how beautiful Kleinbosch really was.

'I was wondering if we might have the wedding here?' Shuna had found her mother on the front lawn, pruning her already-immaculate rose bushes. It was already the second day and, despite an excess of polite formality, things were going better than Shuna had expected. Even the announcement that she and Simon were engaged hadn't provoked the expected reaction.

Shuna's mother didn't turn away from her roses, but Shuna could see her back and shoulders stiffen. She'd known this would be a bad idea, but Simon had been insistent; he'd fallen in love with the place. The pruning shears carried on, moving almost by themselves and with practiced ease while the dead heads dropped to the ground soundlessly.

At last, Shuna's mother turned and looked at her. 'Do you know how long our family has lived here?' she said.

'Of course I do, Mum. That's a stupid, rhetorical question.'

'It may not be such a big deal in England, but traditions and family count here. That's what has held us together through good times and bad.'

'I get that, but I still don't see your point.'

'The idea of a family holding an estate like this in stewardship through the generations is important. Especially these days.'

'I know you believe that. I'm not quite as convinced, but I understand,' said Shuna. 'And what do you mean by "especially these days"?'

'I know we don't see eye-to-eye on these matters, but surely you can see that the country is falling apart? And what can anyone expect with a string of self-declared terrorists running the show?'

Shuna took a deep breath. 'I'm not going to dignify that with a response, Mum,' she said, suddenly wanting to be far, far away. 'I was only asking if we could have the wedding here.'

'... And I was trying to explain how much it saddens me that I will be the last of our line to look after Kleinbosch.'

Shuna could feel the old frustrations reach critical mass as she listened to her mother's self-aggrandising bigotry. 'Isn't that up to you? I'm sorry that you don't have a son to carry on the line, but it's not my fault I'm female.'

Her mother's eyes flared wide. 'Do you think I care about not having a son? My parents lost both of my brothers in the war, but it didn't matter. I was there, and I've taken care of Kleinbosch as well as any man.' A lone airplane flew low overhead, and she took a long breath. 'I always thought I would have you, but you had other ideas.'

'But we haven't talked about this, Mum. I never said that I was leaving for good. I know it's been years, but I've enjoyed my time away and there's nothing wrong with seeing the world.'

'Of course there isn't, and I've never expected you to come home twice a year. It's just that everything's changed now.'

'What do you mean changed?' said Shuna. 'The government and the economy will sort themselves out. Zuma can't last for ever.'

'I don't really care about the government. We've dealt with worse and we'll deal with this one.' She paused and looked at Shuna with something almost approaching affection. 'Do I really need to spell it out, darling?'

Shuna had been away too long and had allowed herself to believe that things had moved on. 'Spell what out?' she said. 'If you've got something to say, just say it.'

'All right,' said her mother, dropping the shears and taking Shuna's shoulders in her hands. 'Let's speak plainly. You're a grown woman and you make your own choices, and so do I. Simon seems nice enough, but he's black. I'm sorry darling, but no-one – living or dead – would forgive me if I allowed a kaffir to be master of Kleinbosch. Surely you can see that?'

Shuna could still remember the white hot flash of anger which actually blinded her for a couple of seconds. How could she have been so stupid? She'd known deep inside that her mother would never change, but it had been so much easier to believe that she might. Too angry even to scream and shout, she twisted out of her mother's grasp and ran down to the edge of the lake.

Simon found her two hours later, still sitting on the damp grass looking at the ducks and listening to the wind rustling the leaves of the gum trees.

'I've been looking for you all over,' he said. 'I spent a couple of hours working in the winery. It's amazing.'

'We need to leave,' said Shuna, 'Now.'

Simon knelt in front of her. 'What's wrong, darling,' he said. 'What happened?'

'I really don't want to talk about it. It's just me and my mum. I can't stand it.'

'But she seems really nice,' said Simon. 'I don't understand.'

'You don't need to understand. This is my problem. You just need to help me pack and get us a taxi. We'll find a hotel in Cape Town.' She stood up, pulling Simon with her. 'Please.'

And that had been that. They were in a taxi less than an hour later and Shuna had never been back to South Africa.

She hadn't even gone to her father's funeral a year later; her mother had insisted that he be buried in the family cemetery at Kleinbosch even though Shuna had told her repeatedly that he wanted his ashes scattered from the East Head at Knysna. Words had been spoken, words that couldn't be unspoken and Shuna had cancelled her flight.

She would never forgive herself – or her mother – for that.

Dan

The last Vicodin was taking its time and Dan's breath was coming in short, tight gasps through clenched teeth. It was supposed to be fast acting, for Christ's sake.

After a few minutes, he felt the pain ease back like a resentful tiger cowed by cracks of the tamer's whip; it would return, but each time it slunk back into its cage, he was a little more grateful – and a little more fearful of the next time.

Rachel wouldn't be long – she was the most reliable person he'd ever met – and Dan sighed gently as he sank back against the smooth mahogany. He felt his breathing returning to normal and his eyelids sagged lazily as he enjoyed the sensation. For a few moments he was able to forget what was growing inside him.

His head sank forward and the in-out, in-out of his gentle snoring was as soft as the memories of the sea inside a beachcombed shell.

Dan could feel the Texas sun beating down as he stood like an island in the sea of people. The noise was overwhelming; the organisers had loudhailers, the police had loudhailers and the voice of the mob was louder than either.

The girl had disappeared, and the crowd was surging back and forth against the police lines with increasing anxiety. Dan came to his senses and pushed his way through the tangle of bodies into the main building; he must have then found his way to the library on autopilot.

He couldn't free his thoughts from the moment when she'd handed him the leaflet; it was replaying itself over and over and over in an almost-hysterical mental loop. Had their fingers actually touched? He thought so. Had she felt the jolt of energy surge through her as well? He hoped so. Was he just behaving like an overworked fool? Probably.

He spread the crumpled sheets of paper out on the table in front of him. They were trying to promote the big march on Washington that everyone seemed to be talking about. The arguments were well-written and self-evident and Dan found himself stuck on one section

WHY WE MARCH

We march to address old grievances and to help resolve an American crisis.

*That crisis is born of the twin evils of racism and economic
deprivation. They rob all people, Negro and White, of dignity,
self respect and freedom. They impose a special burden on the
Negro who is denied the right to vote, economically exploited,
refused access to public accommodations, subjected to inferior
education and relegated to substandard ghetto housing.*

*Discrimination in education and apprenticeship training
renders Negros, Puerto Ricans, Mexicans and other minorities
helpless in our mechanized, industrial society.*

It was so obvious. How could this country, supposedly a beacon of
light to the world, still be treating so many of its citizens with less
respect than had been shown to nineteenth century Russian serfs?

There was a blue stamp on the back cover:

*UT Organising Committee meeting - Tuesday 2nd June, 7:00
p.m. at the Riverbend Church. Come and register your support.*

Dan had gone to the meeting of course.

He convinced himself that he went to show solidarity, but it was
all about the girl. During the days after the demo, he'd not stopped
thinking about her. He couldn't sleep more than an hour or two in
the night; all food tasted dry and barren in his mouth and burned
acid in his stomach and a constant "she loves me, she loves me not"
pendulum swing threw him back and forth between joy and despair
hundreds of times a day. As always, Dostoevsky had it right – *To love
is to suffer and there can be no love otherwise'.*

At first he'd been terrified she wouldn't be there. He would
probably have been beaten to a pulp if he'd walked up to one of
those passionate, inflamed activists and said 'Do you remember a
girl from the demonstration last week. Mexican-looking, black hair,
brown eyes …? She was handing out leaflets.'

But, if she hadn't walked through that door at a quarter past
seven, he would have walked up to every last one of them and damn

the consequences.

Dan hadn't been able to talk to her straight away as the meeting had already started. Four or five African Americans, or Blacks as they were still known back then, had stood up in turn and described their lives. The purpose wasn't to pick out extreme examples – no stories of rapes or Klan lynchings – but rather the struggles and indignities of ordinary daily life.

As he sat there, Dan realised how easily he'd turned a blind eye to the reality around him, hiding behind his smug Canadian liberalness. For half an hour, he almost forgot why he was there as he let the simple, eloquent truths flow through him.

Almost forgot, but not quite. He thought he saw her look at him once or twice, but it may have been wishful thinking.

She was sitting behind a long trestle table, along with two others, taking down the names and contact details of everyone who wanted to march on Washington in August. As Dan took his turn and scribbled his name with hesitant fingers, he looked up. She was more beautiful than he'd imagined; his memory had served him poorly.

When he'd finished writing, he held out his hand. 'I'm Dan,' he said, leaning against the table for balance as the adrenalin coursed through his veins.

'Rosa,' she said, looking him in the face with no hint of shyness. 'Pleased to meet you, Dan.'

'Could I …? Could I … speak to you afterwards,' he said. He could hear his voice was trembling even more than it had when he'd invited Angela Babinski to the High School Prom.

'Sure,' she said. 'I'll be half an hour or so.'

Nadia
Nadia had made an effort that morning – smart trousers, sky-blue silk blouse and a half-length jacket from Hobbs. By her usual work standards, she was dressed up, although after six months wearing nothing but shalwar kameez and dupatta, anything normal was an improvement.

Her usual standards were clearly not up to South Kensington

expectations and, as she walked into the restaurant, she felt as though every eye was on her – she was slim, fit and pretty enough but, as she looked around the room, there was no doubt that she was coming up short. As for Ed, with his floppy, badly cut hair and crumpled jacket, the two of them might as well have been wearing flashing lights on their heads.

She'd forgotten what it was like. Her civil servant's salary was just enough to cover a small flat in Balham, but once upon a time South Ken had been home. Nadia had spent her teenage years living with her aunt in Onslow Mews and, for seven years she'd studied at the French Lycee just up the road from Muriel's Kitchen.

Leila – calling her Auntie Leila was strictly forbidden – was her mother's younger sister although it was difficult to imagine they came from the same family. Nadia's mother hadn't been a strict traditionalist – she'd married a Catholic Frenchman after all – but no-one would ever have accused her of being a rebel either; she'd been modest and sensible, well-educated without showing it, conservative with a small "c", full of fun without needing to be the life and soul of the party and devout without making it a big deal.

Leila couldn't have been more different. She was much too young to be a true child of the '60s, but that didn't stop her trying to be. Her frizzy hair hadn't seen a headscarf since the day she left Lebanon and she wore her intellectual feminist credentials proudly on her sleeve. She smoked weed in front of teenage Nadia, probably took cocaine when her niece wasn't around and seemed to believe that the best way to get even with the patriarchy was to party harder and sleep around more than most men.

As for her faith, it seemed to Nadia that Leila was only really Moslem when it suited her. Religion for her was like an umbrella or one of the Burberry trench coats she loved so much. When the sun was shining, it would sit alone at the back of the cupboard, but when it rained …

Strip away all the over-intellectualised bullshit and Leila was, even at forty, not much more than a selfish child who loved to party. A million miles from the mother figure Nadia had missed and needed. That had been clearer than ever the last time they'd seen each other face-to-face.

Leila had flounced into Nadia's bedroom while she was knee deep in history revision.

'Nadia?' she'd said. 'Nadia, darling?'

Nadia had looked up and seen the make-up and excited eyes. Leila was off partying again by the looks of her ... And then Nadia saw the two big bags in the hall behind her.

'What's going on, Leila?' she'd said, smelling the tension fill the room like ozone after a lightning storm. 'What's with the suitcases?'

'Well, sweetie. The thing is ... the thing is ... I know you've got your A-levels coming up, but I've been offered this amazing job with Vogue in New York ...'

And then, as Nadia sat stunned silent in her chair, it all came out. Leila had a car waiting for her outside and was leaving immediately. The flat was paid for until the summer and Leila had transferred five hundred pounds to Nadia's bank account. After that, she would come into a small inheritance on her eighteenth birthday and would be, quite literally, on her own.

'But you can't just leave,' Nadia had said as reality started to bite. 'Who's going to look after me? You promised Mama that if anything happened to her ...'

'... And I have looked after you,' said Leila. 'For seven years. I've done my best, but you're almost grown up now and I need to get back to my own life.'

'You can't,' sobbed Nadia. 'It's not right. It's not fair.'

Leila had walked over to her, taken her face in both hands and smiled. 'You're so much like your mother,' she'd said. 'Always looking for justice and honour.' She'd dropped her arms to her sides and stepped backwards. 'You need to learn that life isn't fair. People are bastards and you have to step up and take what you want or you'll always be screwed over.'

And with that, she'd walked out and left Nadia alone in the flat, six weeks before her A-levels.

Nadia tried not to think about that time. A part of her had wanted to break the world with her anger – to drink, to sleep with every boy in her class, to trash the beautiful flat, to forget about her

A-levels and university. To show Leila the consequences of being a stupendously selfish bitch.

Unfortunately – or fortunately – Leila had been right. Nadia was her mother's daughter and, in spite of the loneliness and pain, she'd done none of those things. She'd studied hard and had won her place at Oxford as planned.

But, as she packed her bags and locked up the flat for the last time, she'd made herself a promise. She would leave that self-absorbed privileged world behind her, start a new life and never look back.

Nothing about South Kensington had changed while she'd been away; even though Muriel's Kitchen hadn't existed back then, the local clientele was the same. It wouldn't have surprised her to find out she'd been at school with half of these women.

They hadn't changed, but Nadia had. It wasn't much more than ten years since she'd left, but Nadia looked around and struggled to believe that the younger version of herself had ever really existed. What would she have thought of Nadia today? A different person leading a different life.

The middle-aged woman at the counter looked as though she might be the eponymous Muriel. She smiled at Nadia. 'Can I help you?'

'Yes. I hope so,' said Nadia. 'I'm from the police.' She held out an ID card. 'I'm in a bit of a hurry, I'm afraid. We're looking for someone. This man.' She showed the woman her phone with an image of Snowflake enhanced and blown up from the CCTV footage. 'We believe he was in here earlier.'

'Yes,' said the woman. 'I'm pretty sure he was here. Sally served him. Let me get her for you.' She beckoned to a slim attractive girl who was clearing tables. 'I'll leave you to it,' she said, as the girl put down her tray and walked over.

'Hello Sally,' said Nadia. 'Sorry to disturb you. I understand you served this man earlier today?'

The girl looked at the image on Nadia's phone. 'Yes,' she said. 'He left ten minutes or so ago. Is he in trouble?'

'No. No,' said Nadia. 'We just want to find him. Did he say where he was going?'

'I'm afraid not,' said the girl. She looked down at the floor. 'I actually agreed to meet him here after work. We're both from Bradford, see.'

'Don't worry. I'm not going to tell your boss,' said Nadia, laughing. 'What time are you meeting?'

'Three o'clock. When I get off my shift.'

'Right. Well, thanks very much for your help. I'll let you get back,' said Nadia. She handed the girl a business card. 'If you remember anything else, please call this number.'

She was turning to leave when she felt a tap on her shoulder. 'He forgot his bag,' said the girl.

'Do you still have it?' said Nadia.

'Sorry,' said the girl. 'I chased after him and gave it back.'

Nadia felt the moment's rush of excitement and hope evaporate. That would have been too lucky.

'Which way was he going?' she asked.

'Up towards the park,' said the girl. 'The bag was bloody heavy, though. He said it was full of presents for his nephews.'

Nadia smiled. 'Thank you. Thank you very much,' she said before grabbing Ed by the arm and steering him out of the door.

'Police?' said Ed, as soon as they were outside. 'What's that all about?'

'I'm not going to say I'm a bloody spy, am I?' said Nadia. 'Get with the programme. I'm not happy about that heavy bag, though. It's not looking good. I need to post an update.'

Nadia and Ed stood on the busy street outside Muriel's and she felt a moment of panic. Something was definitely happening – there were face matches and reports coming in from all directions, many of them clearly false alarms, but enough of a concentration to be sure he was in the region and on the move. They were also getting reports of increased chatter on ISIS-related websites which couldn't be ignored.

They needed to do something, but she didn't have enough

information to act on and she couldn't see a pattern from the reports.

Nadia looked at Ed and shrugged her shoulders. 'The girl said he was going towards the park, but I don't know how much that means,' she said. 'What do you think?'

'We're close,' he said. 'Assuming Snowflake stays on foot, we might as well do the same. Go up towards the park and wait for more intel?'

'Agree,' she said. 'We'll leave the car here in case we need it later.' She signalled to the driver to wait, and they started to walk up Exhibition Road.

Ed pointed at the scrappy courtyard in front of the Natural History Museum. 'They do skating there in the winter, don't they?'

'Yup,' said Nadia. 'Been doing it for a few years now.'

'Ever been?'

'Just the once,' she said. 'I went last year.' An evening Nadia would never forget. The images flooded her mind in an unstoppable wave; once-treasured memories now pressing themselves upon her like strangers at a funeral. The night had been perfect in every way – renting the badly fitting, smelly skates; James falling over within ten seconds; James sitting on the ice, giggling like a schoolgirl; overpriced drinks at the cocktail bar on top of Harvey Nick's; a dinner they couldn't afford in a place they'd never remember; and all the while they'd both known how the evening was going to end up.

Nadia was certain it had been equally special for both of them, and the relationship had stayed great for the months which followed. She was too scientifically minded to believe in the idea of there only being one perfect match for everyone, but was also old enough to understand that there weren't so many either – and they weren't easy to find. With James, she'd made up her mind that he was the one and had already asked David to authorise her having "the conversation" about her job as soon as she was finished with Birmingham.

She would have explained … and he would have understood. If only the soft impatient idiot hadn't decided to make the great romantic gesture and screw it all up. Maybe she should get the authorisation anyway and see if she could change James's mind? When she had a chance to think properly, she'd consider it, but she was sure it would be too little, too late.

'Tell me more about Unicorn,' she said to Ed, striding forward towards the park.

'I can tell you what I know,' he said, 'but the man's surrounded by so much mystique it's difficult to separate the hype from reality.'

Nadia nodded, happy to be putting distance between her and her memories.

'He joined the Afghan Mujahideen in 1983 when he couldn't have been much older than sixteen or seventeen. We suspect his family were all killed during the Israeli invasion of Lebanon in 1982, although what happened in Sidon was fairly messy and records are poor.'

'That would explain a few things,' said Nadia.

'Yup,' said Ed. 'His brand of fanatical drive has to come from somewhere.' He stopped while Nadia checked her phone. 'Anyway, his name has been popping up again and again over the years. Always in the background, never quite visible, but associated with some of the most successful terrorist operations of the past twenty-five years.'

'Well. Let's see if we can end his lucky streak,' said Nadia. 'Snowflake has just been picked up on CCTV going into the park. Alexandra Gate. It's right up here. We must be close.'

11:36

Jim

It couldn't have been her. Jim shook his head from side to side as he picked up the silver-grey thermos and settled back into his chair. He watched the tea swirl into the cup and took a big slurp. It was turning out to be a weird day. There was something in the air.

He managed to bring his distracted thoughts back to the image of the parakeet. He would normally pass the time until lunch mulling over the image he'd been studying and wasn't going to let that bloody woman take that small pleasure away from him.

There was nothing particularly technical in the shot; it was good because the animal actors were performing perfectly for the camera, right at that moment. Did that make it a matter of luck – leaving aside the fact that the guy had spent two days halfway up a tree – just waiting for the right moment? This was an ongoing debate among wildlife photographers – should you take shot after shot and hope for one to come good or should you wait, finger poised over shutter, until the perfect moment and risk being just a little too slow, a microsecond too late.

He and Alastair had argued about that a lot in Belize. Alastair had been firmly in the second camp. Apart from anything else, in the days before digital SLRs, you had to consider the cost of film, the limited shots in a roll, and the time and expense involved in developing. All of these factors argued against trigger-happy shutter fingers.

They were young men, and it was no great surprise that the arguments had turned competitive. The two of them had been out in a canoe early one morning a couple of months after Jim had begun to take photography seriously. A three-toed sloth was hanging on a branch by the river, her newborn baby draped over her shoulder. Once they were as close as they dared go, they waited, cameras at the ready, for her to move around and face them.

'One shot,' said Alastair. 'You take the whole film and I'll just take one.'

'Well, it's not as though the subject's moving too quickly, is it?' said Jim, laughing quietly.

'Still,' said Alastair. 'Thirty-six against one. The best shot wins. A tenner?'

'You're on,' said Jim, never one to turn down a flutter.

They'd left after an hour – it was important to at least try to give the impression of doing some work to justify their existence. Jim had finished his film and was confident he had some great shots.

Despite that, he'd felt a sense of inevitability when Alastair had brought out the developed prints a couple of days later. Jim did have some great shots, but then Alastair turned over his own photo.

'See!' Alastair said, a huge grin spreading slowly across his face.

Jim remembered smiling himself and reaching for his wallet.

As he drained the last few drops of tea from his cup, Jim tried to remember when he'd last picked up a camera. It was probably over a year but, since he'd started at the museum, it was always too late by the time he got home and he couldn't find the energy to get up for the dawn.

Once the Belize dream was over, he hadn't thought he'd ever take another picture. Photography was hardly an option back in regular squaddie life and he filed it away in the mental "not to be" folder. He didn't believe in regrets. He made his own decisions, and he understood that photography would cost him more in grief and humiliation than it was worth.

It was over twenty years before things changed. He'd been driving the cab for a few years by then and had got into the routine of spending his mornings cruising around Holborn. Depending on the weather, he might drive up and down Old Holborn ten or twenty times before he picked up a fare. There was a big Jessop's camera shop about halfway along on the north side and he found himself checking it out each time he passed, sometimes from the cab but, more often than not, he'd pull over, get out and have a proper look.

The first decent digital SLRs were just on the market and there was always something on offer, but the reasons why it wasn't worth doing were still the same. As soon as anyone found out about Jim's hobby, he'd have to deal with a continuous stream of piss-taking which would never stop. He couldn't face that.

Being a cabbie was different from being in the Army. It was a one-of-a-kind job and there were blokes with all sorts of strange hobbies, but it still wasn't exactly a world where you would strike up a conversation about beauty and colour over a bacon sarnie. In any case, his old friends and his wife hadn't changed at all.

One particular day, he was looking through the window at a particularly interesting package offer. The wheels had just fallen off the dotcom juggernaut and London was full of dazed investors and bankers who hadn't got their money out in time. There were deals and offers in every shop and this was a 50% discount on a package of body and lenses which had been state-of-the-art only months earlier.

As Jim went through the arguments in his head for the hundredth time, he suddenly woke up. Why did anyone need to know? He didn't need a darkroom with digital. There was no need for boxes of prints, he could keep the equipment in the cab and, if he started a bit earlier in the mornings, he could sneak off for a few hours when business was quiet.

The plan had worked perfectly until that bloody South African bitch had come into his life.

After the incident at the airport, Jim had struggled to get her out of his mind. It wasn't as though a bit of a shouting match worried him. He'd always been up for a barney; it got the juices flowing. No – there was something about that bloody woman which had got under his skin and he couldn't figure it out.

Her complaint hadn't been necessary and the whole episode was blown out of all proportion. Everyone tried to avoid the airport hotel rides if they could. It was a wasted hour for a ten quid fare and, if you got stuck in traffic and didn't make it back in time ...

That night he was at the end of a long shift, he was tired and all he wanted was an American businessman in a suit. Full fare into central London and a ten quid tip. On a rainy Tuesday evening at Heathrow, that wasn't too much to ask for.

Instead he'd been lumbered with a tired, grouchy family with huge suitcases only going as far as an airport hotel. Who wouldn't have tried to wriggle out of that one?

He was angry with her – his fists clenched reflexively every time he thought about it – but there was more. Layered on top of the anger were other feelings and emotions which had no place being there. There was something about her that wouldn't leave him alone.

Shuna. Shuna was her name, as he'd found out later. With her silky South African accent and long blonde hair, she was a lioness protecting her family. Much as he hated her, he couldn't help remembering how magnificent she'd looked.

When he first heard that she'd reported him and that there would be a hearing, his outrage had been mixed with a sense of inevitability. They were always going to meet again. He didn't know how he could know that, but the certainty had burned inside him with a white hot flame. Their story wasn't over.

By the time of the tribunal – almost six months later – Jim's life had slipped back into its normal routine. Long shifts, family time, Friday nights with the lads and, whenever he could, hours spent out on the Rainham Marshes, alone with his camera. He still thought about Shuna from time to time, but couldn't remember how she'd got herself stuck so persistently in his mind.

She shouldn't have reported him, but it wasn't as though anything was going to come of it; the worst outcome was that he'd get a proper rap on the knuckles and maybe a hundred quid fine. And, as the money would go to the kiddie's charity anyway, it wasn't much of a threat.

The hearing had been in a small basement office off Fenchurch Street, seven of them crammed into a space not much bigger than Jim's kitchen. The rancid smell of damp paint filled the room, but it was bearable. Even if they'd managed to unjam the dirty sash windows, it wouldn't have been long before the diesel fumes rolling down off the street would have made things much worse. Still, looking on the bright side, back in the day, at least four or five of them would have been chain smoking, stubbing butt after butt into stale, overflowing ashtrays.

The tribunal was nothing more than three retired cabbies sitting behind a brown, formica desk and trying to look serious. The Met always passed on this sort of complaint; no actual laws had been broken, and they had better things to do with their time.

He knew two of the men well enough; they were decent guys, but they would have to go through the motions. The one in the middle was the chairman, and he looked like he must have been from Uncle Don's generation although, in amongst all the wrinkles, his eyes looked sharp enough.

Jim hadn't denied the facts – in any case, they'd probably spoken to some of the other guys who'd been there on the night – but the facts weren't that important. He'd refused the fare, that was the truth. Was he justified in refusing it? That wasn't so clear.

In any case, it wasn't as though they were in a court room with lawyers and wigs. Each of them had given short written statements about that night which the panel read through, occasionally muttering to each other and nodding.

'Do any of you have anything to add to your statements?' said the chairman.

Jim shook his head, hands clasped loosely on his lap. 'Nothing from me,' he said, looking across the room to where Shuna and her husband were sitting.

'I'd like to say something if I may,' said Shuna.

'Of course,' said the chairman. 'Go ahead.'

'I don't want to change anything in the statement,' she said. 'That's what happened.' She looked down at her knees for a few seconds before lifting her head and staring at Jim. 'When I made the complaint, I was very angry. I was tired and jet-lagged and maybe turned the incident into something bigger than it actually was. I wouldn't want this man's career to come to any harm as a result.'

'That's all very well,' said the chairman, not looking impressed. 'But maybe you should have thought of that before bringing the complaint in the first place.'

Shuna didn't reply, but dipped her head again, golden hair veiling her face like a sunlit waterfall. She was stunning and Jim understood how she'd burrowed her way into his thoughts. First the proud, defensive lioness and now this. He'd never come across a woman like her.

The chairman looked around the room. 'Anything else?' he said, shuffling the papers in front of him into a neat pile. The three of them leant in close together and mumbled as they confirmed their agreement with more nodding of heads. The chairman cleared his throat. 'I don't think anyone disagrees that Mr Pritchard refused the fare, and I can't see any convincing evidence that there was reasonable justification for his actions. As London taxi drivers, we take on a set of obligations and we are proud of the fact that we're the best in the world at what we do. The refusal of valid fares goes against that.'

He looked at Jim with hard eyes and lips pressed tightly together. For the first time, Jim worried that things might turn out worse than he'd expected.

The chairman continued. 'As a general rule, we accept that these things can happen and that an apology and a small donation to charity is a satisfactory resolution, but ...' – Why did there need to be a 'but'? – '... In this case, we have learned from a number of other drivers that this isn't the first time this has happened. There appears to be quite a pattern.'

Jim hadn't expected that and didn't know how to respond. His mouth moved, but no sounds came out. Other drivers! The sneaky, cowardly bastards, all anonymous of course. What happened to solidarity? To having a code? It could never have happened in the Army and, in his foolish naivety, he'd assumed that the same values applied to being a cabbie. Shuna and her husband were leaning forward and whispering, his expression dark and angry, hers confused.

'In light of that,' the chairman continued, 'we've decided that you will be placed on a 12-month probation. Any further complaints or issues within that period will almost certainly cost you your license, Mr Pritchard.'

The next ten minutes had been a blur. He hadn't lost his license, but a probation was like being put in the stocks in the Dark Ages; as much as anything else it was punishment by public humiliation. Everyone would know, and whenever he went for a tea or a bacon bap, there would be whispers and sniggers. They were no better than him, but they'd make out they were. Maybe the sour taste would go away eventually, but it would take a long time.

He'd tried to speak to her when it was over, but her husband was there, protective arm wrapped around her and shepherding them out to the waiting Range Rover. He was the Alpha male, hours spent in the gym bulging through his expensive suit and understated superiority screaming silently from his vintage Rolex and his designer sunglasses. What was the story there? Mandela or no Mandela, white South Africans of Shuna's generation didn't marry black guys. Even if they were rich investment bankers. It didn't happen.

They drove off and Jim walked slowly back to his cab, his anger and frustration growing with every step. And that should have been that. It should have been the last time he saw her.

Hassan

If he'd never met Mona …

Hassan walked slowly across the Kensington Road. He was overdressed and needed to avoid getting too hot. There was nothing more suspicious than uncontrolled sweating. They had been very clear about that.

If he'd never met Mona …

He knew there was no point thinking back. No value in dredging up old dirt. But what did it matter now? Surely it wasn't wrong for him to revisit the milestones in his life, to see the steps on the road which had led him to this moment. It was a perfect time to exorcise those demons one by one, in time with the measured pallbearer paces which were leading him on to his destiny.

There were many milestones, but the only ones which mattered were the ones which marked out his time with Mona.

The first term had been coming to an end; the days and weeks had blurred in a grey swirl of activity and he couldn't quite see how time had passed so quickly. He had a few mates on his course – boring geeks like him – and they must have dragged him out for a few drinks from time to time, but when he looked back all he could remember was days and nights filled with studying. He was smart enough, but there was so much to do and never enough hours.

The daily catch-up sessions with Mona made it all worthwhile – each time he spotted her, he stood a little taller, and the exhaustion slid off his shoulders and away. She was a shining metallic flash of silver glinting brightly through the dross of his daily slog.

She met him so she could share his notes and he could help her with work she'd missed, but it wasn't entirely a one-way street and they didn't only talk about their studies. As the weeks passed Hassan began to suspect that Mona might actually enjoy his company, and that they were becoming real friends.

That friendship was an unexpected bonus and he certainly never expected their relationship to be anything other than platonic. Mona was light years out of his league and, if Hassan knew anything, he knew his place in the pecking order of life.

There was nothing different or special about that particular day. A typical grey cold January morning – he and Mona had just spent two hours in Caffe Nero going through the previous afternoon's lecture notes. Mona insisted on paying for the coffees and they set off for their weekly tutorial. Mona was babbling on about something or other as they walked past the Bodleian and Hassan was only half-listening, enjoying the moment and noticing, not for the first time, that they were walking in perfect step with each other.

'Hassan!' Mona stopped without warning in the middle of the

busy street.

'What's up?' he said. 'We're gonna be late.'

'You've got no idea, have you?' she said, looking deep into his eyes.

'What?' She was right. Hassan had no idea what she was talking about. People were flowing around them like river water around rocks, but Mona didn't seem to notice them.

She lifted one hand and slowly stroked his cheek with the back of her fingers, all the while fixing him with that bottomless gaze. Hassan froze. Not breathing. Even his heart seemed to have stopped beating.

'How lovely you are, idiot,' she said, smiling.

And then she kissed him.

There was nothing different or special about that day, but the kiss changed his life forever, bisecting his entire existence into distinct halves – before and after. With the awful clarity of hindsight, the path from that moment to his careful overdressed trudge along Exhibition Road might as well have been laser-etched into his bones.

From the moment Hassan and Mona became a couple, his life revolved only around her. He studied hard so he could help her with her studies but every other moment was spent with her, thinking about her, or dreaming up new ways to please her. He wasn't worried about missing out; he had everything he could possibly want.

Mona had lots of other friends and Hassan understood that he would always have to share her. She was one of those rare spirits who made things glow. Everything, and everyone, who came near her became brighter and more alive. It was an amazing gift and of course she had many, many admirers. That was all right. Hassan was her boyfriend, and he was certain she was faithful to him. Mona couldn't lie.

Whenever Hassan parted from Mona, he would feel a slight shiver run through him, as though a cloud was sliding softly across the sun and he needed to find some warming comfort by thinking about the next time he would see her.

The long holidays had been the worst, especially the summer breaks. He and Mona talked often about him taking a trip back to Cairo with her – to see the pyramids and meet her family – but it didn't happen. Something would always get in the way, either Hassan's obligation to work for his uncle or some family drama of Mona's that made it 'not the best time'.

The subject of going to Bradford to meet the Qureishis never came up.

It was Mona who suggested they share a flat in their final year. It was the last chance to be outside the college accommodation, to have a little more freedom. They were spending most nights with each other, anyway. Why not move in together?

She found a place, which was perfect. A short walk into town and tucked away down a quiet street off the Iffley Road. It was way outside Hassan's budget but Mona rented it in her name and charged Hassan a small rent. It wasn't a big deal; her parents were paying.

She was so excited about having their own love nest and couldn't stop giggling about it. It was exactly like being with an eight-year-old playing "house".

The love nest came with rules, as had their frequent nightly encounters for the previous two years. Mona was a proper girl from a good family, traditional and a devout Muslim in her own way. She wanted to be "intact" when she got married and Hassan respected that. With a bit of imagination there were plenty of alternatives, and neither of them seemed to be short of fresh ideas.

Hassan stood by the side of the road and smiled. There were so many good memories, happy times and moments of physical closeness that could still make his toes curl.

How could it all have been a lie? Surely he wasn't that stupid? He should have figured it out when her parents came to visit. It was understandable that she didn't want her mother and father to know that their precious princess was sharing her bed, but he hadn't even been allowed to meet them. That was a pretty bloody big clue. Sadly, naïve idiot that he was, Hassan had accepted Mona's feeble excuses without question.

A man in a suit brushed past him roughly, the token 'excuse me' signifying nothing. Hassan looked up sluggishly and realised that he had been standing motionless at the pedestrian crossing while the green man flashed at him unseen and ignored. He dragged himself out of his daydream and stepped forward, cursing silently. He was supposed to be keeping a low profile, not standing around like a sleepwalking mental case.

The first sound he heard was the high-pitched scream of protesting tyre rubber, the next was the blaring horn. He barely had time to turn his head and the white van was there, dirty windscreen filling his vision. He started to brace for the impact – much too little and much too late.

But, praise be to Allah, the driver was young, he was watching the road and had lightning reactions. The van stopped with its snub-nosed bonnet half touching Hassan's hip and the white-faced delivery man staring into his eyes from a few inches away.

They held that frozen tableau without breathing until Hassan crumbled. He sank to his knees on the road, gulping short, sharp, sobbing breaths.

The driver climbed down from the cab and stumbled towards him. 'Jesus Christ! Are you all right?'

Hassan looked at him and nodded, afraid to speak.

'What the fuck were you doing?' said the driver, panic and fear fuelling his anger. 'You just walked out in front of me. I had a green light.'

Hassan reached his fingers into the van's radiator grille and pulled himself to his feet. 'I'm sorry,' he said. 'I didn't see you.' He started to walk away down Exhibition Road.

'Where do you think you're going?' shouted the driver, taking a step towards him. 'You can't just bugger off.'

By that stage three or four cars were waiting behind the van and they began to hoot and honk out their impatience. When Hassan looked back and lifted one hand in apology, the driver stopped and shrugged his shoulders. 'Fuck it,' he muttered, as he turned and ran back to his van.

Shuna

Shuna always took a while to settle in to exhibitions. Whatever was on display, and however well it was displayed, there was always too much to see and she found it difficult to decide where to start. Little Anna had no problem. She had studied all the winning entries online and printed out a list of the ones she wanted to visit first. She'd disappeared down the dark avenues before Shuna had even begun to get her bearings.

Where had she got that from? Neither Shuna nor Simon were particularly organised and Zoe left chaos behind her with a natural ease that sometimes left her parents slack-jawed in admiration. Anna was the cuckoo who was going to push them all out of the nest one day.

For want of a better plan, Shuna decided to start at the end and work backwards. Zoe trailed slowly behind, oozing indifference and resentment. The winning image was blown up to cover the whole wall of a small room; an orangutang slowly climbing up a thigh-thick creeper, wrapped around a bare and isolated tree trunk which soared hundreds of feet above the rain forest. Shuna felt her buttocks clench with vertigo. The more you looked at the picture, the more you realised how far it was to fall. Very clever to get the photograph, but was it so clever to make people feel that uncomfortable?

She felt a tug on her sleeve.

'Mum,' said Zoe, pulling her out into the main corridor. 'You have to see this.'

The stopped in front of an image of snail shells piled on a beach and, for a moment, Shuna was confused.

'It's disgusting,' said Zoe. 'So gross. Why would they do that?'

It was only after Shuna had read the information card that her eyes adapted to the real subject of the photo. They weren't snail shells, they were the half-defrosted corpses of pangolins which had been seized in a raid. Over four thousand of them.

'Oh my God,' said Shuna, wrapping a protective arm around her daughter. 'That's awful. I thought they were snail shells to begin with.'

'So did I,' said Zoe. 'When I realised what they were, I was almost sick. They're going extinct and it's just so some rich Chinese businessmen can eat something different.' She looked up at her mother. 'Mum, I don't want to hang around here any more. Can I go and get a Coke? I'll see you in the dinosaur hall.'

'Of course you can, sweetie. We'll be along in fifteen minutes or so. See you then.' Shuna turned, but was stopped by another tug on her sleeve.

'Mum?'

'Yes.'

'Can I have some money?'

Shuna smiled as she handed over a fiver. When everything else was looking dark and teenage rebellion was dominating their lives, there would always be money.

It was a treat to be alone for ten minutes, even though the defrosting pangolins had left her feeling queasy. God, people were such idiots. Couldn't they see what they were doing to the planet? The idea that people were custodians of the natural world was something Shuna had been brought up with from an early age. All use of the land came with responsibility and obligations. Sadly, the values of traditional Afrikaans culture tended to give more respect to the environment than they did to the majority of their fellow countrymen.

The exhibition had a small urban section, wild animals who'd found a home in the city, and one image leapt out at Shuna. The subject was a beautiful dog fox, brush stretched behind him as he sauntered across a zebra crossing perfectly lit by the streetlights and looking like he owned the place. But behind the fox, and waiting for him to pass, was a black cab, headlights staring out of the photograph and the driver no more than a shadowy figure behind the windscreen.

Wherever she went, she couldn't get away from them. Maybe she should suggest to Simon that they move out of London. It wasn't good for her to be continuously reminded of that night. She couldn't decide which was worse, the fear or the guilt but, as the months went by, the fear faded and the guilt didn't.

The tribunal had been bad enough. He hadn't lost his license but Shuna could tell that he hadn't been expecting things to turn out like that. She hadn't wanted to make an enemy and, if she'd been able to take it all back, she would have. But, as the tribunal chairman had told her, she should have thought about that before registering her complaint. Still, what was done was done, and that should have been the end of it.

But, of course, it wasn't.

It had happened just before Christmas. Shuna had taken the girls to get presents for their dad and they'd popped into Muriel's for a treat. She'd been feeling on edge for a few days and, that morning, she'd realised why that was. She left the girls with their hot chocolates and stepped outside the cafe to call Simon.

'I think that taxi driver's following me?'

'What?'

'I think he's stalking me.'

'That seems unlikely. He knows he was lucky to get away with a warning before. He's not going to push it.'

'I've seen him three times in the last week. I'm not making it up.'

'I'm not saying you're making it up, but it could just be a coincidence. Were you a hundred per cent sure it was him every time?'

'Yes. I know his number plate by now,' Shuna said. 'But it's more than that. When I left the house this morning, he was parked across the road and it looked as though he was taking photos of me.'

'Now that's really creepy. Why would he do that?'

'How would I bloody well know? He definitely had a camera though – a big paparazzi one with a proper zoom.'

'Shit. We need to do something about that. Look, I'm just about to go into a meeting. Can we pick this up tonight? Are you going to be OK?'

'Of course. I'm fine. Aren't you coming home first?'

'No. I'll see you at the restaurant at seven. We'll have half an hour before Josie and Adam get there and we can talk about this properly.

If you see him again, try and grab a photo with your phone.'

'I'll do that. See you later.'

She should have said something to Simon sooner. Her sixth sense was working overtime but not fast enough.

After they left Muriel's, she'd dropped the kids with friends for a sleepover, walked home and indulged herself with a long, hot bath. Candles, glass of prosecco, the works. She was excited about the evening; the restaurant they were going to had only been open for three months and reservations were like hen's teeth. Luckily Simon knew someone … who knew someone … who was a friend of the chef's wife and he was feeling very pleased with himself. He loved to fix things.

After her bath, Shuna had almost an hour to get ready and, for once there was no-one to tell her to hurry up. She had the same cheesy '80s playlist running at full volume on every speaker in the house and was singing along. It was great to not have to worry about anyone else for a little while.

She would have had time to spare if her house keys hadn't disappeared. She always left them in the bowl on the hall table, but they'd chosen that evening to hide somewhere else. After fifteen minutes of checking and double-checking every possible location, they'd eventually turned up under her scarf in the kitchen. And Simon wasn't even there to be blamed.

It didn't matter how the keys had found their way there; the result was that her good mood was shattered, and she was running twenty minutes late by the time she threw on her long, black coat, locked up and ran up to the Gloucester Road to look for a cab. For once, luck was on her side and she saw an orange light behind her straight away. She held out an arm, watching as the taxi indicated and pulled over.

'Chez Alice, please,' she said, breathing hard as she slid into the back of the cab, taking care to lift the hem of her new coat. 'It's a new restaurant on Blandford Street … and quick as you can, please. I'm terribly late.'

'Right you are,' said the driver.

Shuna checked her phone for messages from the kids before

zipping it back in her bag and leaning back in the seat to catch her breath. She would only be ten minutes late, and it was set to be a wonderful evening. The couple they were going with, Josie and Adam Gardner, were great fun and they'd not been out for ages. She closed her eyes and began to feel the warmth and relaxation from her long bath seeping back.

When she opened her eyes, she noticed the taxi driver looking at her in his mirror and, without quite knowing why, the first tendrils of panic started to snake into her stomach. Her eyes flicked down to the permit on display. Jim Pritchard. It was him.

Dan

Rosa's half an hour at the registration desk had ended up being more like an hour and a half, but eventually she was done.

'Sorry about that,' she said. 'We weren't expecting so many people to be interested.'

'Maybe things are really starting to change?' said Dan, watching as she piled up the boxes of pamphlets and forms.

'Maybe?' she said. 'But, if you ask me, it's going to get a lot worse before it gets better.' She tried to pick up the tottering pile of boxes.

'Let me give you a hand with those,' said Dan. 'Where do they need to go?'

'They let us use a cupboard out back,' said Rosa. 'I'll show you.'

They walked around behind the altar to a room full of wardrobes and storage cabinets. They were the last people to leave and Rosa carefully locked up the cupboard, before taking a look around the room.

'OK. I think we're done,' she said, flashing him a cheeky smile. 'Now what is it you wanted to talk about?'

After they left the church, Dan and Rosa went to an all-night coffee bar and sat chatting for hours. She was passionate, smart and opinionated. Dan learnt very quickly that his logic of *I'm Canadian – Canadian's aren't racist – US Deep South racism isn't my problem* wasn't going to get him far with Rosa.

She believed that it was everyone's job to stand up and join the fight. Just because you weren't racist didn't mean that leaving the fight to the victims of racism was an acceptable option. By the end of the evening, Dan was a convert, and not only because he was becoming more in love with every breath he took.

They didn't only talk about civil rights, they explored the differences and similarities of growing up in small-town Mexico and small-town Canada. They both described stifling, small-minded communities dominated by religion and net-curtain-twitching gossip and scandal. They'd both been in a hurry to escape and for identical reasons.

She even pretended to be fascinated by Dan's work and, by the end of the evening, he'd convinced her to read The Brothers Karamazov, his favourite Dostoevsky.

He walked her home and was rewarded with a chaste kiss on the cheek and the promise of a proper date the following week.

Rosa and Dan had started dating and, for Dan, it was like being seventeen again. Rosa was a very well-brought-up girl and their relationship developed slowly and along very traditional lines. There was no chaperone, but there might as well have been.

Dan hadn't minded. Even though he could still remember wanting her with an aching which threatened his sanity at times, it was worth it just to spend time with her. They were both busy, Dan with his PhD and Rosa with both her undergraduate studies and preparations for the March on Washington. Every spare moment they had was spent together.

By the time the day of the march arrived, there was a craziness in the air. Dan had handed in his final thesis, Rosa was on summer break and, if any preparations hadn't been made by then, they weren't going to get made.

Dan had rented a small, seedy hotel room with the last of his grant money and they arrived back there late in the evening filled with the euphoria of Martin Luther-King's amazing speech and the mass adrenalin buzz of a crowd which was estimated to be a quarter of a million strong.

Neither of them had planned it, but the stars must have aligned for them. There was no thought of chaperones as Dan kicked the door closed behind him and they fell into each other's arms.

After they came back from Washington, everything was different. Rosa moved into his small apartment and Dan got into the habit of pinching himself several times a day. It must be a dream. No-one had the right to be that happy.

Like most of his generation, he could still remember exactly where he'd been a few months later, on that fateful day in November 1963. He and Rosa had talked about driving to Dallas to see the President, but decided to take a day's holiday instead. They would spend the day in bed, reading books and drinking wine like decadent Parisians. It would be easier to watch the motorcade on TV, anyway.

Dan had lost a bet – he couldn't remember what it was about – and the penalty was to get up and make brunch. As he walked back into the bedroom carrying a tray piled high with pancakes, coffee and juice, he saw Rosa sitting at the edge of the bed, eyes wide and staring as though she'd seen a ghost. He put the tray down and ran over.

'What is it?' he said.

Rosa just pointed at the television where the same terrible images were looping over and over – an open car and a man collapsing into his wife's lap. Like hundreds of millions of people around the world, Dan and Rosa sat silently, wrapped in each other's arms, wondering if this was going to mean the end of everything good.

A single gunshot which changed the world and which changed Dan's life.

'Let's get married,' he'd said, later that evening as they were lying in bed. 'Let's do it now, before the world collapses.'

Rosa had kissed and hugged him for an age, her tears wet on his cheek. 'Yes. Let's do it. Whatever happens, we'll have each other.'

'Hey, you.'

'Hnnnh.' The bed was rocking, and he thought he would fall out

'Dan?'

'What?'

'Dan, it's me. Rachel.'

The rocking bed faded away, taking Rosa with it and Dan felt Rachel's hand on his shoulder, gently shaking him back and forth.

He opened his eyes and blinked. 'Sorry, Hon. I was asleep.'

'No kidding,' she said, sitting down next to him on the bench. 'You were a long ways away.'

'Yeah,' said Dan, desperately trying to hold on to some fragment of his dream memory. It had been so real. Every smell, sound, taste and touch had been vivid and true. But now it was all disappearing into a black funnel, swallowed up by the aches and pains of the real world. He looked up at Rachel and smiled. 'But I'm back now. How was your shopping?'

Rachel pointed to the stack of carrier bags on the bench and arched her eyebrows. 'I'm never going to fit all of this in the suitcases, but I had such fun. Everyone was so kind and helpful.' She laughed. 'You would have hated it.'

'What, by pointing out that they're paid to be kind and helpful? Stuff like that?'

'Exactly,' said Rachel. 'Thanks for letting me go on my own. I hope you weren't too bored.'

'I was fine,' he said. 'I had my book … and I met a very nice young Spanish girl called Ramona.'

'Really?' said Rachel. 'I leave you alone for less than an hour and that's what happens. You're incorrigible, Dan Bukowski.'

They sat quietly for a while, holding hands and sharing familiar, conspiratorial smiles.

'There's something I have to tell you,' said Dan once the silence had come to a natural end.

'That sounds serious.'

'I guess it is. But it's not just that.' He shifted around further on the bench. 'I've been thinking about things a lot over the past few weeks, and I've decided that I want to tell you about the years before we met.'

Rachel put her hand on his arm. 'You don't have to, you sweet man. I know it's painful for you and we've managed this long without talking about it. We can let it lie.'

'No,' said Dan. 'You've been so wonderful, right from the start. Accepting me with all my baggage. I know it hasn't been easy and I owe you this.'

'But I don't want you to feel obliged …'

'… I don't feel obliged. I want to tell you. I want you to understand. I have to tell you about Rosa.'

Nadia

'Hang on, Ed.' Nadia's phone was going crazy in her pocket. Beeping and buzzing as alert followed alert. She flicked through the messages but focused on one which she read three times. Ed was standing in front of a big map of Hyde Park and she tugged on his jacket. 'Come on,' she said. 'Someone's called in a suspicious package. At the sports club. It's only a couple of hundred yards from here.'

Nadia noticed that Ed was gasping by the time they got there, even though she'd slowed down for him. People should really keep themselves in shape.

There was a young man in a wheelchair waiting inside the gate. He looked like a soldier. He must be the one who'd called in.

'Captain Wilson,' she said, registering his crisp nod of recognition. 'Nadia LaRoche.' She held out her hand. 'And this is Ed Bailey.'

The young man shook her hand and smiled. 'Sorry to be a pain,' he said. 'Can I see some ID, please?'

'Of course,' said Nadia, handing over her police warrant card.

He looked at it and smiled again. 'You're not really police are you?' he said.

'More or less,' said Nadia with a shrug of her shoulders. 'Anyway, we're up against the clock here. The ones with the hats and the blue flashing lights will be here soon. In the meantime, can you show me what you found, please.'

'It's in here,' he said, wheeling himself ahead of them and through the double doors into the sports club. After pushing open the door of the disabled toilets, he pointed to the far corner. 'Over there,' he said. 'I didn't touch it, but I saw what it was and called it in.'

'What is it,' asked Ed.

'Packaging for a detonator control unit,' said the soldier. 'We were briefed about them after the Americans managed to mislay a couple of hundred units in 2010. A favourite option for IEDs.' He patted the armrest of his wheelchair and looked up at Nadia.

'That's a bad break,' said Nadia, as she bent down and picked up the cardboard box with a pair of tweezers. 'I'm sorry.' She'd met quite a few veterans over the years and had always been impressed by the way they maintained that rugged humour after something so traumatic.

She held the packaging up to the light and beckoned to Ed. 'You ever seen anything like this?'

'No,' he said, 'but it's definitely military and definitely American.'

Nadia turned back to the soldier. 'You sure about this?' she asked.

He nodded. 'A hundred per cent. I briefed my troop on them a few days before I copped it.'

'And you think it might have been left by the guy who was in here before you?'

'I think so. He was taking forever.'

Nadia held out her phone. 'Is this him?'

'Yes. That's him.'

Nadia almost had time to ask herself where the hell the real police were, when two fully kitted-out SCO19 officers burst in, guns at the ready.

'You're late,' she said, recognising the first one.

'Good to see you too, Nadia,' he said. 'What've we got?'

'Suspected detonator packaging,' she said. 'And confirmation that Snowflake was in here ten minutes ago. We've definitely got a situation, we just don't know where. The camera routing has been patchy and unclear, so he might have been briefed on CCTV locations. Are forensics here?'

'Outside,' said the SCO19 officer.

'Great,' said Nadia. 'Ask them to get on this straight away and ping me field fingerprints as soon as they can. I need to call this in.'

Ed followed her outside, tugging on her sleeve. 'Nadia,' he said.

'Hang on,' she replied. 'I have to speak to David.'

'That's fine,' he said. 'But before you do, you should understand that Unicorn is behind this. The technology, the preparation, avoiding CCTV, losing the tails … this is him. I know it.'

'I believe you,' she said. 'I'm not sure how that helps though. We still don't know where the target is, and we're running out of time.' She looked at him. 'You know this guy. try to come up with something concrete we can work with.'

Nadia called David, desperately hoping he would have some inspirational insight to lead her to Snowflake. She could tell straight away he had nothing to add; they were both stuck in the same circular groove, frustrated and panicking, but powerless to move forward. Meanwhile the certainty of an attack grew and grew.

Nadia was normally a clear decisive thinker under pressure – shooting Stu Ronson was evidence of that – but she was emotionally and physically exhausted. As she spoke to David, she could feel her mind turning to mush, important thoughts and ideas floating out of reach like dandelion seeds in a summer breeze. The whole time they were speaking, Nadia had a nagging feeling she was missing something. Something which would give her the clue she needed.

After she'd come out from undercover, Nadia had travelled the country, retracing Snowflake's life in the hope that someone from his past would be able to help find him – or at least give her some useful intel. Apart from his friend in Birmingham, no-one had seen or heard from him, in most cases not for years. His father had refused to speak to her; his son was apparently "dead" to him after he'd dropped out of university.

His mother had been more helpful, telling her how her son had been bullied, not least by his father, and how she'd always known he was too clever to stay at home. She'd shared stories of how he'd been reading by the age of three and about his precise, beautiful drawings; she'd been close to tears as she described the way his father had hated and resented his son's intelligence and how he'd once gone so far as to throw Snowflake's only book in the fire. It was a sad story – not so unusual – and she clearly blamed her husband for everything which had gone wrong afterwards.

Nadia had also found a few of his old school friends to speak to and had built up a picture of a bright young man, going up to Oxford full of hope and insecurity – mixed with some anger and bitterness, but nothing out of the ordinary for a working-class Asian boy from Manningham who wasn't good at cricket.

She replayed the conversations over and over in her mind, but there was nothing there which could help her as she stood in Hyde Park watching the precious minutes tick away.

11:42

Jim

'Excuse me, madam.'

'Yes. What is it?' The woman was from somewhere in the Middle East and had that way of talking that made people feel like servants. She wasn't one of the strict ones, all covered in black felt. Or at least she wasn't one of the strict ones when she was in London. Who knew what they got up to back home?

A few years earlier, Jim had read somewhere that almost fifty per cent of Victoria's Secret's sales were in Saudi Arabia. Almost certainly a bullshit statistic, but there might be some truth in it and he'd enjoyed imagining what might be going on under all of those tent-like burkas.

'I'm sorry. Could you ask your daughter not to climb on the glass fence, please? It's dangerous.'

'He's my son,' she said, now talking to him like a servant who'd stolen the DVD player. She wasn't bad looking, but a sneer is never pretty, especially when it's directed at you. 'Can't you tell the difference between a boy and a girl?'

'I'm sorry, madam,' said Jim, feeling his blood pressure soar. 'My mistake. But if you could do as I ask, please. It's dangerous to climb on the glass as you can see from the sign.'

The woman pushed her designer sunglasses up onto her headscarf and looked at him with disdain. 'Do you really not have anything more important to do? Shouldn't you be checking for terrorists rather than wasting your time harassing six-year-old children?'

Jim took a slow, deep breath, turned and walked back to his chair, leaving the outraged woman muttering behind him. If she didn't stop the bloody kid, he'd tell Will to go over and sort her out. He couldn't be bothered.

His father had fought at El Alamein and had brought back a capful of stories about the 'bloody rag heads'. They weren't all bad, according to his dad, but it was hard to keep an open mind these days, what with everything that was going on. And the brazen cheek of the woman. 'Checking for terrorists?' It was her bloody lot behind all of the trouble in the first place. Who did she think she was?

He wasn't in the mood for that sort of hassle. The day had started badly and his thoughts had been racing since he'd got back from the exhibition. He was half-tempted to ask Will to cover for him while he went to check and see if that really had been Shuna standing in front of the photograph. She'd probably be long gone, but the shape of her face in profile was stuck in his mind.

He had always processed images slowly, especially if they were at the edge of his vision. Half-seen images would gradually come into focus as time passed, even half an hour or an hour afterwards. It was like a face emerging from old-fashioned developing liquid as the photographic paper floated back and forth.

He'd needed to make a conscious effort to manage that delay when he was in the army. There were times when it was useful, but not on watch duty where sharpness and quick decision-making were critical.

The more he thought about the woman in the exhibition, the more certain he was that it had been her. What were the odds of that? And what if she hadn't left already and decided to come into the hall?

The terms of the restraining order had been crystal clear; he wasn't under any circumstances to be within a hundred and fifty yards of her or any of her family. How did that work if he was stationary? Was he supposed to get up and run away, leaving Will to defend the Empire against the horrors of six-year-old jihadis?

He still wanted to see her. Even if the bitch had ruined his life.

She hadn't really meant to. It had just been the way things had turned out.

In any case, it wouldn't hurt to give Will a heads up.

'Hey Jim. What's occurring?' Will's attempt at a Welsh accent was a mess and Jim couldn't stop himself smiling.

'All good,' said Jim. 'Just stretching my legs.'

'What was that with you and the tasty woman in the headscarf,' said Will. 'Were you making a move? I knew I was right about you.'

'Don't be a prat. I went to tell her to keep her obnoxious brat off the barrier and she got all snotty with me. Really pissed me off.' Jim could see that the boy had stopped climbing. 'If he does it again, she's all yours.'

'OK. No problem,' said Will, his cheery smile untouched by Jim's sourness. It was like he was covered in a suit made of Teflon; all the shit storms of daily life slid past him without sticking. Jim would have given a lot to be able to borrow that suit for a while.

'I'd better not hang around,' said Jim. 'You-know-who will be back soon.' He turned to leave and then span back, leaning close to Will. 'One more thing. When I was on my break, I think I saw this woman I used to know. If she comes in here, I might need to make myself scarce. OK?'

'OK. No problem.' Will was clearly interested and Jim knew that he wouldn't let this slide by. 'So. Who is the lucky lady? A blast from the past?'

Jim leant closer and gave Will the look. Eyes hard and unblinking, face set in a tight, humourless mask. It took a few seconds, but the young lad got the point soon enough and backed away, showing the whites of his eyes. Jim patted him on the shoulder and smiled. 'Good lad. Just cover for me. All right?'

Will nodded and Jim turned away.

He pulled his chair round to face the passageway leading to the exhibition. He could picture her stepping out into the hall in such detail that it felt like a regular event. It was like the anticipation of waiting for someone at an airport, or a moment back in the

Christmas Eve excitement of childhood.

Before the girls had been born, he'd been posted for a couple of years to Cyprus, and Julie would come out and visit for the weekend every few months. He could still remember the churning hungry feeling in his stomach as he waited for her to come through customs. Ten minutes would seem like an hour as figure after figure walked out and, one after the other, turned out to be someone else's wife or girlfriend. Until, when he'd suffered enough, the shape that had looked like Julie had turned out to actually be Julie and Jim could start breathing again.

A lot of water under the bridge since then. They'd been good times. Uncomplicated times. A shame things couldn't ever stay simple, but what could be done?

The exhibition was popular and people flowed in and out, but none of them was Shuna. He thought he saw a girl who looked like her daughter, but he'd never paid much attention to the girls and they changed so fast at that age. Maybe he'd imagined the whole thing? The power of wishful thinking should never be underestimated, as he'd learnt to his cost.

He'd only wanted to talk to her and there hadn't been a better way. He could understand now why she'd been frightened, but if she could only have stopped to listen to him, everything would have been different. Why did people find it so difficult to listen? He could get their attention well enough with the threat of aggression – look how young Will had buckled – but he was tired of it.

Perhaps the wind had changed suddenly one day and left him frozen as an aggressive, curmudgeonly old git? He lifted his hand to his mouth to cover the involuntary snort of laughter. Who was he kidding? He'd always been an aggressive, curmudgeonly git; the only new element was the added bonus of getting old.

He'd been working hard to put that evening, and everything that came later, behind him; in spite of his ongoing anger or panic attacks, the doctors thought that he was doing well. Seeing Shuna, or an imaginary ghost of Shuna, had dragged him straight back into the thick of it and reminded him that, whatever progress he was making, he had a lot of work ahead of him if he ever wanted to properly make it up to Julie.

The days and weeks which followed that incident in the cab had blurred into a rolling nightmare with new disasters striking on an almost-daily basis.

Julie, in particular, had lost the plot completely, especially when the police came sniffing around looking for his cameras, laptop and hard drive. It was strange, but the fact that he'd kept his photography hidden had seemed to hurt her more than anything else. Their marriage had never been smooth, but Jim had always been certain that they'd find a way through. These days, he wasn't quite as sure. They were moving forward, but something was still badly broken, and he wasn't the world's greatest fixer.

'Jim. Are you planning on telling me what the fuck's going on?' Julie had stood at the open front door, spitting the words out onto the street like shrapnel. 'The police were round this afternoon, looking for cameras and computer equipment.'

'OK, Luv,' said Jim. 'Let me just get inside.'

'Don't fucking "Luv" me. The whole street was out. I've never been so bloody humiliated.'

Jim had then pushed her gently back into the hall, closing the door behind him. 'I'm sorry. It's something – not actually a big deal – which is being made into something much bigger than it actually is.'

'That's not the impression I got from the police.'

'Why? What did they say?'

'That you've been following that woman from the tribunal. And taking photos of her. I told them that you didn't even have a camera, much less know how to use one. They looked at me as though I was a sad idiot. The copper was only about twelve and I could swear he felt sorry for me.'

'Well, there's an element of ...'

' ... What?'

'It's partly true. I do have a camera and I was taking photographs of Shuna, but they won't find them.'

'Shuna? It's fucking Shuna now is it?' Julie was pacing up and down the narrow hallway, stiff arms barely moving and fists clenched. 'And how come you've got a secret camera? Are you some sort of pervert?'

'Don't be fucking stupid,' said Jim. 'I take photos of wildlife. Mostly birds. I've been doing it for years.'

Julie had stood looking at him with her mouth hanging open before spinning around and letting out a guttural sob. Half a second later the kitchen door had slammed in his face and the glass vase on the hall table had started rocking back and forth in sympathy; once, twice and then the dull crack as it fell, broken in two.

Hassan

Hassan didn't look back to see if the van driver was following him. He either was or he wasn't. Hassan had moved beyond caring as his feet led him closer and closer to the museum. He was on schedule and would have enough time to look at the diplodocus. That would be a fitting end to his fucked-up journey. There was a tidiness about the way it would close a circle going back to his childhood.

Did it make sense to see life as a circle or was it a series of choices, branching out into multiple futures in a dizzying pattern of ever-thinning threads? Or was it both? Did anyone really have any choice about what they did, or was every step ordained by the Fates from the beginning, with every branch already drawn out?

To begin with they'd pretended that the ultimate decision was his, but that pretence had stopped as soon as he'd started sharing his views about violence, and whether it was ever the best option. Choice either sat in their hands, or that of the Fates. Hassan, as for so much of his life, had none.

Could Hassan really decide to go back to the park, take off the vest and then go to meet that girl outside the posh cafe? Would she be waiting for him at three o'clock with a smile on her face? Or would it turn out to be another humiliating disaster in his failure-filled life? How could he know and, even if she were waiting for him, how could he live with the consequences of that decision?

Sally. That was her name. It was calming to imagine meeting her.

They could go out for a quiet drink and Hassan would find himself content with just one, or maybe two, whiskies. They would laugh and tell stories about home before strolling back to her place as the sun was fading. He wouldn't need to go back to Bradford ever. He would find work making the best cappuccinos in London and no-one would know where to find him.

Maybe he would contact his mother, but not for a long, long time. Perhaps to send her photos of her grandchildren, little Hassan and baby Fatima. She would want to know that he was all right, but she would need to swear never to tell his father.

Why couldn't that be his future?

Did he really need to ask that question? Maybe his future had been mapped out from birth, maybe not. But, whatever had come before, his future had been fixed at that moment in time when Mona had told him about Anwar. The path from that morning to a young man in a vest walking down Exhibition Road was scored so deeply into the fabric of the universe that nothing could have changed it.

It had been half way through the second term of his third and final year at Oxford.

Hassan and Mona had been having such a great time; they were partners in every facet of daily life, they could talk about anything, they would cook together and laugh together, and the sex (even with the self-imposed restrictions) was amazing. Every morning, Hassan woke early just so he could spend a few extra minutes watching Mona breathe softly through gently parted lips. She was even more beautiful asleep and her relaxed half-smile told tales of exotic dreams filled with sand and spice.

It was during these moments – no more than five or ten minutes every day – that Hassan thought about the one subject which appeared to be taboo. The future.

It wasn't as though they'd specifically agreed not to talk about life after Oxford, it was simply that Mona always skilfully avoided any attempt to discuss what happened next. Hassan didn't want to create a big issue because his life was closer to perfection than he'd ever dreamt of; he didn't want to jinx things, but the future was now less than three months away. They would take their final exams in May. And then what?

He couldn't picture what would come afterwards, but he definitely couldn't imagine a future without Mona. She completed him; she brought out everything that was good in him and allowed him to feel – for the first time in his life – that he had a place in the world.

Eventually, he'd found a solution. It had taken every ounce of courage he could scrape together and every last penny in his bank account, but he had a plan and on that particular March morning, as he watched her lying next to him, he'd known everything was going to work out.

Saturday mornings were always relaxed. Study wasn't allowed and they would walk into town and have a late brunch at Quod on the High. Hassan was doing his best to relax but, as Mona dithered back and forth between the blue scarf and the green scarf, he felt his resolve crumbling.

'The green looks great,' he said. 'Come on. I'm starving.'

'All right. Keep your hair on.' Mona wrapped the blue scarf around her neck and opened the door. 'It's only eleven. You'll probably survive.'

'Of course I will, but I wanted to take you to the botanic gardens on the way. I know how you hate our English winters and I thought the spring flowers might cheer you up.' He bustled her outside and pulled the door closed. 'Y'know? Remind you that summer's on the way.'

Mona wrapped an arm around his waist. 'That sounds great,' she said. 'You are a sweetie.' She lifted her hand to her mouth in mock horror. 'As long as you won't collapse from starvation before we get there.'

Hassan laughed. 'I think I'll make it.'

The Oxford Botanic Gardens were only ten minutes walk from the flat and they seemed to be the only people there. Most of the flower beds were still bare, and it was only when they got to the far end towards the river that the reason for their visit became clear. A carpet of tiny, blue scilla spread out under the trees, a light blue sea surrounding beds of hellebores, papery flowers pink-veined and modest against the vibrant freshness of their leaves.

'It's beautiful,' said Mona, squeezing him tight. 'What a lovely idea. You were right. I was getting a bit fed up with the greyness of everything.'

Hassan knew that the moment was right and he kissed her gently on the lips before sinking to one knee in front of her and holding out the small red box which held all of his hopes.

'Mona,' he said, smiling as he saw her hand go to her mouth in mock horror again. 'Mona El Masry. Will you do me the honour of becoming my wife?'

Mona's hand stayed over her mouth as the two of them held their cartoon tableau. Neither was breathing.

Eventually, she spoke. 'Oh, Hassan,' she said. 'I thought you understood.'

'Understood what?' Hassan hadn't moved from one knee and didn't know what was happening. Whatever it was, it wasn't what he'd been hoping for.

'Stand up,' she said quietly. 'Come over here and sit down.'

Hassan allowed himself to be led to the waiting bench like a spring lamb. 'Understood what?' he said again, trying to keep the rising panic from his voice.

'I'm already engaged,' she said. 'I've been engaged since I was seventeen.'

'Engaged? Who to? How can you be?'

'His name is Anwar. He's twenty-six. His parents are friends of my parents.'

'Do you love him?'

Mona glared at him. 'How could I? I hardly know him. We've only met once or twice since I was a kid.' She moved closer to Hassan, confusion tracing tiny wrinkles in the corners of her eyes. 'Surely you know how this works? Love has nothing to do with anything. It's just how it is.'

'But you're different,' he said, hearing the notes of pleading creeping into his voice. 'You're not from some poor village family, hanging onto old traditions. Your father's a doctor and your mother's a university professor. It's different.'

Mona rested her cool palms against his cheeks. 'No,' she said. 'It's not.'

Hassan's sluggish mind was still unable to keep pace, and he kept the ring box wrapped in his fist like a talisman. 'But I love you. Don't you love me?'

'I don't know what to say. If I tell you I love you, does that make it better or worse?'

'If you love me, we could find a way. I don't know how, but we could find a way.'

Something broke then. An invisible thread that had been joining them together. Mona took her hands from his face and pulled away. 'No. We couldn't,' she said, an imperial hardness filling her words. 'I love my family and my country. My life is there. You and I have had such a wonderful time, but when I leave Oxford, it's over.' Her lips were set tight and he could see the implacable certainty in her eyes. 'I'm so sorry, but I really thought you understood.'

Hassan didn't know what to say. Should he have known? Why? She'd never said a word about bloody Anwar. Was he supposed to be psychic? He'd been nothing more than a toy for her. Why was he surprised?

Mona looked at him, waiting for him to respond, but he didn't trust himself to speak. An elderly couple were making their way towards them along the path, arm in arm. They looked as though they'd been married for a lifetime. 'Well, if you're just going to sit there,' she said, eventually. 'I'm going to brunch. Are you coming?'

'Of course I'm not coming to fucking brunch.'

'Suit yourself,' she said, before getting up and walking away, her back stiff and the blue scarf flowing behind her.

As Hassan sat alone on the bench, head resting on his hands and the misery washing over him, he realised he was greeting an old friend. He'd allowed himself to believe that he could be happy, but the reality was that this was all there was. All there had ever been, waiting at the end of every tunnel.

Failure. Pathetic, weak and oh-so-familiar failure.

Shuna

It had to be a coincidence.

Of course it wasn't a bloody coincidence. Shuna could remember how she'd pressed herself back in the seat of the cab that night as though it would help her to keep away from him. She'd wanted to scream, but all she could manage was a whimper.

'Please don't hurt me.'

'I'm not going to hurt you. What makes you think I would want to do that?' His disembodied voice crackled over the intercom and Shuna wanted to scream out the list of reasons why she didn't believe him – his aggression at the airport, his face after the tribunal, the fact that he'd been following her and taking photos, the fact that he'd abducted her and locked her in the back of his taxi. What did he expect her to think?

She didn't say any of those things. She knew that she needed to stay calm. 'Please let me out,' she said. 'Just pull over here and open the doors. I won't tell anyone.'

'I will. I promise,' he said. 'But not quite yet. I want to talk to you first.'

'Talk about what?' Shuna could see his eyes in the mirror, watching her as she reached for her phone.

'No. Don't do that. Don't call anybody.' The taxi stopped sharply, and the phone flew out of Shuna's hands as she was slammed into the seatbelt, the coarse webbing cutting through her thin coat and dress and biting into her right breast.

She sat back, shocked and aching and the taxi pulled away again. She could see her phone on the floor, too far to reach with her foot.

'Shuna. Can I call you Shuna?' His voice was hoarse and grating or was it the speakers? He sounded desperate, pleading, a different man from the oaf at the airport. 'I just want to talk to you for five minutes. No more.'

The click of Shuna's seatbelt releasing was unnaturally loud and his eyes widened. 'Stop that,' he shouted. 'What are you doing?

164

Don't …'

But it was too late. Shuna threw herself onto the floor, grabbing her phone and bracing herself for another sudden stop. His voice was still booming from the speakers, but she wasn't listening.

Simon picked up on the second ring and Shuna blurted out the words in a stream. 'Simon … It's me … No, just listen … I'm in a cab … On Piccadilly … It's him … I'm locked in … Call the police … Help me …'

Simon hung up. He was always calm in an emergency and she knew he would be calling the police, giving them complete precise information. He would call her back when he was done. There was nothing else she could do, and she lay curled up on the floor, her nostrils full of the stale stench of London which lingered in the carpet.

The taxi stopped. She heard the clunk as the door locks released. Was he coming into the back? Should she fight back? Why was he doing this?

Paralysed by indecision, Shuna lay there shivering, eyes closed and both hands clasped together in desperate prayer.

'Get out.' The noise of his voice condensed into those two small words. The doors were still closed, and he hadn't moved from his seat. What was happening? Was this some sort of trick?

'Get out. Now.'

Shuna scrambled to her knees, pulled open the door and rolled out onto the pavement. They were in a side street in Shepherd's Market, nobody in sight, but close to the middle of the busy West End. She saw his face appear at the open passenger-side window. He wasn't angry, and she saw something broken and beaten in his eyes.

'I only wanted to talk,' he said. 'You didn't have to do that.'

And then he was gone, the open door swinging closed with a final thunk as the sound of screeching tyres faded.

Shuna never found out why he'd been following her.

She'd had a complete breakdown a few weeks later and the drugs they'd given her had disengaged her from reality. Medication had taken the edge off her fear and controlled the panic attacks, but for several months, she'd lost interest in everything; it wasn't only the police action against Jim Pritchard which she avoided, every element of her life had been reduced to lifeless clockwork.

She hugged Zoe and Anna when she remembered, but took no pleasure from it. Food and wine, which had been her passion, were reduced to fuel and sedatives and, wherever she looked, beauty seemed to have faded quietly out of the world.

Sex was off the table. More than just a lack of libido, she couldn't control the myriad dark images which filled her mind whenever the subject arose. Simon had been wonderful, although she could see that the strain of it all was making him unhappy. It was probably causing permanent harm to their relationship, but she struggled to care.

He was angry that she'd refused to press charges; they fought often about that. He couldn't understand how much she needed it to simply go away. None of it made sense, but she didn't want revenge. All she wanted was her life back and persecuting that man wouldn't help. She could see that Simon was trapped by his memories of that evening. His failure to protect his wife still gnawed away at him and he needed something to tip the scales back.

Despite her reticence, the police charged Jim Pritchard with attempted abduction although, in the circumstances, she was excused from making a court appearance and they relied on her written statement. The offence was potentially very serious, but there was no real evidence of the stalking and they hadn't been able to find any photos on either of Jim's cameras nor on his laptop. Nothing had actually happened to her in the taxi and the defence lawyer had apparently been very good.

At the end of it all the judge gave him a suspended sentence, subject to a strict restraining order, and that was that. Unsurprisingly, the taxi licensing authorities were less understanding; he was banned from driving a taxi for life.

Simon had been in court for the verdict and, even after the drive home, he was livid.

'What's the point?' he shouted, banging his fist on the table. 'What's the bloody point?'

'It's done,' said Shuna. 'That's what's most important. If they'd given him jail time, his lawyer would have appealed and it would have carried on. I'm much happier this way.'

'But what about justice?' said Simon. 'Anything could have happened that night. Look what he's done to our lives.'

'The thing is,' said Shuna. 'Nothing did happen. And I can't imagine his life's looking great either.'

'But he brought it on himself. He deserves to pay.'

'We started it, darling. If I'd been a bit less obsessed with my rights back then, none of this would have happened.'

'But that's no excuse for …'

Shuna had suddenly remembered why she loved him and smiled. '… Let's stop worrying about right and wrong for now. I'm happy it's over and I'm going to stop taking those stupid drugs. It's time we got our lives back.'

'Mum?'

'Yes, Anna?'

'That man over there's giving me a weird look.'

Shuna wasn't really listening to what Anna was saying. The colossal majesty of the dinosaur had caught her by surprise and she'd been standing and staring in disbelief for over a minute, her lips slightly apart and eyelids heavy and drooping.

All those months working on her uncle's game reserve as a fifteen-year-old fed her imagination; memories of elephants and hippos ponderously crunching their way through the bush gave her mental tools which allowed her to clothe the skeleton in sheets of heavy, wrinkled hide – grey and bulletproof. She could imagine the massive feet reaching up and out with deceptive slowness before pounding down to crack the red terracotta tiles and send minor earthquakes rippling out in splintering starbursts.

'MUM!'

Shuna was jolted a hundred and fifty million years forward – back to the real world. 'I'm sorry, darling. I was miles away. What did you say?'

'I said that the man over there was giving me a weird look.'

'Which man?'

'The old man in the purple fleece. In the corner behind the dinosaur's foot.'

'But, he's a museum guard, sweetie. I'm sure he was just checking to make sure you weren't touching anything.'

'No. It was different. I might only be ten, but I'm not blind. He looked surprised and then angry. Look. He's still staring at us.'

Shuna looked over at the guard. There was nothing special about him. He was about sixty, short grey hair under a baseball cap, plenty of wrinkles and a nose that had probably been broken one time too many. Aside from that, just an ordinary man. His face was shaded by the cap, but she could see he was angry and there was no doubt that he was staring directly at them. There was something accusing about that look and the way his head was hunched down into his shoulders looked familiar.

The context was completely wrong, but something was tugging away at her memories, teasing out the woollen thoughts, strand by strand.

As she turned back to Anna, she realised what that something was.

'It's him,' she said, pulling her daughter by the hand and looking around for Zoe.

'Who?'

'That bloody taxi driver.'

Dan

'Rosa?' said Rachel. 'In my heart, I always knew it must have been about a woman.' She looked at Dan and he wondered if she would understand. 'Rosa. It's a beautiful name.'

'She was a beautiful person,' said Dan. 'I've never talked about her since that day. Not to the counsellors. Not the police. No-one. I wanted to keep my memories of her all to myself.'

Rachel didn't say anything. She always knew when to speak and when to remain silent.

'I'm going to start at the end,' said Dan. 'I'm not sure whether I'll manage to get through to the beginning, but at least you'll know how it ended.'

He took out his wallet and opened it on his lap. His fingers were clumsy, and he found himself struggling to tease out the small piece of soft, yellowing paper. He unfolded it slowly and, without looking up, handed it to Rachel.

That small piece of paper had been in his pocket every day for half a century. He'd felt a jagged knife plunge into his heart every time he'd looked at it and had lost count of the number of times he'd almost torn it up or thrown it in the fire. Almost, but not quite. He couldn't allow himself to forget. His memories were all he had left.

But his memories weren't real any more. They were memories of memories, layered one upon another, day-by-day for fifty years. He couldn't recall anything they had spoken about as they walked, there was no continuous record of their journey into town that morning. There were only disconnected images: bright sunlight and flickering shade; the tall oaks dappling the sidewalk under their feet; simple white strap sandals and delicate brown ankles, the yellow cotton of her dress; white teeth, happy laughter and dancing eyes. Dan no longer knew what was real and what was imagined.

It was all so long ago.

THE AUSTIN DAILY OBSERVER *August 2nd 1966*

One and a Half Hours of Terror

Yesterday morning, just before noon, the unthinkable happened. A young student and former Marine opened fire on innocent bystanders at the University of Texas.

Over 96 minutes, the sniper shot forty-four passers-by from on high in the University of Texas tower, killing 14 and seriously wounding many of the others. Earlier in the day, Charles Joseph Whitman, 24 had also murdered his wife and mother with a knife and handgun.

Whitman successfully defended his position from police marksmen until two policeman eventually killed the shooter by climbing to a platform above him and blasting him with revolver and shotgun fire.

Four of the wounded have since died, including a young pregnant woman; her six-month-old unborn son was killed instantly by yesterday's bullet which today also claimed her as a victim.

Three years after President Kennedy's assassination, Texas is again the centre of a firearm-related tragedy. Never, in our proud history, has anything like this occurred.

Will our great nation ever be the same again?

They sat in silence while Rachel read the article.

Dan didn't trust himself to look at her and it was only when she gave him back the refolded newspaper cutting that he dared to lift his gaze. He saw the love and anguish in her eyes which was more than he could bear, as he'd known it would be. He dropped his head onto her shoulder and, when she wrapped her warm arms around him, the tears came.

'Maybe I should have chosen a slightly less public place for this?' he said eventually, his trembling voice ill-suited to humour.

'Screw them,' said Rachel and the profanity sounded stranger on her lips than the fact that her husband was bawling his eyes out in a British museum.

'Yeah,' said Dan. 'Screw them.'

'So, Rosa was the young pregnant woman?' said Rachel.

'Yes,' said Dan.

'And the unborn baby,' said Rachel. 'That was your son?'

'Yes,' said Dan.

'You poor man,' Rachel sobbed. 'You poor, poor darling.'

Nadia

Nadia looked at her watch. Almost quarter to twelve and still nothing. She left two messages for the waitress at the cafe, asking her to see if she could remember anything else and then gave her phone to Ed in case he was able to pick out some sort of pattern from the hundreds of updates to the Snowflake thread. It was crazy that MI5 and MI6 didn't have open data sharing. Weren't they supposed to be on the same side?

He looked up. 'Are you aware you're literally hopping from one foot to the other?' he said. 'I didn't know people ever really did that.'

Nadia glared at him. 'I can't stand this waiting. I know we're running out of time.'

He handed her back the phone. 'I don't think you've missed anything here,' he said, 'although you won't want to hear the latest from GCHQ.'

'What is it?'

'Seems you're right about timing. They've just intercepted an encrypted message referring to a glorious event at twelve o'clock today.'

'Oh Christ,' said Nadia, feeling her shoulders sag and the nervous energy drain out of her body. 'We're too late.'

She felt Ed's arm around her. 'Let's not get ahead of ourselves,' he said. 'It ain't over 'til it's over … And who knows? … His watch might be slow.'

Nadia laughed in spite of herself. 'A poor moment for humour,' she said. 'But you're right. Nothing is over until the fat lady sings. Let's sit tight and give the forensics guys a few more minutes. We know he's close and there's no point in chasing off in the wrong direction.'

Ed took his arm away. 'I was a desk analyst for my first five years at GCHQ,' he said. 'It was a strange job. There were moments of huge excitement when things were going down. Maybe someone had called the wrong number on a burner phone and we suddenly got access to a dozen other targets, or a simple tip-off released a cascading waterfall of new intel. At times like that, we worked until we couldn't see straight, living off Red Bull and pizza.

'And then, the flow would stop as though a tap had suddenly closed. No warning and no explanation. There was nothing anyone could do about it. The only option was to wait. I guess we used humour to defuse the tension.'

Nadia nodded. 'I get that,' she said. 'It's not so different on a stake-out. Even though most of the time nothing happens, I'm normally OK with it. I don't know why this one's getting to me so much. I suppose I've just spent six months watching thousands of people going to the mosque every Friday. I had a good view from my window and could watch them as they arrived and left. They were just ordinary people, coming to worship peacefully. I know I don't believe in God, but I still felt happy to be a part of it, somehow. I felt proud of my roots.'

Although Ed didn't speak, Nadia watched his features soften, and she saw kindness and understanding in his eyes.

Nadia felt her built-up anger and frustration pushing to the surface. 'Maybe I'm just fed up,' she said. 'Fed up with a tiny minority of idiots giving all Moslems a bad name and I can't cope with the idea of another incident making it even worse. I may not be religious, but that doesn't mean I'm ashamed of who I am and where I come from.'

'You don't need a Moslem background to feel that way,' said Ed. 'Fingers crossed we get lucky this time.' He sat down on the low wall behind him, leaving room for Nadia. 'For now, I think we just have to wait. Even though they're one step ahead of us, we're close.'

'I know,' said Nadia, joining him on the wall. 'The other thing that's bugging me is Snowflake. He really doesn't fit the usual profile.' She knew that her own personal issues were probably making her over-sensitive, but she became almost tearful as she thought about the things she'd uncovered. He'd only been a few years after her at Oxford and, apart from being a little naïve, he'd done nothing to deserve the perfect shitstorm of bad luck which had hit him.

'Tell me what you found out,' said Ed.

'He grew up in Bradford,' said Nadia. 'Bright, but wimpy, nerd with a stupid bullying father. Somehow managed to defy the odds and get a place at Oxford to study biochemistry. An uncle – who happens to be a known drug dealer – agreed to fund his education in return for a commitment to work for him. He was doing OK until his final year, on track for a high 2:1 or even a First, but there was a complication.'

'A "complication"?'

'Yes,' said Nadia. 'I tracked down his old tutor and a few of his contemporaries and apparently he fell in love with an Egyptian girl, Mona El Masry. The way I heard it, she was already engaged back home and just wanted to have a bit of fun while she had the chance – to enjoy her final years of freedom. She was wealthy and beautiful and Snowflake was either too stupid or too blinkered to see the truth. He fell head over heels and they were together for two years.'

'Poor bloody idiot,' said Ed. 'It's not only men who are arseholes, is it? So, what happened?'

'Well, it was all a bit predictable, I guess ...' said Nadia, who hadn't stopped staring at her phone. She paused in mid-sentence. 'Hang on. They've got a first pass on the fingerprints ... it's definitely our man, a twenty-two point match ... three other sets ... and one of them is an eleven point match for Unicorn.'

'He must have brought the detonator unit with him from Pakistan,' said Ed. 'That fits completely.'

'But it doesn't bloody move us forward at all, does it?' Nadia could feel the events of the past few weeks catching up and black despair sinking over her. What was the point? 'All it means is that we now know for sure we're dealing with a highly experienced terrorist who never fails.'

'It means he's here somewhere,' said Ed. 'If we could find him, it would be a major coup.'

Until that moment, Nadia had been pleasantly surprised by Ed, who appeared to be a decent man, maybe even someone worth going out for a drink with. It was, she realised, inevitable that his true colours would shine through sooner rather than later. 'So, there's a central London suicide bombing,' she snapped. 'Dozens of people are killed and injured, bigots around the world are given another gift-wrapped excuse to be racist and anti-Moslem, hundreds more jihadists are inspired to join the cause … and all you give a damn about is a major career coup?'

Ed stepped backwards, eyes wide with shock. 'No,' he said. 'No. That's not what I bloody meant and you know it.'

Nadia looked at him. He was standing in front of her, arms by his sides, looking at her like a smacked puppy. He'd just opened his mouth to say something else – probably some sort of pathetic justification – when her phone started to ring. She lifted one hand which stopped him dead.

'Hello …? Hello …?'

11:48

Jim

Luckily – or unluckily – Julie wasn't the type to sit and stew for hours and Jim barely had time to pick up the broken halves of the vase – which had cost a bob or two – before the kitchen door swung open and Julie filled the doorframe, gloves on for Round Two.

'What's wrong with you?' she screamed at him. 'Where did you get all of that bloody equipment? How much did it cost? Why would you keep it a secret?'

The whole saga with Shuna had done something to Jim. His standard M.O. would always have been to go straight onto the offensive and bulldoze any resistance into the ground, just like the Rio police had done to those favela slums before the World Cup. It had always worked for him and he'd never thought twice about it.

But something had changed inside him over the previous days and weeks. As he looked at Julie's clenched fists and face flushed with anger and pain, he actually understood that she deserved an explanation.

'I'm sorry, luv. I didn't think you'd understand.'

'What are you crapping on about?' Julie's nostrils flared wide as she took a step towards him. 'Understand what?'

'About the photography and everything. I thought you'd think I'd gone soft. Take the piss or something,' Jim mumbled, unable to look Julie in the eyes. '… And there's no way you'd have kept it to yourself.'

He staggered backwards, off balance for a second as she planted the flat of her hand into his chest. Once. Twice. Hard. Punctuating her words with the short jabbing pushes. 'Are – you – fucking – serious?' She grabbed his chin and forced him to look at her. 'You think I married you because you were a hard man? You think I like it when you shout me down?' She let go of him and took a step backwards, biting her lower lip. 'Or slap me around?'

It probably hadn't been the best moment for Jim to show his caring, listening side. Julie may have been slightly surprised to have the opportunity to say her piece, but she didn't show any signs of slowing down.

'I don't know. I just thought ...'

'No ... No ... You fucking didn't.' Julie had stopped shouting and was looking at Jim as though he was something she'd scraped off the bottom of her shoe. 'If there's one thing you didn't do, it was think. God, you men are so bloody up yourselves.'

'But ...'

'Do you really *think* I would have minded you having a hobby like that? Is that what you *think* of me? We've been together for more than forty fucking years. D'you really *think* I'd rather find out about your dirty secret from some smug copper?'

'It's not a dirty secret. I just take photos of waterbirds, for Christ's sake.'

'Blonde South African ones if the police aren't lying.' Julie looked as though she'd shouted everything out of her system and there was nothing left. She crumpled back against the wall, eyes blank and unfocused. Her face was sagging and Jim noticed the wrinkles around her eyes and mouth for the first time. 'Honest, Jim,' she said at last. 'What do you fucking expect me to believe?'

Jim had never been lost for words, but, for the first time, he understood how this situation might look to other people. Even worse, he began to realise how frightened Shuna must have been in the taxi. Why should she have believed he really only wanted to talk? He'd locked her in for Christ's sake.

He could remember the hostage and captivity training they'd had to do when he was in Belfast. It had been called SERE – Survival, Evasion, Resistance, and Escape – and he'd hated it as much as anything he'd ever done, before or afterwards.

The real killer had been the feeling of powerlessness, of being trapped and at someone else's mercy. It was something out of his experience and, for some reason, brought back thoughts of his father and the way he would suck up to Dave Vickers in the pub.

He'd failed the course twice before scraping through.

And he'd put Shuna through that! It was as though his brain had turned to mush and he couldn't see anything properly any more. In just a few weeks, his life had changed completely, he'd changed completely, and, in a flash of clarity, he'd known nothing would ever be the same again.

Jim squeezed his eyes tightly closed; he could still relive that moment of revelation in high definition even though it had been almost a year earlier. Julie had stood sagging in front of him like an empty carrier bag, the anger gone and nothing left to hold her up. And it was all his fault. All because of his stupid, pointless male pride. All because he wanted to show everyone he was a real man.

Worse than that, after everything he'd done to his wife, the person who was dominating his thoughts was Shuna. As he'd watched Julie breaking down in front of him, all he'd been able to do was worry about a woman he hardly knew. He really was a git.

Since then, he'd done what he could to make it up to his family. The new Jim would carry on trying, but after so many years it was hard to change and the old Jim wasn't going anywhere in a hurry; there were two men battling inside him and, despite the pills he was taking, trying to find a balance was wearing him down.

He looked around the hall which had emptied out again. He'd been right about one thing back then; it was after he'd picked Shuna up in his cab that his life had changed forever. That was when the hard shell which always protected him had been broken.

No sign of Shuna. What with everything else that was going on his head, it was definitely possible he'd imagined seeing her in the exhibition. During the weeks after the first tribunal, he'd seen her everywhere, in shops, pubs, on the street, in the West End, in the East End and even on the marshes when he'd been out with his camera.

That was why he'd decided to find out where she lived and started working that patch; once he began to see her in the flesh most days, the imaginary sightings began to fade away. As for the photos, he always had his camera in the car and it passed the time. It had seemed harmless enough.

Will caught his eye and waved to indicate he was off on his break. Jim gave him the thumbs up and watched as the young lad strolled out past the entrance to the exhibition. He really would have liked to have had a son. They'd decided to stop after the second girl – the pregnancy hadn't been easy for Julie and the doctors had been quite clear it was time to call it a day. In spite of everything, he'd done his best for his girls but he was a bloke's bloke and, looking at Will, he could imagine all the things he and his boy might have done together.

Spilt milk. Too much worrying about that these days. It didn't help anything.

A man was standing by one of the stone pillars, a bit of a non-entity, mousy hair and a pale blue anorak. There was something odd about the way he was pressed against the wall, almost as though he was trying to hide from someone.

Jim had noticed him when he first came in and since then he'd been stuck in the same spot, looking around nervously; not interested in the dinosaur or anything else in the museum. For about ten minutes, the poncey little bloke had been jabbering into his phone and waving his free hand around like an overexcited hairdresser, but when he saw Will walking towards him, he seemed to panic, finished his call and started pretending to read some sort of leaflet.

As soon as Will had walked past, Jim saw the man's shoulders slump, he smiled a smug smile and tucked the brochure back into his pocket. Jim didn't give a toss about his job, but he didn't like the look of him. Something wasn't right and, as he didn't have anything better to do …

He pushed himself up from the chair, stretched out his back and started walking across the hall.

Jim smiled as he saw the frightened-rabbit look in the man's eyes. He was hiding something without a doubt. From closer up, the guy looked like even more of a loser than he had at a distance. It was difficult to imagine him being any sort of threat, but Jim had learnt to avoid making too many assumptions; you only had to look at some of those high school killers in the States to see what total nobodies could be capable of.

'Good morning, sir,' said Jim, wondering why that particular floor tile was so interesting.

'Oh. Good morning.' The man looked up from the ground in a pathetically transparent attempt to pretend he hadn't noticed Jim walking towards him. 'Can I help you?'

'It's just a random security check,' said Jim. 'You know how it is?'

'Yes, of course,' said the man.

Jim looked at him and shrugged his shoulders, but the penny obviously hadn't dropped.

'Well, could I have a look in the bag, please?'

'Aha. Yes. I see. Sorry. I'm really not with it this morning.' He opened his brown leather shoulder bag – something designer by the look of it – and handed it to Jim. 'Here you are. Just some medicine and a couple of books.'

Jim took out the books and checked the bottom of the bag. Nothing else. No need to worry. He was just one of those sad, lonely blokes who were creepy and suspicious by nature.

'Thanks,' he said, as he put the books back in the bag and handed it back. Now that was strange – he was reading the Twilight books. Jim could remember Brooke, his youngest, being obsessed with them when she was thirteen or fourteen. Hardly standard reading material for a man in his mid thirties. He sighed. It really was nothing to do with him what the bloke chose to do in his spare time. After all, who was he to talk?

He'd not seen Brooke for over two years. She'd never forgiven him for the last time he'd whacked her mother. Brooke wasn't supposed to be there and Julie hadn't had a chance to tell him she was staying over. Jim had just pulled an all-nighter – the third on the trot – and everything had gone wrong. Nothing out of the ordinary, just a perfect storm of idiot punters winding him up one after the other.

The icing on the cake had come at after four. He'd been cruising somewhere around Harley Street hoping to get one last fare. There were loads of girlie bars and all-night drinking clubs hiding away in the basements of the posh houses and lawyer's offices, and he'd been hoping to catch some pissed businessman staggering out of one of them.

Jim had been about to give up when he saw his man – sharp suit, but barely able to walk straight. A ten minute fare to some posh West End hotel, a decent tip and Jim could call it a night … until the guy had poured himself into the back of the cab and leant forward.

'Tooting, please,' he'd said. 'Eswyn Road.'

Tooting! Bloody Tooting. At four in the morning! Jim couldn't believe his luck. No juicy last fare for him. He'd have to dump the guy and go straight home.

'Sorry, mate,' he'd said. 'I'm just finishing my shift. Can't go south of the river at this time of night.'

'Not my problem,' slurred the man. 'You've accepted the ride. You have to take me.' And then he'd leant forward and taken a bloody photo of Jim's ID.

Jim could remember the anger rising and was surprised he hadn't actually broken the steering wheel. But it was only three weeks after he'd been put on probation. The last thing he needed was to be reported by some smug investment banker.

His teeth were still clenched tight by the time he got home ninety minutes later and the rage was pumping in and out of his nostrils in sharp bursts as he stormed into the house.

Julie worked an early shift on Thursdays and was sitting in the kitchen having a cup of tea. Jim had no idea what she'd said – if she'd actually spoken at all. It didn't matter. He needed an outlet for his rage and there was no-one else around.

As she'd backed away from him, holding a finger to her bleeding lip, Jim had realised her panicked stare wasn't aimed at him, but over his left shoulder. He'd turned to see Brooke standing in the doorway, holding baby Josie and staring at him with tight lips and narrow eyes.

Since then, neither Brooke nor her big sister had wanted to have anything to do with him. Even after he'd written to them both, apologising and swearing never to do anything like that again.

Luckily Julie had persuaded them to let him see his grandkids – Kaylee was about the same age as Shuna's oldest and little Josie was the cutest little thing imaginable. Jim was continuously surprised by the warm swelling glow in his stomach which appeared every time he saw them. It might be too late for his daughters to forgive him, but at least he had time to get one thing right.

Jim settled back in his chair and scratched his head. It had been a lively half hour what with the imaginary sighting of Shuna, that creepy guy and the old man who didn't die. That was more activity than he could expect in an average week – and it was still only Monday morning.

The creep was slinking off down the corridor towards the cafe – something definitely wasn't right with him – and the old man was still on his bench, now hugging an older woman like his life depended on it.

He should have stuck with the young Spanish girl. Much tastier.

This was what Jim's life had become. Every day a pointless, pathetic routine where the most trivial action was a highlight. And it was all Shuna's fault. If the stupid cow hadn't been at the airport that day, things would have stayed in place. She'd humiliated him in front of the only people who mattered to him. Why couldn't he stay angry with her? He wanted to be pissed off with her.

He could accept that locking her in his cab and driving off had been a bad idea, but he'd told her he'd stop, he'd explained that he only want to talk. She could have bloody listened. She wasn't in the cab for more than a few minutes before he let her out. Nothing happened.

But, just like with the airport pickup, she wouldn't let it drop. And then the police had turned up with a search warrant. It was her fault that his life had gone down the pan. She hadn't needed to be so bloody vindictive. He felt the first stirrings of rage boiling in his belly. Screw keeping calm. Screw the doctors with their bloody pills.

He wanted to be angry with her. She deserved every bit of it.

Hassan

The Natural History Museum loomed in front of him. The massive, monumental facade was no more than a symbol of colonial hypocrisy, a salmon-pink statement of Imperial might, built on the bones of millions of subjects across the colonial world, his ancestors included.

Hassan waited for a moment before slowly walking up the steps to the massive entrance door, his mind replaying everything he'd been taught over the past two months. He'd known for years that people like his father were foolish victims of establishment propaganda and he'd taken little convincing as the government's lies had been exposed one-by-one like wriggling earthworms, pink-bellied and vulnerable in the light of day. He'd grown up; the boy had become a man.

But, for a moment, the small boy was still there, and he couldn't suppress the feelings of awe which welled up inside him as he caught his first glimpse of the central hall. The architects had built the hall itself to impress and to intimidate but, for Hassan, the diplodocus skeleton at its centre was so much more overwhelming – a breathtaking reminder of what God can achieve without the meddling of man.

But, as they'd reminded him again and again, the age of the dinosaurs was no more. That was the way of the world and part of Allah's infinite plan. Now it was time for the blinkered and hidebound imperialists to learn that all ages and empires are built on foundations of sand, and that they are destined to crumble away and to be replaced.

First, however, he needed to get through security. He had studied dozens of photos of the entrance set-up and knew the odds. The guards were poorly trained – ticket collectors really – but they had a policy to do a full pat-down search of one in every forty people in the queue. Odds in his favour of ninety-seven and a half per cent. He would have to live with that.

Nevertheless, as he approached the young girl in the purple

fleece, he kept his right hand close to his pocket.

Just in case.

There was never an actual argument. After all the time he and Mona had been together and the humiliation of the proposal, there should at least have been a few screaming, arm-waving, coffee-cup-smashing attempts to apportion blame. But Hassan wasn't like that; his new status of naïve, humiliated, single fool fitted him like an old, worn leather jacket. There was nothing to fight about. He should have known better. The world didn't simply change overnight.

Even when the enormity of his failure had eventually sunk in, he'd held his rage and sense of loss deep inside as he'd done all of his life. In those first moments, however, as he'd stood alone in a sea of blue flowers, he was a mindless, emotionless zombie, unable to properly understand what had just happened.

He left the botanical gardens, went back to the flat – Mona's flat – and packed his stuff. Two big sports bags were all he needed, and it took him less than an hour to cut himself out of her life. He took nothing to remember her by and left no letter or note – what would it have said? He placed his keys carefully on the hall table and walked out, squeezing his eyes tightly shut as he heard the solid thunk of the front door closing for the last time.

Hassan found himself homeless, broke and with a diamond ring worth three thousand quid in his pocket. His third-year exams were only two months away, and he was actually a long way beyond broke, but all of these problems could wait. He would take the ring back the next day and sort everything out, but right then, as he stood on the Cowley Road with his world in two bags at his feet, he needed a drink.

The barman at the Rose and Crown was a fellow biochem student. Not really a friend, but someone he knew well enough. He agreed to stash Hassan's bags in the back room and had a generous heavy hand with the spirit optics. The hours passed, people arrived and left, and Hassan sat quietly in the corner drinking whisky after whisky without feeling a thing. He wasn't drunk, and he wasn't sad; he was trapped in a frozen slice of time where his mind was still protecting him from truly understanding what had happened with Mona that morning, and how his dreams had turned to slush.

By early evening he'd started to realise that the whisky was winning the battle, but he kept on drinking, regardless. It was a one-off. He needed to get it out of his system and would figure out how to rebuild what was left of his life in the morning. Eventually, drunkenness claimed him. Unfortunately it wasn't a gentle slide into oblivion, but more of a retching, bile-filled collapse into pain and self pity. The barman found him passed out on the wet toilet floor and Hassan solved his accommodation problems by spending the night at A&E recovering from a stomach pump.

He wasn't up to much the next day. They hadn't had any beds in A&E but, as there had been no-one to look after him, they couldn't send him home. Once they'd finished turning him inside out, they stuck him in a chair to wait until they were sure his body had stabilised. It was during that miserable night, at half-past three in the morning, that Hassan realised it was over.

The nightly parade of walking wounded had slowed by then and a young nurse came over and sat beside him as he crumpled.

'It'll be OK,' she said, patting him on the shoulder. 'Plenty more fish in the sea, eh?'

But there weren't, and it wouldn't be. Hassan knew that.

By the time he got out, it was late afternoon and the jeweller's shop was already closed. A friend from his course had offered to let him crash on his sofa for a few nights and Hassan went back to the pub to pick up his bags. The same barman was there and Hassan mumbled a few words of thanks and apology, all the while looking fixedly at his shoes. The whole department would know the sordid story already; it seemed that there was no end to the number of ways in which he could humiliate himself.

He was still feeling terrible and wasn't even slightly tempted by the thought of a quick whisky while he was there. At least he'd learnt his lesson and wouldn't be repeating that fiasco in a hurry. The sofa was surprisingly comfortable and Hassan's fears about not

184

being able to sleep were unfounded.

As he walked into the jeweller's the next morning, he was filled with determination. He'd made a mistake, but he couldn't let that drag him down. Mona had been the love of his life, but it was over. He had to pick himself up and get on with things.

'Good morning, Mr Qureishi,' said the assistant, just as slimy as when he'd sold Hassan the ring. 'Have you come to have the ring resized? As I said to you last week, it's always best to start too large. That way ...' His voice tailed off when he saw the expression on Hassan's face.

'Oh,' he said, eventually. 'Things didn't go as planned?'

'No,' said Hassan. 'You could put it like that.'

'I'm very sorry. I hope it wasn't anything to do with the ring?'

'No. Of course not.' Hassan did his best to smile. 'We didn't get that far.'

The two young men faced each other across a polished glass cabinet filled with glistening symbols of hope and promises. Neither wanted to speak first.

Hassan gave in. 'So. I need to sell it back to you.' He took the ring out of his pocket, opened the box and set it down on the counter. 'It's never even been tried on. I paid three thousand, two hundred and fifty. I get that you'll want to apply some sort of handling fee, but it shouldn't be a lot as I've only had the ring for a couple of days. To tell you the truth, I couldn't really afford it in the first place.'

The assistant was shifting from leg to leg like a toddler in denial about the contents of his nappy. 'I'm afraid it's not quite as simple as that, Mr Qureishi,' he said. 'You see, we're in the business of selling jewellery, not buying it back.'

'Of course,' said Hassan. 'But in the circumstances ... I only bought the bloody thing three days ago.'

'I do understand, sir, but we have a very strict policy on returns and my hands are tied. I would need to make a call.'

'What are we talking about here?' said Hassan, feeling the floor start to shift and tilt underfoot. 'How much will I lose?'

'As I said. I'll need to make a call.'

'Well, make the bloody call then.' Hassan was never normally rude or aggressive, but his body was still full of poison and the assistant was being stupid as well as slimy.

The call went on and on with long periods of silent listening interspersed with grunts and exclamations; 'Aha', 'I see', 'Oh, I see', 'And that's the best we can do?', 'No, I do understand', 'Yes, I'll make that clear'. None of it sounded good.

Eventually the assistant put his phone down on the glass counter and looked up.

'Well?' said Hassan.

'Not great news, I'm afraid.'

'Just tell me how much, will you?'

'The best we could offer for a second-hand ring like that would be seven hundred and fifty pounds.'

'What?!' The foundations of Hassan's world were already cracked and crumbling and he now felt the walls folding in and the roof collapsing down, crushing him into the floor. 'Seven hundred and fifty quid? It's not fucking second-hand. I bought it from you three days ago.'

The young man stepped back from the counter, the whites of his eyes bright in the halogen lights. 'I do understand, sir. I've tried as hard as I can, but it's the best we can do. You may want to look around and see if you can get a better price somewhere else.'

'Too fucking right I will.' Hassan swept up the box and its not-so-precious contents and barged through the door, scraping a blunt gash on the back of his hand as he went.

It hadn't taken him long to realise that seven hundred and fifty quid was the best he was going to get but, even though he had no money at all, he couldn't bring himself to take it. The pawn shop had offered him five hundred; all he needed was to come up with an extra hundred within ninety days and he could have the ring back. That felt better. He'd have a bit of breathing space so he could figure out how to get a better price. Maybe his uncle would want it.

The thought of his uncle had sent shivers down Hassan's back. He'd already taken out two big overdrafts which were basically advances against the following year's allowance. What if Uncle Sami found out? Hassan may have only been an office boy, but after two summers working there, he'd heard enough stories to know that the boss knew everything before anyone else ... and crossing him was an extremely bad idea.

He toyed briefly with the idea of putting some or all of the five hundred on a horse, but he'd never even been inside a betting shop and he couldn't exactly claim to be on a winning streak. The best thing would be to focus on his revision and piecing together what was left of his life.

And so began the darkest period of Hassan's short life.

Nothing worked. He couldn't concentrate for more than a few minutes at a time. He tried, but his mind was spinning through the broken dreams of what might have been, and panicking about the terrifying realities of his current finances. A small glass of Famous Grouse from the bottle on his desk helped a little to calm those racing thoughts, but didn't help much with the concentration. He found himself craving the company of other people and closing his books earlier and earlier every day.

The only time he felt good was when he was drunk and in the company of other drunks. In that environment there was no need for honesty, or realism, or even to listen to anything anyone said. There was a conversational protocol of sorts: each of them would take a turn to mouth off about something – either how brilliant they were, or how badly the world had treated them – while the others waited for their turn, nodding and grunting approval automatically. And so it had gone on until either the drink or the money ran out.

As Hassan stood outside the museum, overdressed for the morning sunshine, he struggled to remember that time. Not because of alcohol-induced amnesia, although there was plenty of that, but because it hurt too much. With the benefit of hindsight, the events which had dragged him into that sucking cesspit were not so massive, but at the time ... He felt his fists clench tight as he let the memories in; the pain, the emptiness and the numbing sense of worthlessness had been so intense. It was no surprise that he had fallen.

And he'd kept on falling. Eventually, he'd lost the few friends he had and, in retrospect, it was amazing that they'd stuck by him for so long. He argued with anything and everything, and droned on and on, repeating himself in endless cycles. He kept his hard-studying, over-tolerant hosts awake for hours with his rambling soliloquies or woke them up when he arrived back in the middle of the night having lost his keys again. And he started to protect his dwindling bundle of cash like a dog with a bone. He took food from the fridge, bummed drinks and cigarettes whenever he could, and contributed nothing.

To begin with, he would still go to the library or to revision tutorials – almost out of habit – but it didn't take long for him to decide that he was wasting his time. He'd be fine. He'd worked hard all year and the exams would be easy. He would be over this bad patch in a week or two and then get his head down again. The "week or two" flew past and nothing changed.

As he sank down further and further, he stopped looking after himself. Personal hygiene had become a low priority and the scrape on his hand from the jeweller's door was swollen red and oozing. No-one had wanted him on their sofa any more. No-one had even wanted him on their floors.

Shuna

Shuna glanced over her shoulder once more, holding Anna protectively in front of her. It was definitely Jim Pritchard, and he was dressed as a museum guard. What were the chances of that? Her mind was racing. Where had Zoe got to? Should they try to sneak out without being seen?

'Owww!' Anna squealed. 'Let go. You're hurting me.'

Shuna looked down at her daughter and realised that she'd been squeezing her wrist as hard as she could. She let go and bent down to stroke Anna's cheek. 'I'm sorry, sweetheart,' she said. 'I didn't realise I was holding you so tightly.'

Anna pulled away from Shuna's touch, rubbing her wrist and oozing resentment. 'I thought it was all over,' she said. 'But now that man's here again.' She seemed close to tears. 'I just want things to be normal.'

For a moment, Shuna didn't know what to say. She'd also believed her life was on track again, but seeing him there had brought everything back and, like before, all the people around her – even Simon and the girls – would be shunted into the background, shut out behind a wall of fear, rage and guilt.

'Things are back to normal, princess,' she said. 'I was just surprised for a second.'

'That's rubbish, Mum,' said Anna. 'You should see the look on your face. It's just like when you were ill.'

Shuna knelt down and this time Anna allowed herself to be hugged. Shuna couldn't get the image of Jim out of her mind. He looked so much older and somehow pathetic in his baggy, purple fleece. This was probably the only work he'd been able to find, and it was all her fault. She realised she wasn't afraid of him any more, and the anger had long since faded. But she couldn't shake the thought that her arrogant and entitled behaviour had destroyed this man's life.

And for what?

She felt a tap on her shoulder and looked up to see Zoe standing over her, silhouetted in the bright lights. Shuna stood up and turned around, wiping the back of her hand across her eyes.

'What's wrong?' said Zoe. 'Is Anna being a loser again?'

'It's got nothing to do with me,' said Anna, always on the defensive. 'It's Mum. She's seen that taxi driver man. He's over there.' She nodded theatrically in Jim's direction. 'And you're the loser, anyway.'

Zoe turned to look across the hall. 'OMG,' she said, covering her mouth with her hand. 'It is him. What's he doing here?'

'He's a guard,' said Anna. 'When Mum recognised him, she freaked out.' She held out her hand. 'Look what she did to my wrist.'

Zoe ignored her and looked at Shuna who was now staring over her shoulder across the hall. 'Oh, Mum,' she said. 'That's crazy. Are you OK?'

Shuna nodded. 'I'm fine,' she said. 'It just came as a bit of shock. He was the last person I expected to see here.'

'But isn't there some sort of law that says he mustn't be in the same place as you?' said Anna.

'Yes. There's a restraining order that means that he can't be within a hundred and fifty yards of any of us.' Shuna snorted with laughter at the absurdity of the situation. 'But he can hardly be blamed if he's only sitting there doing his job and we walk in, can he?'

Anna was looking at her like a cornered deer, big, brown eyes wide and full of fear. Zoe's expression was more difficult to read, but she wasn't happy.

'Don't worry, girls, I'm not about to lose it again,' said Shuna, smiling. 'I know you've been worried about me and that's not fair. It's my job to worry about you, not the other way around.'

The tight smile on Zoe's face softened and Shuna could see that both of them were relaxing.

'But I am going to go over and talk to him, though.'

'No!' said Zoe, her words echoing around the hall. 'No, Mum. You can't.'

Shuna lifted both hands, palms outward. 'Shhh,' she said. 'Calm down and listen to me.'

'But you've only been better for a few weeks,' said Zoe. 'It's crazy to stir things up again. It's not fair on us ... or Dad. Let's just go.'

'I do understand,' said Shuna. 'But you don't have to worry. And I am thinking about both of you and Dad. Will you let me explain?'

'OK,' said Zoe, and Anna nodded her head silently.

'Right,' said Shuna, consciously keeping her back to Jim and sheltering her children. 'I know I've been much better for the past month or so ... and I can see that I must have been a terrible mother for a while ...'

'... No, Mum. That's not what we're saying,' said Zoe.

'... Never mind,' continued Shuna. 'That's not my point.' She looked closely at her beautiful girls, trying as hard as she could to project feelings of love and confidence. 'I'm better, but I'm not quite "good" yet. I can't get over the feeling that I ruined that man's life. And for what? To satisfy my stupid ego? I really don't know what to believe any more but I think I need to tell him I'm sorry.'

'But he was horrible to us,' said Anna. 'And then he locked you in his taxi. I don't understand why you want to be nice to him.'

Neither do I really,' said Shuna. 'But I'm pretty sure it's something I have to do if I want to move on.'

Zoe had been staring at Shuna with what appeared to be total disbelief. 'I don't get you, Mum,' she said eventually. 'But you're not going to listen to us, are you?' She picked up her bag. 'Well, you're not dragging us with you. Me and Anna will go and look at the dinosaur.' She drew herself up to her full five foot four. 'And I'm telling Dad, whatever you say. Come on Anna.' Zoe grabbed her sister's hand and stalked off towards the centre of the hall, leaving Shuna open-mouthed and alone.

Dan

'You could have told me before,' said Rachel. 'I might have been able to help.'

'You did help,' said Dan, using the backs of his fingers to gently wipe the tears from Rachel's cheeks. 'You were always there for me when I needed you.'

'But I meant if …'

'… I know what you meant,' he said. 'But it just wasn't possible. I couldn't. Sorry.'

'Don't apologise, you idiot. It just hurts to think of you carrying that wrapped up inside for all of these years.'

'Honey, it's hard to explain. I've had a good life. We've had a good life together. I know I haven't always been everything you wanted me to be, but a part of me died as well that day. I always hoped it would somehow grow back, but it didn't.'

'You really are an idiot,' she said. 'I didn't need more. You've done OK, you big lump.' As she started to smile, Dan saw a lightbulb flick on at the back of Rachel's eyes and the smile faded. 'But why now?' she said. 'Why here, and why now?'

'Ah. There's the thing,' said Dan. 'I'm afraid there's more.'

'What? Tell me.'

'You know that I went to see the oncologist for my check-up a couple of weeks before we left?'

'Uh-huh. He gave you the all clear.'

'Well, I lied,' said Dan.

'What do you mean, you lied?' said Rachel. 'I don't understand.'

'I lied about the results.' Dan could feel the emotion rising to the back of his throat. The moment he spoke the words out loud, everything would become real and there would be no reprieve. 'It's back. And it's spread everywhere.'

Rachel looked more confused than shocked. 'But why didn't you tell me? Surely you should have started chemo straight away? Why didn't we cancel the trip?'

'It's too far along,' said Dan. 'Like I said, it's everywhere. There's nothing they can do.' He smiled and pointed at the shopping bags on the floor at Rachel's feet. 'And I didn't want to cancel the trip. We've been looking forward to it for ages.'

Rachel was quiet for a long time and Dan knew he needed to give her the space to absorb what he was telling her. It had taken him more than three hours after the doctor's appointment. Three hours of pacing up and down in the park before he truly understood what he'd been told.

What was it Doestoevsky had said to his wife, Anna, right at the end? 'Hear now—permit it. Do not restrain me!'

There had to be a moment of acceptance. A time to stop raging against the dying of the light.

He looked across the hall to where a blonde woman was talking animatedly with her two daughters. He was certain that Rachel would have been a great mother. Had he denied her too much?

At last, Rachel lifted her head. Her mouth was set firm, lips pursed in determined self-control. 'How long?' she said.

'A month. Maybe two.'

'Are you in a lot of pain?'

Dan shrugged. 'It's OK when the drugs are working, but I'm taking more and more every day. I think I'll need something stronger soon.'

As the world turned and people busied themselves with their daily lives, Dan sat silently on the bench, watching his wife of forty-five years struggling to turn his words into a reality she could cope with, and wondering if Rosa was watching on from somewhere, happy that her long wait was almost over.

Nadia

'Thank you, Sally. Thank you very much.'

Nadia put her phone back in her pocket and turned to Ed. 'That was the girl from the cafe. She just remembered Snowflake told her he was going to the Natural History Museum.' As the adrenaline kicked back in, the jolt almost lifted her off her feet. 'That's it! That's our target. The main hall at the Natural History Museum.'

Nadia could tell Ed was struggling to catch up, but there was no time.

'You call it in,' she said. 'Then follow me. You'll never keep up, anyway.' Then she turned and started to run, ignoring his protesting voice fading behind her.

How far was it? A bit less than a mile? She should be there in five or six minutes. It was going to be tight.

As she threaded her way between hooting cars on Kensington Gore and started down Exhibition Road, she remembered the missing link which had been bugging her. When Hassan's mother had told her about his dad throwing books in the fire, it hadn't been just any books. The actual words replayed in her mind in Hi-Fi quality – 'The bitter old man threw his dinosaur book in the fire. My poor little Haso. He loved his dinosaurs. Fascinated by them, he were.'

Of course. It was a great target for them. High profile, low security and plenty of international tourists. If only she'd figured it out twenty minutes earlier.

Nadia settled into her stride. She could maintain a steady eight and half miles an hour for a couple of miles without overexerting herself – there was no point in getting there and being too out of breath to think straight. In an ideal world, SCO19 would have an armed response vehicle there before her, but there were roadblocks everywhere and traffic was jammed up. At least she was on foot.

Although finding opportunities to exercise while she'd been working at the mosque had been challenging, she'd worked out a routine she could do in her tiny bedroom; one hour's cardiovascular, morning and night. In any case, she'd needed the endorphins to keep her sane.

Nadia felt bad about the way she'd jumped down Ed's throat. He'd done nothing to deserve it and she would definitely need to consider some suitable grovelling later.

It had been telling Snowflake's story of thwarted love which had tipped her over the edge. The more she'd learned about him, the more she'd started to like him and to feel sorry for him. It was easy to forget how many normal lives were filled with tragedies of Shakespearean proportions. Even so, only a tiny minority of those ordinary people were prepared to give their lives for a cause, and even fewer were ready to kill and maim others in the process. Snowflake wasn't one of them. She was sure of it.

Her feet pounded rhythmically on the hard paving and she could feel the Glock bouncing against her left breast. Would she need to use it? Would she be forced to shoot Snowflake? She hoped not, but she wouldn't hesitate if she had to. Hesitation cost lives.

She was already almost halfway there, and she started to run through the protocols in her mind. She would need to identify herself to security; those valuable seconds were necessary to avoid interference coming from behind. Standard procedure also mandated a final check of her authority status; she'd been given the authority to take her own autonomous decisions, including using proportionate force, but that could change at any moment. There might be hostages or additional targets and co-ordination was key.

Only then would she be ready to move forward, fully assess the situation on the ground and use the remaining seconds to do whatever she could to prevent a disaster. If Ed and GCHQ were right about the timing, it was going to be very tight. Snowflake would already be past security and she'd have one or two minutes to spare at most. But she would make it in time - *insha'Allah.*

Despite Nadia's uncompromising secularism, she'd retained her childhood habit of saying *insha'Allah,* if God wills it; the words had replaced 'hopefully' and 'maybe' in her daily vocabulary. During the last six months, when she was actually supposed to be a practising Moslem, she hadn't said much else on most days. 'Will the imam's office be cleaned before he returns?' – 'insha'Allah'; 'are you going to be here to make coffee on Saturday?' – 'insha'Allah'.

It was almost like saying 'yes' although it allowed for uncertainty and could also be used to avoid saying 'no' if that was uncomfortable. There was also an implicit abdication of responsibility. It didn't necessarily mean that the speaker wouldn't try their hardest, although it did imply that it wouldn't be their fault if things didn't work out as planned.

Those were the last words her mother had said to her, before Nadia started running. Running as she was running now. Running against the clock.

They'd been on holiday in Brittany, near the village where her father had grown up. He'd borrowed her grandfather's old Mercedes and the three of them spent a wonderful day by the sea, Nadia dashing back and forth collecting shells from the beach while her parents sat in a small restaurant on the edge of the sand, working their way through a towering seafood platter.

Maybe her father had drunk too much wine, maybe a tyre had blown out – Nadia would never know. She was only ten years old and was much more interested in the pile of beautiful sea shells glistening in her lap. She remembered feeling a sudden lurch and hearing the harsh shriek of metal grinding against metal. And then a frozen, almost-magical instant as the shells hung weightless in the air. The car was rolling, over and over, Nadia tumbling like so much laundry as they crashed down the rocks to the edge of the sea.

The Mercedes had ended up on its side with Nadia lying against the door, the window handle digging into her back. She could see her father in the drivers seat, hanging motionless from his seatbelt. She couldn't see her mother.

'Mama!' she'd cried, as she struggled to pull herself upright. 'Mama!'

'I'm here, Cheri,' came her mother's voice from behind the

passenger seat. 'Are you hurt?'

Nadia managed to pull herself upright and leant forward to see her mother. 'I'm OK,' she said. 'Are you all right?'

'I think so,' said her mother, 'but I can't move and your father's unconscious. Can you open the window?'

'I can try,' said Nadia, hearing the shiver in her voice. Although the handle was stiffer than usual, she managed to open the window above her, letting in the wind, the salt spray and the booming of the waves.

'Good girl,' said her mother. 'Now I want you to listen very carefully. The tide is coming in and you need to get help. Climb up to the road, turn left and run as fast as you can to the next village. There's a garage there. Tell them what's happened and tell them to come quickly.'

Nadia hadn't wanted to leave the safety of the car. She hadn't wanted to go off on her own, but she'd known it was important and so she'd climbed up and managed to squeeze out of the window. She'd looked back into the car one more time.

'Don't worry, Mama,' she'd said. 'I'll be back soon.'

'*Insha'Allah,*' said her mother, as Nadia jumped down.

She'd been a podgy, unathletic child, always last to be picked for any team, but she'd tried so hard. She'd dragged herself up the rocky cliffs and onto the road and then she'd run as fast as she could, her breath rasping, the blood pumping in her head and her feet rubbed red raw in her light beach shoes.

Running against time ... as she was once again. This time she would get there before it was too late – and the will of God would have no say in the matter.

11:54

Jim

It wasn't hard for Jim to stir up a minor thunderstorm of rage if he thought about what had happened to his life. He only needed to look around him. To look at the stupid, plastic dinosaur and the idiot tourists who visited the museum because it was on the list of things to do in London.

Tourists were fine when you could see them as walking taxi fares, each one an opportunity for exploitation; once they were in the back of the cab – your cab – they belonged to you. They would listen to you, smile and laugh at your stories, however exaggerated and untrue, and then, best of all, they'd pay you for the privilege and give you a massive tip often as not.

There'd been an informal monthly competition amongst the cabbies for who could get away with the most outrageous story and Jim was disappointed if he wasn't shortlisted. Some foreigners were so gullible, it was like taking candy from a baby.

In the museum it was different. Here, they just cluttered up the place.

Jim wasn't particularly racist – a few of his mates had pretty good tans when it came down to it – but he had no problem with racial stereotyping.

It made sense after all. If someone grew up somewhere hot like Cyprus, it was natural they'd end up lazy and, if they came from somewhere poor like Africa, why should anyone be surprised if they had light fingers? It was about survival after all. Human nature.

It was the Chinese who really got up his nose though. It had been bad enough when they kept themselves to themselves – living illegally, ten-to-a-room above restaurants and food shops in Soho. Back then, there were hardly any Chinese tourists, they'd almost never take a cab and they would never, ever leave a tip.

The other thing was that there was always this sneering expression on their faces, like they were looking down on you. That's what really got Jim's goat. Whose bloody country were they living in, after all?

Thinking about those superior looks had been enough to wind him up every time he'd worked the West End, but at least the facts had been clear. The UK was First World and China was Third World. There might have been billions of them but, with an average wage of a couple of quid a week, they weren't in a position to look down on anybody.

After the idiot government gave Hong Kong back, it had all changed. Everyone started kowtowing to them rather than the other way around. Even the Americans. The world was different. And it wasn't going to change back in a hurry.

These days, it wasn't just the odd diplomat or businessman. Chinese tourists were everywhere, busloads of them: shouting and squawking at each other, wearing dressing-up-box clothes and stupid floppy hats, and taking photos of themselves with those bloody ridiculous selfie sticks. If all they wanted to do was to take pictures of themselves, why didn't they do it at home?

They were in the museum all the time. There'd been about forty in earlier that morning. Still wearing stupid floppy clothes, still taking bloody selfies and still not actually interested in anything apart from saying that they'd been there.

He leant back in his chair with a grunt. What difference did it make to him? Museum guards didn't get tips, anyway.

The hall was almost empty. A brief lull before the lunchtime rush. That creepy bloke had finally disappeared, the old couple hadn't moved from their bench and the schoolgirls were back, giggling in the corner. Jim noticed a young guy who had just come in. He wasn't an Arab – he might have been a Paki, or maybe an Indian – and he was standing just inside the hall looking at the dinosaur with his mouth sagging open and wide eyes glistening. He must have been in his late twenties, but he was behaving like an eight-year-old school kid, come up to the big city for the first time and impressed by everything.

Looking at the open childish joy on the young man's face washed away the righteous anger which Jim had worked so hard to stoke up only moments before. He was almost jealous of the lad. Was it too late to find a bit of wonder and awe in his own life? If he wasn't careful, the time that he had left would be completely filled with cynical bitterness and resentment. He didn't want that scratched on his gravestone.

As he watched the young man walking slowly around the huge skeleton, Jim made a silent pledge – not for the first time – to find a way to change, to forgive and forget, and to find happiness in being a good husband, father, grandfather and friend. That shouldn't be so hard, should it?

Julie was slowly beginning to come around. The last year had been terrible, but things were getting better. He'd take her somewhere. Somewhere where they could spend a bit of time just the two of them, away from the museum and away from bad memories and the ugly words which were still hanging in the air at home. Maybe they could go back to Cyprus?

There was no point in pretending nothing had happened and they'd both said a lot of things that would have been better unsaid, but it was his responsibility to find a way to move past that.

Megan and Brooke would always take their mum's side, but if he squared things away with Julie, they'd come around. As for the grandkids, Kaylee was at the age when she wasn't talking to anyone anyway and little Josie was only three and she loved her Gramps.

It wasn't too late. Jim squeezed his eyes tightly closed and clenched his fists. It wasn't too late. There had been too much nonsense. He would fix everything.

He smiled as he opened his eyes. It felt good.

And then he saw her.

It was her. He hadn't been wrong.

She was facing away from him, but he could see her kids behind her and he would always recognise her from the way she was standing, anyway; her head would usually tip over slightly to one side and she would drop her left hip when she stood still.

She looked over her shoulder and he was certain. Shuna was staring right at him and he knew she'd recognised him too. Jim didn't know what to do. He toyed again with the idea of running away, but realised that there was no chance. His legs wouldn't have obeyed him.

She was having some kind of argument with her daughters. He couldn't hear anything, but her arms and hands were waving around like a crazy orchestra conductor. It went on until the oldest girl shook her head violently, grabbed her sister's arm and dragged her away, leaving Shuna standing alone, watching them leave.

Then she turned around slowly and their eyes met across the hall. She started to walk towards him.

Hassan

'Could I see your ticket please?' The girl at the security desk was smiling at Hassan; he could have sworn that the girls in London were looking at him differently? Of course his overstimulated mind was playing tricks, but then again, there had been that waitress. Had something about him changed during his time away? It had been a transformational year, but could it be that now, of all times, he'd become attractive to women? Wouldn't that add a final ironic twist to his short life?

'Here you go,' he said, handing her his ticket. She was pretty, and her friendly smile was definitely directed at him. Hassan stretched a little taller and pulled back his shoulders.

What was he playing at? These delusions were almost certainly a combination of absence and isolation messing with his head. He'd only been back in the country for two weeks and, while he'd been away, he'd met dozens of young guys with even more delusional ideas about women. No actual experience. No means of knowing any better. No idea.

The worst had been at the beginning when one of the other teachers – who'd travelled abroad and who was supposed to be wise – was sharing some Western realities with a few young students.

Hassan had stood open-mouthed while the teacher explained that eighty-five per cent of girls in the UK lost their virginity before they were thirteen years old and that, on average, they would have more than forty sexual partners before they were twenty; the majority of those would be as a result of drunken one-night-stands.

The teenage audience – mostly sixteen-year-olds – lapped it up, none of them questioning for a second the truth of the statistics. The problem was that it was what the boys wanted to believe, but not for the reasons the teacher intended. He was hoping to demonstrate the decadence of Western culture; the young lads were only thinking of the scantily dressed girls, softened by one drink too many, offering themselves willingly one by one.

Hassan suspected that, after a year away, that type of thinking had worked its way into his own subconscious as well – a bit like one of those nasty river worms which managed to wiggle through cracks in your feet and spent years slithering their way through your body to your eyes, where they eventually laid their eggs. He hadn't been blinded but was happy to accept that he might have become somewhat short-sighted.

'Here you go.' Her fingers brushed his lightly as she handed back his ticket. 'Enjoy your visit.'

'Thank you.' The sensation of their fingertips touching stayed with Hassan as he walked slowly past the security desk and into the hall. He shivered.

What did it matter, anyway? The girl had smiled. Nothing more. She had smiled, he had smiled in return, and then he had walked on.

He'd always known the diplodocus at the National History Museum was a replica, but it hadn't bothered him and it was the only one of his "one day" childhood ambitions which had endured. Just to stand there and look up at that majesty would be enough. There had never been enough time or money though; even when he'd been at Oxford, the opportunity to go to London had never come up.

And standing there looking up at "Dippy" really was enough,

even after all those years.

He still didn't care that the skeleton was a copy; it was pure magic to be so close. He'd needed to fight hard to convince them that this was a good target, but it had been worth the effort. Being here made everything easier and there was an elegance and tidiness about the way that his circle was closing. He had no choice. He'd never had a choice.

Hassan didn't have many memories of the two years which followed his departure from Oxford. The university authorities had such a predictably snooty word for dropping out. As his ability to function on any level evaporated, the powers-that-be decided he should be "rusticated" – an archaic concept where the basic idea was that a temporary rest in the countryside would be enough for a sick or struggling student to recover and return.

Hassan didn't have a country estate to be rusticated to, he didn't actually want to recover, and he had no intention of returning. All he wanted was to find a dark corner to creep into, preferably one where his uncle wouldn't think to look. From the few memories which surfaced from time to time, he'd found plenty of dark corners and, either his uncle hadn't been able to find him or – more likely – he hadn't bothered to try.

He did remember waking up in the Queen Elizabeth hospital, but had no idea how he'd ended up in Birmingham. They'd told him his liver was failing and he would die within weeks if he didn't stop drinking. Worse than that, they refused to let him leave for a fortnight.

In amongst the sickness, pain and biting thirst, Hassan had been surprised to discover that he didn't actually want to die.

'So. Hassan. How are we doing today?' Dr Mustafa Zaidi, came from the same region in Pakistan as Hassan's father and had no difficulty identifying with Hassan's shame and the fact that he refused to allow the hospital to contact his family.

'Not great,' said Hassan. 'I still can't stop shivering. It's getting worse if anything.'

'It's going to take a while,' said Mustafa. 'You're a scientist. You must be able to understand what you've done to your body?'

Hassan nodded.

'I had the shakes for over three months,' said Mustafa.

'You had a drink problem?' said Hassan, genuinely surprised. 'But you look so ... so ...'

'Normal and respectable?' said Mustafa, white teeth shining through his beard.

'Exactly.'

'It wasn't easy,' said Mustafa. He was standing beside Hassan's bed looking out of the window. 'It still isn't.' He reached down and took Hassan's hand. 'If you have the right help, though ... anything is possible.'

Hassan could feel the warmth and strength oozing into his palm and looked up at the short, dumpy man standing beside him. 'Will you help me?' he said, eventually.

Luckily for Hassan, guardian angels came in all shapes and sizes and a few days later, Mustafa had agreed to be his personal sponsor at the Muslim Recovery Network. The programme was based at the Birmingham Central Mosque and, with the help of the imam, Mustafa also managed to find Hassan a clerical job there. It wasn't paid, but came with a small room and three meals a day.

It had continued to be a brutal journey and Hassan had wondered many times if he would have been better off allowing fate to take him. There actually had been times when he'd been tempted to give fate a helping hand, but Mustafa had a knack of turning up exactly when he was really needed and, after six months or so, Hassan had begun to feel human again.

Although the physical withdrawal was a continual torture, at least it had a recognisable shape and Hassan knew what he was fighting against. The religious side of the programme was perversely more challenging, at least to begin with. The Islamic Twelve Steps had their basis in the Koran and, even more than AA, religion was an integral part of every step. Personal willpower was vital, but the magic ingredient was faith; it was only by putting yourself freely and openly into the hands of Allah that a recovering alcoholic could hope to find true recovery and peace.

That was difficult; Hassan had always been a fair weather Muslim at best and, since Mona, had spent a lot more energy cursing Allah than praising him. Luckily, the team of volunteers at the mosque had been blessed with superhuman reserves of patience and continued to match his anger and cynicism with reason and calm faith.

There must have been a moment when he stopped fighting and felt the warmth of true belief fill him, but Hassan couldn't remember it.

There was a time before and a time after. It was as simple as that.

By the time Hassan approached his twelve-month milestone, he was a different man. As part of the programme, he'd reached out to make amends to all the people he'd harmed during his lost years. A curiously therapeutic process, he'd been humbled by the gracious way that each of them had accepted his apologies and wished him well even though he'd used them so shamefully. There were a few outstanding exceptions; some of his worst offences were still lost in the fug of his memories and he wasn't quite ready to face his family or Uncle Sami.

The excoriation and evisceration of his grief and despair (not to mention the alcohol) had left him cleansed and fresh, a newborn child ready to begin again. The empty canvas which had once been a weak Bradford boy destined for eternal failure was now being filled by faith and certainty.

He became increasingly involved in the work of the mosque and continued to study his Koran with the singular passion of a newly enlightened convert. He had some good friends amongst the other students and, for the first time, life was simple and good.

When Mustafa wasn't around for support, Hassan would often turn to Sadiq, who had become his closest friend at the mosque. Sadiq was everything Hassan aspired to be – devout, clean-living, knowledgeable and kind. The fact that he was the Imam's eldest son probably helped.

Sadiq worked with Hassan in the small administration office and one evening as he was switching off his computer, Hassan looked up to see him standing in front of the desk.

'You got plans, Hassan?' Sadiq said.

'Nah,' Hassan replied. 'I'm knackered. I'm just going back to my room.'

'Me and a few guys get together on a Tuesday night,' said Sadiq. 'Why don't you come?'

Hassan had a sharp vision of a small group sat in a noisy pub, half-full glasses and wet sticky rings on the battered wooden table. He knew how he would be feeling – strong, confident, brave – and lusted after that feeling. A shiver ran through him.

'Nah. You're all right,' he said, through clenched teeth. 'I'm better off keeping away from temptation. You know.'

Sadiq had laughed and slapped Hassan hard on the shoulder. 'Don't worry,' he said. 'It's not that sort of thing. We just meet up at a friend's house, drink tea and talk. Strictly no alcohol.' He narrowed his eyes. 'You know I don't drink, don't you?'

'Course,' said Hassan, still recovering from the wave of desire which had flooded through every cell of his body. 'Talk about what, anyway?'

'This and that,' said Sadiq. 'What's going on in the world. What's going on round here.'

Hassan had never cared much for politics; he could see how the world was full of injustice, but had always known deep down that nothing he said or did would ever change that. His father was a stupid man who believed he was an important figure supporting his community. Hassan wasn't stupid and, by his early teens, had spotted that for the bullshit it certainly was.

That was the old Hassan, though. He was leaving him behind and the new Hassan was different.

'OK,' he said. 'Sounds all right. What time are you off?'

'Grab your coat and we'll go straight away,' said Sadiq. 'I'll lock up.'

Was that conversation with Sadiq the real catalyst which had set his feet on the road to South Kensington? It was part of it, of course, but he wouldn't have even met Sadiq without Mona. Whichever way he looked at his life, she was there at the start of everything.

As he walked across the huge hall, towards the dinosaur, Hassan reached around to the back pocket of his jeans and slipped his fingers inside. He could feel the folded photograph smooth under his fingers.

Mona had been there at the start of everything, and she would be there at the end.

Shuna

'I'm not allowed to be near you.' The taxi driver took a step backwards. 'I can't have any more trouble with the law.'

'I think it's OK if it's me walking up to you,' said Shuna. 'Rather than the other way around.' As she got closer to him, she had the sensation of pushing through a soft, permeable membrane until, with a final step, she slipped inside a massive bubble leaving the two of them isolated in space and time.

'I don't know,' he said, no sign of the aggressive ex-soldier as he flinched and shifted his gaze from side to side, focusing everywhere but on Shuna's face. 'There's been too much grief all round. And anyway I'm not allowed to talk when I'm on duty.' His face hardened. 'Do you want me to lose this job too?'

Shuna felt the bitterness and resentment like slaps. 'No. Of course not,' she said. 'I didn't want you to lose the last one either. I still don't know how things got so blown up out of all proportion.' She moved closer. 'It wasn't what I intended.'

'But I did end up losing my license, didn't I?' he said, looking at Shuna for the first time. He pulled at the sleeve of his ridiculous purple fleece. 'I lost it and now look at me. I suppose you came here to gloat?'

'No. That's not it at all. I came to apologise. I know it won't help, but I wanted you to know that I'm sorry for everything that happened.' Shuna could feel her eyes prickling and the roughness in her throat; for a brief, crazy instant she thought about kneeling down in supplication. 'I wish more than anything that we could just rewind the clocks and make it all go away.'

It was silent inside the bubble and the two of them stood face to face, close enough to reach out and touch each other, but separated by an unbridgeable gulf. Shuna looked at his crumpled figure and couldn't see the obnoxious, aggressive taxi driver anywhere. This was simply an ordinary man; a sad old man, called Jim.

Eventually he spoke, his voice cracking and the strain visible on his face.

'I know it wasn't really your fault,' he said, bending his head forwards. 'I shouldn't have done what I done. Not before and not after.'

Shuna understood that she should stay silent. There was something about the expression on his face. It was hurting him to say the words but, at the same time, she could see that he needed to rid himself of them, to squeeze and spit out the rot which had built up inside him.

'At the airport, that was just me – the old me – up to my usual tricks. I didn't mean anything by it. I was knackered after a long day and all I wanted was a good fare back to London, a couple of whiskies and my bed. Your stupid airport hotel detour was going to add at least an hour onto that.' He scratched his chin and looked up at Shuna. 'Should you have made a big deal out of it? Probably not. That was unnecessarily arsey of you. But I started it and rules are rules.'

Shuna could see his eyes losing focus as he stared past her, over her shoulder and into the distance.

'No. The real problem came after,' he said. 'At the tribunal.' A small smile played at the corners of his mouth and Shuna suspected that he was thinking back to that day. She hadn't forgotten it and could still remember how disappointed with herself she had been when she saw the consequences of her spoilt vindictiveness.

Jim continued, the smile enduring and an unexpected tenderness coming into his voice. 'I don't know how to say any of this,' he said, eyes and attention back to the present moment. 'It's not the sort of thing that blokes like me talk about ... Or even think about, to be fair.' He cleared his throat with a short cough. 'When I saw you at the tribunal, it was as though you were something from a book or a film. I remember thinking you were like a lioness, proud and confident, queen of everything.'

He stopped talking and stood there, looking at the floor and furrowing his forehead as though he was in physical pain.

Shuna waited a few more seconds before speaking. 'Go on,' she said, her voice not much more than a whisper.

He coughed again. 'I suppose I sound like a right plonker, but I couldn't get it out of my head. I tried for months. I worked extra long shifts – fourteen, sixteen hours until I was almost too tired to walk to my bed. Even then, as soon as my head hit the pillow, the dreams would start. I couldn't stop thinking about you, waking or sleeping. It wasn't that I fancied you. You know? Like that?' He looked at Shuna carefully to make sure she understood. 'Although I'm not saying you're not tasty. No. It was something else, and it was driving me nuts.'

Shuna didn't know what to think. She hadn't seen this coming at all. None of the guys she knew were open with their emotions and she certainly hadn't expected anything so candid from Jim Pritchard. From the look on his face, the rawness of the confession was equally surprising to him.

'About three months before I picked you up that last time,' Jim continued. 'I thought it might help if I saw you from time-to-time to help get it out of my system. That's when I started working your area. Most days, but only for an hour or two. It worked. Even if I just caught a glimpse of you, it made me feel more peaceful and then everything was OK.'

'But what about the photos?' said Shuna.

'Oh. That was nothing,' said Jim. 'Wildlife photography's my hobby, and I kept my cameras in the cab. I started taking photos of people while I was hanging around waiting for you to show up.'

'So they weren't only photos of me?'

'Nah. Course not. I wanted to try to capture how different people moved, just like with animals and birds. It passed the time, and I started to enjoy it after a while.'

Shuna began to feel that the ground under her feet was less solid with every word that came out of his mouth. It was as though she was standing on a thin, hard crust which covered a dark and sucking swamp. If she moved, it would break and she would be dragged down.

'And the taxi?' she said. 'How do you explain kidnapping me in your taxi?'

Jim actually hit himself on the forehead with the flat of his hand like a bad actor in a school play. 'I didn't kidnap you,' he said. 'I only wanted to talk to you, but then you panicked so quickly and I didn't know what to do. Honest. All I wanted to do was talk.'

Shuna didn't know how to respond. She couldn't help feeling sympathy for this surprisingly vulnerable old man. He was clearly miserable and hated what he'd become. On the other hand, the matter-of-fact way he described his strange obsession and the months he'd spent stalking her was much more disturbing than anything she'd heard during the trial. The prosecution had painted him as a resentful, vengeful bitter man and it had been easy enough to turn her fear into anger back then. But after his explanation, the intrusion, the violation, felt much deeper than before.

She looked for her girls. Anna was sitting next to an elderly couple across the hall; she looked so tiny and helpless with her legs dangling from the massive old wooden bench. Zoe was standing next to the dinosaur talking to a young man. How had she managed to meet someone in five minutes? Shuna sighed. That girl really was going to be trouble.

She turned back to Jim. 'I'm sorry,' she said. 'But I'm running late. We're meeting my husband in a quarter of an hour and it's quite a walk.'

Jim shrugged. He wasn't going anywhere.

Shuna continued, 'I don't quite know what to think about what you've just told me, but could we maybe talk again?'

'Why?' said Jim. 'What's the point?'

Dan

Rachel was sitting, hunched forward, misery and confusion painting dark shadows on her face. Dan looked at her and smiled. Their story wasn't quite over and Rosa could wait a month or two longer.

He'd been almost sure about his decision, but the last hour spent sitting and thinking had allowed him to clarify everything in his mind. Funnily enough, it had been that Spanish girl, Ramona, who had helped to push him off the fence. She had been so alive, brim-full of hope and dreams. And fun. She'd reminded him that, when it came to the final reckoning, most people couldn't claim to have made such a huge difference to the world, anyway.

Human nature seemed to have evolved one evolutionary skill which dominated all others — the ability to believe that one's own life, and the goals and results of that life, actually mattered. For a very few, it might be true — although the value of progress could always be questioned — but, for the vast majority, the result of all of that effort and striving seemed to count for very little.

As he'd moved around and got older, Dan had come to the conclusion that most achievements either didn't matter, or could probably have been achieved by some other worker ant. What was it that Flaubert had said? '*Travel makes one modest. You see what a tiny place you occupy in the world.*'.

It was fine to have a genetically imposed drive which tricked people into doing whatever possible to refine and improve the species, but bacteria did that as well. There had to be something else to take away from a life lived.

That was where Ramona's youth and positive passion had come in to the equation. Would it be so bad to measure a life in terms of happy experiences, of honest joy and laughter? If he met his Rosa again in some uncertain hereafter, would she want to hear about his research, his loneliness and misery or would she rather listen to a few, simple stories about the good times in between.

'Rachel?'

'What?'

'It's not so bad, you know?' he said, resting one hand on her shoulder. 'I'm seventy-eight, I've had a good life and we still have a little time.'

'But one or two months,' she said. 'Is there nothing they can do?'

'Maybe,' Dan said. 'With aggressive treatment, they might be able to stretch things out for another month or so.'

'Well …'

'But I've decided that I won't do it,' he said. 'I'm not going to spend my last days dipping in and out of hospital and feeling sick the whole time. What's the point in that?'

'But you need to fight. You hear all these stories of miracle cures. Why shouldn't you be one of them? You can't just give up.'

'I'm not giving up. I've looked at all my options and I've made some decisions that I think will be best for me … and for us. I have a plan.'

He could see her face twisting as she fought with her conflicting emotions. He had come to know her so well over the years. She was a dogged fighter and believed that almost anything could be overcome with willpower alone. Giving up was an alien concept for Rachel. But, at the same time, she had a deep respect for individual liberty and free will and, her rational reasonable calm self won the battle as it always did. 'I'm listening,' she said. 'Tell me your plan.'

'OK.' Dan took out the folded sheet of A4 paper which he'd been using as a bookmark. 'I've made a few notes.' He smoothed out the paper in front of him. 'Let me explain my thinking first and then we can discuss. Is that all right?'

'Of course it is, sweetheart,' said Rachel. 'I'm all ears.'

'Good. The first bits are boring, but we need to get them out of the way. I've spoken to the doctors and they see no reason why I shouldn't be reasonably mobile until quite close to the end. The pain will get worse, but they say that can be managed. The other boring thing is about money. I've spoken to my advisor, and he says you'll be fine. Half of my pension will transfer to you, we don't have a loan on the house and you have your own pension coming in any case.'

'You don't need to worry about that,' said Rachel.

Dan leant forwards and placed two fingers gently on her lips. 'I do and I have,' he said. 'Now, you promised not to interrupt.'

'I'm sorry. Go on.'

'I've made a list of places I always wanted to see,' said Dan. 'And I guess now is as good a time as any.' He chuckled as he looked down at his scribbled notes. 'I've put together an itinerary which I hope will work. It's sort of a writer's pilgrimage, but I want us to have a good time, to see the sights and to have fun together. Will you come with me?'

'Of course I will, you great lummox. You think I'm going to let you go without me? I know what you're like.'

'There's one part which you might not find such fun though ...'

'Let me be the judge of that.'

'OK. So we fly to St Petersburg and spend a few days there doing the tours and visiting Dostoevsky and Pushkin's graves, before taking the night train to Moscow – very romantic. From Moscow, we go to Beijing on the Transsiberian Express – I know I don't have much time and it takes over a week, but I've always dreamt of crossing Russia and I have a plan to re-read every word that Dostoevsky wrote during that week.' Dan looked at Rachel over the top of his glasses and attempted a cheeky, boyish grin. 'You might find that part a little boring.'

'I'll be fine,' said Rachel. 'I almost did it when I was a student, but a friend cancelled on me at the last minute. It's kinda on my list too. I'll knit and look out of the window.'

'Wonderful,' said Dan. 'So, from Beijing, we fly to Japan for two weeks. I haven't figured out what to do yet, but I do want to go to Mishima's grave in Tokyo. I thought I might leave the rest of the Japan itinerary to you. Then, from Japan, we fly to San Francisco, take a tram, eat some sourdough and then home.' He paused for a few seconds. 'Via Austin if you don't mind?'

'Why would I mind?' said Rachel. 'I'm too old to be jealous. That all sounds wonderful.'

As he leant forward to hug her, he saw a small girl – the youngest of the two he'd seen earlier – walk over and sit on the end of their bench. He would have sworn she was crying too.

Nadia

Nothing seemed unusual as she reached the junction of the Cromwell Road and Exhibition Road. There were no ARVs in sight. SCO19 must be snarled up somewhere. She was on her own.

Nadia ran along the path between the railings and the ice-rink courtyard. Groups of families and tourists were ambling along, oblivious to the reasons why this crazy, red-faced woman was pushing them out of the way.

She stopped at the top of the steps and took ten deep breaths before pushing open the door and stepping inside.

The security and bag check area was just as Nadia expected. Low key, no scanners, almost certainly staffed by amateurs. There was a metal table where some, but not all, bags would be checked and that was it. Only two guards were on duty; both were wearing scrappy purple fleeces which did nothing to make them look even slightly serious. One was a pimply adolescent boy, all Adam's apple and bulging eyes; the other was a young woman, maybe mid-twenties with a big smile and a blonde bob. Of the two, she had to be the one in charge.

'Hi,' said Nadia, holding out her police warrant card. 'I'm from the security services.'

The girl didn't even look at the card. 'Yes, I know,' she said. 'I just had a call from the police. They said you were coming. What's going on?' Her lower lip was trembling.

Nadia smiled. 'Great. There's no need to worry,' she said, doing her best to exude calm confidence, despite her racing heart and the sweat running down the back of her blouse. 'We're carrying out a routine investigation of a possible terrorist threat. I can't say more at this stage. Armed police should be arriving any time. They will give you further instructions, but for now, please don't let anyone else into the museum.'

'Should I press the alarm button?'

'No,' snapped Nadia. Was the girl deaf? 'Whatever you do. Please don't do that. Wait here for the police and then do what they tell you. I need to take a look inside.'

The girl nodded obediently and walked towards a small group of Chinese tourists who were waiting at the doorway.

Nadia checked her phone for updates. SCO19 were on their way. Ed was almost there and there was a direct message from David.

Do not approach the bomber, whatever the circumstances. SCO19 are securing the area and we're waiting on new intel. Do not approach directly. Stand down. This is a direct order.

Nadia hunched forwards gripping the metal desk with both hand. 'Shit. Shit. Shit,' she said, to no-one in particular.

'You all right?' The girl had turned to face Nadia. Her face was chalk white and her arms were crossed tightly in front of her.

'Yes. Of course,' said Nadia, her mind racing. 'I'm fine. Please wait for the police as I asked.'

She looked at her watch. Just over two minutes remaining. She had to do something. She couldn't just stand there and watch as disaster struck. Not again.

Bloody David. He knew her too well – he knew her background, and he knew her psych profile. And the new smartarse comms system would register that she'd opened his message. How could he have deliberately put her in this position?

That ten-year-old girl had done her best. She'd run until it had felt like her heart was bursting. She'd found the garage and the owner with his tow truck. He'd called the police and then they'd raced off together with one of his mechanics.

But, by the time they reached the accident site, only the upper half of the car was showing above the water and big waves were crashing over it. As the men scrambled down the cliffs, dragging a cable behind them, Nadia could remember hearing someone screaming hysterically. For a while, she'd thought it must have been her mother crying for help, but then she'd realised it was her own voice. Beyond that her memories were blank.

The men from the garage had tried, they'd really tried, and so had she. But they were all too late

Nadia read the message from David one more time. He understood the way she thought, but then he also knew that, orders or no orders, she wasn't going to run and hide while there was still a chance to help in some way.

Guilt had left her with painful memories which never stopped glowing within her. The guilty memories were like hot coals, ready to burst into flame at the slightest hint of fresh oxygen. During her teens and early twenties, her burning desire to right wrongs and save the day had led her into plenty of trouble.

The worst incident had been shortly after university. She'd been driving back from a party with her boyfriend of the time when they'd seen a couple arguing on the street. Just as they'd passed by, Nadia had been stunned to see the man slap the woman so hard that she'd fallen over. Nadia had told her boyfriend to stop and, despite his protestations, he had. She'd then leapt out of the car and run towards the man screaming and shouting.

He was clearly very drunk and staggered away from her, looking sheepish and apologetic. He hadn't hit his girlfriend that hard ... she was pissed ... he hadn't started the argument. Nadia was fired up and wasn't intending to let him off that lightly, but wanted to check on the woman first. She was turning to see how she was when she half-saw a white shape flying towards her. The fist hit Nadia clean on the end of her nose and she fell backwards. The woman was on her immediately, swearing, punching, screaming, threatening to scratch her eyes out.

Nadia might have been much more badly injured that night if it hadn't been for a passing police car. Even though the police hadn't stopped, the man had grabbed his girlfriend's arm, pulled her up and dragged her away down an alley. The last Nadia had seen of them – through her rapidly swelling eyes – they'd been staggering off arm-in-arm like the happiest couple in the world.

It was only then that Nadia's soon-to-be-ex boyfriend had run up to see if she was hurt. Would he really have sat cowering in the car while she was beaten to death? Luckily he hadn't actually said 'I told you not to interfere'. If he had, Nadia would have probably slapped him, as well as dumping him.

Coming at the end of a string of other, less traumatic, events, the drunken couple had taught her two very important lessons – firstly, that being a knight in shining armour was a dangerous occupation and, secondly, that people didn't always want to be helped.

MI5 had proven to be the perfect balance for Nadia's mission to save the world. She'd briefly considered the police or the army, but ten minutes into her first interview with David, she'd known exactly where she needed to be.

Her inner flames burned as strongly as ever, but were now tempered by years of experience and training. She understood why David had given the order and she appreciated that the situation was both complex and delicate.

She wouldn't exactly obey the direct command, but she wouldn't ignore it either.

Nadia walked slowly to the nearest pillar and slipped behind it, cheek pressed against the cold stone. She took out the Glock, checked it one more time and flicked off the safety. Then she peered around the edge of the pillar and carefully scanned the hall.

It wasn't that crowded, thirty people at most. The nearest security guard was an old man, standing about fifty feet away, talking to a blonde woman. There was no sign of Snowflake. Maybe she'd got it all wrong. Maybe it was the wrong place.

She looked more carefully. There was something unusual about the young couple talking next to the dinosaur's head. The girl was too young, and she wasn't talking. It looked as though her boyfriend was shouting at her, waving his arms and pointing across the hall.

It was him. Snowflake was standing right there together with a young girl. What was that all about? He was leaning over her, telling her something, but he was mumbling too quietly for Nadia to hear.

She looked behind her. Ed had just walked in and was standing in the doorway talking to the security girl. He saw Nadia and beckoned for her to come over. She shook her head, signalled for him to stay where he was, and turned back to the dinosaur.

11:58

Jim

Jim looked at Shuna and watched her shoulders sag forward. In resignation? Sadness? Shame?

What had she expected from him after all? As he'd told her, there was actually nothing to forgive. He knew he'd brought everything on himself and, if it hadn't been her, it would probably have been some other balls-up that delivered him his well-earned comeuppance.

What he wanted most of all was to stop caring what she felt. He'd begun to put it all behind him and then she showed up out of the blue, wanting to talk. Talk about what? There wasn't anything to talk about.

But there she was, spotlit in the lone shaft of sunlight which streamed down from the high windows, head bowed and golden strands of hair falling over her eyes. What was it about the woman?

Jim forced himself to turn away. He'd opened up to this woman more than he had with anyone before, even himself. No good would come of it. If he ignored her for a minute or two, she'd bugger off and never come back. Then he could get on with rebuilding what was left of his life.

The Paki lad who'd been looking at the dinosaur like a little boy was still there, but now he was chatting to a girl. He was much taller than her — she was only a kid — and he was bending over her, arms waving.

He turned to Shuna who hadn't moved. 'Is that your girl talking to the young guy in the anorak?' he said, pointing towards the

217

dinosaur.

Shuna's head jerked up. 'Yes. Why?'

'Is he a friend of hers? She looks upset.'

She shaded her eyes with one hand and squinted. 'No. He's not a friend. He's just someone she met in a cafe earlier today. I saw them talking just now.' She stepped back to get out of the sun. 'She doesn't look happy, does she? I'll go over and see what's up.'

But, before she could move, Zoe broke away and started walking – half-running – towards them, eyes wide open and clearly distressed. Jim watched carefully as the young man turned and carried on walking around the dinosaur, head down and hands in his pockets.

Something wasn't right; Jim felt the hairs on his arms prickle and the once-familiar rush of adrenaline kick in. Zoe was running now, but the lad continued to pace around the dinosaur, no longer looking at anything but the floor. His lips were moving as though he was talking to himself.

Something was definitely off.

Hassan

She was only a child. And she'd been kind to him in the cafe.

Hassan knew he shouldn't have warned her. As they'd drummed into him over and over, sympathy was a weakness, and weakness would risk everything. This was war and the other side didn't have any scruples. Their bombs and missiles didn't care about protecting women and children. The spotty young drone pilots sitting in Las Vegas had no idea of the misery they left behind them with their "surgical strikes". Afterwards, they would leave the office like any other day, laughing and joking with friends as they went off to drink and womanise.

He understood all the reasons why he needed to harden his heart, even in the face of those nagging feelings that more violence would only feed the vicious cycle. He'd accepted the inevitable, and had worked hard to convince himself that what he was about to do was God's will. Even so, he couldn't help smiling as he watched the girl rush over to her mother. He had tried to spare one life and it wouldn't make a difference. Nothing could stop him now and she would either be far enough away or she wouldn't.

He would do what he had to do and God would decide the rest.

Life had been simple and good in Birmingham until, one day, the imam had called him into his office.

'It's been twelve months now,' he said. 'I had my doubts when you first came to us but, Allah-be-praised, you have been blessed with the strength to find your way back. I'm proud of you Hassan.'

Hassan bowed his head, wallowing in the warm glow which filled him. 'Thank you,' he said. 'I also believe it's a miracle I'm here.'

'Good. Do you believe you're now ready to show gratitude to your God?'

'Yes. Of course. What can I do?'

'Let me start at the beginning,' said the imam, leaning back in his chair. 'I know you meet with your fellow students and I also know that many of you aren't happy with the way the mosque works with the local community.'

Hassan focused on breathing regularly. How much did Imam Khan actually know? Sadiq was his son, after all.

The imam continued. 'It's difficult for your generation to understand why we do what we do. You were born here and you can't see how far we've come over the past fifty years.' He slowly traced a snaking line across the tabletop with his forefinger. 'We've always tried our best to walk a narrow path to protect everyone's interests as much as we can.'

'But, with respect, it's not enough. Look at what's going on.'

'Whatever you might think, your parents and grandparents feel the shame and divided loyalties more than you do. For them, the tragedy of the Middle East affects cherished family members and the homes they can still remember personally.'

'Of course. But it's our government's policies we're talking about. Policies is too soft a word – it's war. And it's a war against Muslims. Surely you can't buy in to that.'

'It's not about what I support or don't support. It's about finding a balance. About protecting everything we've achieved. It's also about living in a democracy.'

'But there's so much more to be done. Even though I was born here, I still grew up as a "bloody Paki". I accept that things are probably better than they were, but we can't just give up.'

'No. And I understand that you and your friends are fired with the passions of youth. However this is a time for patience.' He laid both hands palms down on the table in front of him and leant forwards. 'Since 9-11, Islam has been losing the propaganda war. Al Qaida and ISIS have achieved many of their own narrow goals by firing up outrage and calls for Jihad amongst the faithful across the world, but it's a double-edged sword. Being a Moslem is becoming synonymous with being an ignorant terrorist. If we don't take great care, we risk going backwards rather than forwards.'

'Isn't that exactly what they want us to think?' said Hassan. 'To push us onto the back foot and make sure that we stay in our place.'

'Maybe. But I doubt it,' said the imam, suddenly looking old and tired. 'In any case, my job is to help the ordinary people in my community. I don't believe Allah put me here in order to foment hatred and conflict. How can that help the workers, mothers and children who just want to get on with their daily lives? It becomes a political problem as well as one of faith, but in any case, both require pragmatism.'

Hassan could see the truth and sincerity in his words, but the vein of bitterness and humiliation ran deep in his gut. 'I understand,' he said. 'But it's difficult to sit by and watch without doing something.'

The imam smiled. 'And that is why I wanted to meet with you today,' he said. 'We would like you to do something. We would like you to help us cross bridges with young Moslems in Birmingham, to make sure that they are listened to and, hopefully, to work with them to ensure that daily life does continue to become easier rather than the opposite.'

'What?' Hassan looked up to see if this was some form of joke. 'I'm sorry, but what exactly are you talking about?'

'We believe you would be an ideal candidate to represent your community in local politics. First as a councillor and then …who knows?'

'But I know nothing about politics. I'm totally unqualified.'

'You're young, bright, well educated, a good Moslem and you can identify with the issues of the ordinary members of our community.'

Hassan could remember sitting there gulping like a freshly landed trout. 'But … but …'

The imam laughed and reached over to pat Hassan on the shoulder. 'Don't worry, young man,' he said. 'We're not just going to throw you to the sharks without some preparation. The first thing is to get your religious education up to speed. You've been accepted for a one year placement at the Deobandi madrasa in Peshawar, starting in September. You'll help to teach the younger children and also study the basics of Islamic law directly under the mullah. I know him well. He is a good man and a formidable scholar.'

Hassan didn't remember what was said after that. They probably discussed all sorts of other details, but he was too shocked and confused to register much. He remembered walking out of the office realising that he'd just agreed to go and study in Pakistan for a year, but not much more.

The other thought that stuck in his memory was that, before he took that step out of the shadows and stood for the council, he would need to find a way to resolve matters with Uncle Sami. Not a pretty thought but, as he didn't have a better plan, Hassan would have to accept that Allah would provide.

He'd only been back from Peshawar for two weeks, but it was already a world away.

Nothing in Hassan's previous experience had prepared him for life in the madrasa, nor for life in Pakistan for that matter.

It wasn't the dirt or the poverty – he'd seen plenty of that during his drinking days. It was the heat that had got to him and the constant inescapable weight of the humid, pollution-filled air had made life almost unbearable for the first few months.

There were three other students from the UK, but he suffered much more than they did. When he was first admitted to hospital, the doctors had told him that alcohol had damaged his thyroid as well as his liver. It appeared they'd been right; his body wasn't able to slow down its metabolism enough to cope with the sweltering climate.

However, since his welcome into the true faith, he'd developed an almost masochistic asceticism and found himself welcoming the discomfort; sleepless sweat-sodden nights spent tossing under his mosquito net weren't endless purgatory, but opportunities for self-reflection and prayer. He had a purpose in his life for the first time and the true path was never supposed to be easy.

Days were identical. Study, prayer, teaching, food, sleep, combined in strict routines and then repeated over and over. Hassan soon lost any sense of beginning or end, before or after. There was only now, today, the next task. He must have been growing in knowledge and understanding, but there were no landmarks, milestones or any way to measure his progress. He spent half an hour every day with the mullah but, whenever he'd asked him about progress and the future, he was met with an enigmatic smile.

Mullah Akthar ul-Haq was in his late seventies, but still ruled his fiefdom with an iron rod, uncompromising with failure or laziness, although he was also quick to praise when praise was well earned. Hassan liked and respected him and could see why he had been friends with the imam of his Birmingham mosque.

Apart from mealtimes, there was little time or energy to socialise and Hassan made few friends during the months he spent at the madrasa. Luckily, as a teaching assistant and senior student, he didn't need to sleep in one of the main dormitories and had the luxury of a small room which he shared with only one other teacher. As the months passed, they became close friends.

Ibrahim was originally from Lebanon although he looked like the postcard image of an Afghani tribesman – full black beard, a hawk's beak of a nose and startling green eyes which missed nothing. He was secretive about his background and personal life but, like one or two of Hassan's friends in Birmingham, he was defined by his anger which must have come from somewhere. That inner rage wasn't obvious at first glance as Ibrahim was remarkably self-controlled but, as Hassan got to know him better, he could see that the fury was always there, boiling furiously and struggling for release.

Ibrahim wasn't interested in Mullah Akhtar's slow, political road towards peace and equality. For him, Islam was always under attack and had been fighting – and losing – the same war for centuries. Talking and compromise would only play into the hands of the West. The ideas of divide and rule – so cleverly used by the British – were still working and it was only by making a stand and fighting back that Islam would survive.

And then Mullah Akhtar died.

It was October and the cooler temperatures had begun to release Hassan from his overheated daze. His brain was functioning again and he watched from the sidelines as the madrasa struggled to deal with the sudden, unexpected loss – without their leader, fractures and factions had appeared as if from nowhere and there was no clear successor ready to take charge.

During this period, when the lessons were disrupted, Hassan had time to think about the plans which had been made for him and began to have doubts. Would he actually be able to make a difference by being one of the token Moslems on the council? The Moslem councillors he'd met so far seemed more interested in furthering their own business interests than in changing things for the better. Could that really be why he'd been saved?

As the weeks passed, he found it more and more difficult to imagine himself going back to a career in local politics. He would always be grateful to the mosque and everyone who'd helped him, but that wasn't a role for him. A politician needed to work with hope and to believe in a shared future and Hassan didn't have that any more – at least not for himself.

He shared his feelings with Ibrahim and, over the course of dozens of late night discussions, began to realise that his friend was not exactly what he'd seemed to be. Hassan had always assumed that Ibrahim's angry politics were similar to those of his radical friends back home. Youthful passion and righteous fervour. Words not deeds.

He was wrong.

As the madrasa changed from a peaceful place of learning to a mess of bitter in-fighting, Ibrahim chose to reveal his true self.

It turned out that he was very much a man of deeds. He was a militant radical as well as a politician in training and was an active member of the Tehrik-i-Taliban, the Pakistani Taliban. He wouldn't share much about his past, although Hassan began to realise that everyone else at the madrasa was afraid of Ibrahim; his roommate was definitely much more than he appeared to be.

Once the truth was out in the open, Ibrahim lost no time in explaining that he and his superiors had become convinced that Hassan would be an ideal candidate to mount an attack on UK soil. To do something that would make a real difference.

Hassan didn't take him seriously initially, but he was insistent and very persuasive. Being at the madrasa wasn't the first time in Hassan's life when he'd dared to believe he might be able to control his future and even have some sort of purpose. And it wasn't the first time that he'd found that vision snatched away from him.

It wasn't the first time, but it was definitely the worst.

'If I have to do this, I want it to be the Natural History Museum,' said Hassan.

They were alone in the madrasa's library and Ibrahim was standing with his back to a wall of books. Many of them dated back to the fourteenth century and, despite the librarian's constant efforts, the spines were white-spotted with mildew.

'Why there?' Ibrahim said, eventually.

'Mostly because it's a soft target and you've made it very clear what happens if I fail,' said Hassan, hating himself for his transparency and weakness. Ibrahim had known exactly which button to press, and how.

'But also because it's a perfect location.' Hassan took advantage of Ibrahim's silence to press his point. 'Think about it. It's a symbol of colonial hypocrisy, there are always lots of tourists and there's limited security. No-one will expect it, but they'll never forget it.' Hassan had spent days agonising over the right location. He couldn't risk failure. The consequences were unthinkable.

'That's true, but the Sheik was thinking of something more

political. The Houses of Parliament, maybe?'

'Too obvious,' said Hassan. 'And too much security. I wouldn't be able to get close enough. Think about my idea and ask them to consider it … Please.' As he looked at his former friend, Hassan wondered if Ibrahim actually needed to consult anybody.

'I will,' said Ibrahim. 'But wherever it is, they want it to happen at exactly midday. That's important.'

'What difference does it make?' said Hassan.

'It's a play on words,' said Ibrahim. 'Noon the time and noon the Arabic letter.' He was standing still with his hands clenched into fists. Hassan could feel the righteous zeal burning off him and wondered if that was what evil really looked like. 'But noon is also for Nasara,' he continued. 'It will be another red mark on the houses of the Nazarenes, just like in Mosul.'

'No-one's going to understand that,' said Hassan, briefly wondering if killing Ibrahim would set him free. 'Journalists don't know the Arabic alphabet and it's too obscure.' Killing Ibrahim? Who was he kidding? The man was made of stone.

'They'll understand when we explain,' said Ibrahim. 'But anyway, the Sheik has decided that the time is auspicious, so you should accept it.'

'Of course,' said Hassan. 'It's as good as any other.'

Hassan looked at his watch. Not long now. Once more around the dinosaur and it would be time.

He wasn't afraid any more. He'd never been afraid for his own life, but he'd been terrified that something would go wrong. Although getting caught, arrested and dragged out for public shaming would be terrible, that wouldn't be the worst thing. He reached into the back pocket of his jeans and felt again for the folded paper, the talisman which kept him moving forward step-by-step.

At the beginning, imagining the price of failure had made him feel physically sick, but he'd moved past that. He wasn't going to fail.

The hall wasn't as full as they'd hoped it would be, but this wasn't about absolute numbers of casualties, it was about the symbolic act and there was no doubt that today would be a day for the history books.

He looked up at Dippy's massive tail as he passed underneath. How many millions of people had stared at the skeleton in wonder over the past hundred years? It must be millions. The irony was that the museum was planning on taking the dinosaur away and swapping it for a blue whale. The exchange was only a few weeks away and Dippy had a nationwide tour planned. Unfortunately, he wouldn't make it out in time.

Hassan had a few seconds left to mumble his last prayers. His faith was the one good thing to come out of his life and he would keep that whole whatever Allah had in store for him.

Even if there was nothing afterwards, even if there was only blackness, that would be preferable to any earthbound future he could imagine.

Shuna

'What's wrong, darling?' said Shuna. 'You're white as a sheet.'

'It's that guy from Muriel's. The one outside the loos.'

'What about him? Take a breath and tell me.'

'He was covered in sweat and shaking. He told me to leave.'

'Why would he do that? Did you say something?'

'No you don't understand. He wasn't angry with me. It was like he was begging me to go. I don't know why … the way he was looking at me scared me.'

'What exactly did he say?' said Jim, his strong voice surprising Shuna, who had forgotten he was there.

'What I just said,' said Zoe. 'He said, "Leave now. Please. You have to go." and then he said it again.' Zoe was flicking her eyes back and forth between Shuna and Jim. 'But it wasn't only what he said. It was the way he said it. I told you. It scared me.'

Shuna turned to Jim who had magically transformed into a different man – ten years younger, inches taller, his eyes sharp and scanning the room. 'Do you think he's some sort of nutter?' she said.

Jim's voice was also that of another man. 'Lie down, both of you.

Facing the wall. Hands over your heads.'

Shuna felt her arms and legs complying without question until her brain kicked in. 'Why?' she said. 'What's wrong? I need to get Anna.'

'Do what I say and do it now,' Jim said, and this time there was no questioning the command. 'I'll look after your other daughter.' Shuna found herself sinking to the floor, pulling Zoe with her and watching from the corner of her eye as Jim began to walk slowly away and towards the dinosaur.

Shuna wrapped her arm tightly around Zoe and pulled her close, feeling her daughter's skinny body trembling. The tiles were hard and cold and the acrid smell of some sort of industrial cleaner scratched at the back of her throat with ammonia claws.

'What's happening, Mum?' said Zoe. 'I'm frightened.'

'I don't know, little one,' said Shuna, her own fear and confusion smothered by the primal need to calm and protect her child. What about Anna? Should she have gone to get her? Jim had said he would look after her, but why trust him? 'I don't know,' she said again. 'But the museum guard used to be a soldier. I'm sure he knows what he's doing.'

Shuna could hear Jim saying something as he walked away. He was speaking slowly and calmly, in deep bass tones, but she couldn't make out the words.

Dan

Dan continued to hug Rachel and felt the relief fill him. He hadn't noticed how much his shoulder blades had pulled themselves tightly up towards his ears or how hard he'd been clenching his teeth. Over the past five months, his whole body had been steadily building tension in every muscle like a thousand springs in the testing department of a Swiss watch factory and, as he looked at Rachel smiling with acceptance and agreement, every one of them sprung free in perfect synchronicity. He sagged forward with a gasp.

It was going to be OK. Everything was going to be fine. Well, maybe not exactly fine – he was still going to die – but now that

227

Rachel knew and understood about the cancer (and about Rosa), Dan felt at peace in a way that he hadn't for a long, long time. He knew his new tranquillity might not last – there was still plenty of time for fear and doubt – but right at that moment, it was all good.

'Are you OK, hon?' said Rachel.

'I'm fine,' said Dan, spluttering as a burst of uncontrollable coughing doubled him over. That would teach him to try to smile, laugh and talk at the same time. He could feel Rachel patting him on the back with firm confident blows as he struggled to get the coughing – and the laughter – under control.

Eventually he managed to calm himself and sat motionless for a few moments, bringing his breathing back to normal. On the edge of his vision, he noticed that the small girl who'd sat down at the end of the bench was staring at him with wide, frightened eyes. She probably thought he was about to keel over. He smiled at her and turned back to Rachel.

'You sure you're OK?' she said.

'Uh-huh,' said Dan, still enjoying the euphoric sense of relief. 'I actually feel great. It's so much better to have everything out in the open. I hate keeping secrets, especially from you.'

'And you're rubbish at it,' said Rachel. She lifted one eyebrow. 'You do know that, don't you?'

'I guess.' Dan wasn't interested in learning just how poor a keeper of secrets he was. 'Anyway, the most important thing now is to get moving on organising that trip. It's going to be incredible.'

'I think it will be,' said Rachel. 'And there is a lot of planning to do.' She picked up Dan's book and put it in her bag. 'But maybe a couple of hours rest first?'

Adrenaline and excitement could still give Dan a rush of energy which allowed him to remember how it was to be young. Unfortunately, these days, the tingling rush lasted for seconds rather than minutes and, when it passed, he felt diminished, as though he'd eaten into precious, irreplaceable reserves. He nodded and his tired voice croaked and rasped like a ninety-year-old's. 'A couple of hours rest first wouldn't be such a bad idea,' he said eventually.

Dan shifted himself into a position which would allow him to stand up. He had his hands on his knees, ready to push, when Rachel tapped him on the shoulder – two urgent taps. He sank back down, aborting the operation.

'Hon?'

'Yup,' said Dan, trying to hide his irritation. Standing up always hurt – somehow things inside him became shifted about – and he'd got his mind in the right place just as Rachel had stopped him. 'What is it?'

Rachel leant forward and whispered close to his ear. 'That little girl,' she said. 'I think she's crying.'

Dan turned and looked at the girl. She was only three or four feet away along the bench, dressed in the sort of inappropriate party clothes that most children seemed to be wearing. Jeans covered in rhinestones and some sort of pink, glittery, spangly top. She was ten years old at a push and she looked like she was dressed for a night out with Mick Jagger at Studio 54. Her arms were crossed, straitjacketing around her chest and her chin was tightly tucked in. He couldn't hear any sobbing, but her narrow shoulders were definitely shaking. Not a happy bunny and way too young to be sitting there on her own.

He slid along the bench, halving the distance between them. 'Hi,' he said. 'Are you OK?'

The girl turned to him, her eyes shining in the bright lights. 'I'm fine, thank you,' she said. 'Just annoyed with my stupid family.'

Dan smiled as Rachel walked around and squatted down in front of the girl. 'Are you sure you don't need any help?' Rachel said. 'Are you with your Mom?'

'Yes,' said the girl, pointing across the hall. 'She's over there talking to that stupid old man.' She looked back at Dan and her cheeks reddened. 'Sorry,' she said. 'I didn't mean ...'

'That's OK,' said Dan, laughing. 'I know I'm past my sell-by date.' He was quietly disappointed by how easily those three words flowed together. He was old, but he wasn't stupid. At least not yet. He stretched out his right hand and left it hanging in the air at a respectful distance. 'I'm Dan,' he said. 'And this is Rachel.'

The girl looked at the proffered hand and Dan imagined the thoughts whirring around in her head. *I'm not supposed to talk to strangers. But he's only an old man. Mum's just over there. He seems nice. And there's a lady with him. It's probably OK and I'm not supposed to be rude …*

Dan was on the point of accepting defeat when she reached out her own hand and politely shook the ends of his fingers. 'I'm Anna,' she said.

'Pleased to meet you, Anna,' said Rachel. 'Now, do you want to tell us why you're upset?'

'Not really,' said Anna, taking a deep breath. 'It's just that my Mum decided to go over to that man and she's not supposed to and then my sister went off in a huff and started talking to the boy who was in Muriel's and I just have to sit here and wait for them and I'm always hanging around waiting for them and I'm fed up with it.'

'Is that your sister over there?' said Dan, pointing towards Zoe.

Anna nodded her head.

'More interested in boys than hanging around with you these days?' he asked.

Anna nodded again.

'Well,' said Rachel, standing up. 'That's probably more than enough chit-chat. I think we'd better get you over to your Mom, don't you?'

Anna looked up at Rachel and shrugged her shoulders. 'I suppose so,' she said in a quiet voice.

As Rachel reached down to take Anna's hand, Dan looked up and saw the older sister running across the hall. She reached her mother, who was still talking to the museum guard, and grabbed her by the shoulder. The girl was excited about something – her arms were waving and she kept pointing back across the hall towards the dinosaur.

The discussion lasted for a few seconds and then, all of a sudden, something changed. It was like one of those Victorian still-life tableaux where the lights would flash off and, when they came back on a second or two later, the scene would be different. In the blink of an eye, the guard had turned and was walking towards the dinosaur, while behind him Anna's mother and sister were on their hands and knees and then, moments after, lying down flat on the floor.

Dan felt the air buzz with static electricity and the hairs on the back of his neck rising like the hackles on a dog's back. He was thrown back through time – fifty years snatched away as though pages torn roughly from a book – and left standing once again on a hot August morning in Austin, Texas.

'Wait!' he said to Rachel and Anna as he pushed himself to his feet. 'Stay here. Keep behind the bench.'

Nadia

Nadia no longer cared what was happening behind her or about the almost constant buzzing of new alerts from her phone. Everything important was happening straight ahead, in the centre of the massive hall. If she looked away, even for half a second, she might miss an opportunity to intervene, to make a difference.

She needed to be focused and ready to act, but not yet. Although hesitation often did cost lives, blundering in without a plan could be even worse. She was a great shot with a handgun, but all studies had shown that pistol rounds, even from close range, were unlikely to be traumatic enough to prevent a bomber pressing a trigger. Standard procedure mandated either armed police or special forces with their SIG 516 semi-automatic rifles loaded with hollow point ammunition. Any attempt to reliably neutralise a bomber required enough force to cause an immediate loss of nervous function.

And so, despite her race against time, Nadia understood that there may well be nothing she could do to help. It was tearing her apart, but at least she was there.

She watched as the girl span around and started half-walking, half-running towards the blonde woman and the security guard. Snowflake watched her progress for a second or two, before turning away. Then he began to pace slowly around the huge skeleton as though in a trance. He was wearing a thick black hoodie and she could see how much bulkier he appeared to be. He was definitely wearing a belt.

Snowflake looked up at the dinosaur's tail as he passed

underneath it and then he was walking back towards Nadia. His head was bowed and she could see his lips moving, although she couldn't hear anything. Was he praying?

The young girl had reached the blonde woman – her mother, probably – and was waving her arms like an Italian, pointing towards Snowflake. He must have said something to her. But what?

Suddenly, the old man pulled himself upright and loomed over the girl and her mother. They froze as the man spoke to them and pointed firmly to the floor behind him. He pointed a second time and the two women dropped down and lay flat. The old security guard waited until they were lying down, before turning to face Snowflake. Nadia was puzzled for a second until it clicked. Snowflake must have warned the girl and given her time to get away. Nadia had been wrong all along. He was going to go through with it.

Snowflake had almost reached the dinosaur's head when he looked up and saw the guard moving towards him. Nadia heard the guard gently repeating the same words over and over, 'It's OK. Take it easy. I just want to talk to you.'

Even from forty feet away, Nadia could see the anguish on Snowflake's face as he backed away and the panic as he looked over his shoulder and saw another even-older man approaching him from behind. Who were these men? There was no questioning their guts, that was certain.

She didn't know what to do. Snowflake looked as though he was being torn apart by internal conflict as his moment of truth approached, and meanwhile the two brave men were closing in. If she joined them, would she upset the delicate balance and push Snowflake over the edge? Or would a third presence – with brown skin – be enough to help his better angels prevail?

Nadia stopped breathing and stood – paralysed by indecision – as the slow-motion endgame played itself out in front of her.

12:00

Hassan

Hassan completed his final circuit, stopped and took three long deep breaths.

In the corner of his eye, he saw the old museum guard walking slowly towards him, arms by his sides. He was saying something, but Hassan couldn't hear him. The blood rushing through his head was deafening, as though he was standing in the middle of a busy motorway.

He smiled at the man, looked up at the massive bony dinosaur head one last time and reached into his pocket.

The light would come before the sound but both would come too slowly for Hassan. Before the huge hall filled with smoke and anguish, there would be one brief moment of frozen beauty – a tiny sun bursting into life below the huge skull and blazing orange before invisible hands would reach down and tear the skeleton apart, scattering the pieces in all directions.

Two hundred and ninety-two enormous plaster bones would tumble through the air in a slow motion death dance. By then Hassan would have already disintegrated body and soul and it would be too late to see the horror of his misplaced devotion come to life.

Too late to hear the screaming begin.

The old man was closer now, black eyes fixed on Hassan and glinting in the bright lights. He was still mumbling the same unintelligible words over and over and his arms were now spread wide, palms facing outwards. Hassan took a step backwards. He could feel the sharp plastic edges of the trigger cover against his fingers and the soft smoothness of the button under his thumb.

One firm push, a rush of electrons and it would all be over. He looked around the room one last time. The girl was lying on the floor next to her mother, but he could see another man walking towards him from behind.

It had to be now.

As he started to press down, a searing white light flashed in front of Hassan's eyes. He was torn roughly back in time, transported back to being a small boy, desperate to please his father, watching a cherished book burning on a coal fire, tears streaming down his cheeks as the thick cardboard blackened and twisted in the flames, the dinosaurs twisting and stretching like living beasts.

What was he about to do? Everything became clear. There would be no virgins, no houris. No praise for his faith and bravery. He wasn't a killer. He was still a small sad boy who didn't understand what had become of him. They'd started by insisting he had a choice, but then they'd crawled inside his head with all of their bitterness, threats and twisted values and taken that choice away.

Whatever the consequences, this wasn't the solution. This wasn't who he was.

The force of the revelation was like a physical blow and Hassan gasped before sinking to his knees. He bowed his head, released his grip on the trigger and stretched both hands out in front of him, palms flat on the cold hard tiles. In prayer or submission? Or both?

No Choice

The slim bearded figure stood at the corner of Cromwell Road, leaning against a wall and holding a street map open in front of him. He looked at his watch, a gold Rolex, all his attention focused on the second hand as it crept slowly upwards.

He shrank back against the wall and squeezed his eyes tightly closed as the thin gold needle reached the zenith, his body tense and his hands clenched into tight fists. Nothing.

He kept his eyes closed as he counted the seconds silently in his head ... twenty ... forty ... sixty ... but still nothing happened to disturb the routine bustle of a busy South Kensington morning.

When his count reached a hundred, the man opened his eyes and sighed, before reaching into his jacket pocket and taking out a mobile phone.

Afterwards

Shuna

The silence left her first of all. Shuna took a deep sucking breath, and the clouds disappeared in an explosion of adrenaline. The realisation that she had woken from a dream was a temporary relief before the room filled with the sound of a thousand pounding waterfalls and blinding light burning magnesium white.

The memories of the last few seconds in the museum flooded back into her bruised mind like a tsunami. No structure or sequence, just a confused tumbling jumble of words and images loosely held together by flailing threads of uncontrollable terror.

'Zoe? Anna? Are my girls all right?' Shuna's voice was raw as a raven's croak and her shoulder screamed pain at her as she tried to sit up.

'They're fine,' said Simon's voice. 'They're both fine, but you need to lie still or you'll tear those stitches again.'

'Oh, thank God,' said Shuna, eyes stretched wide as she tried to bring the room into focus. 'Where are they?'

'They're sleeping now,' he said. 'They've been up and about already. Just a few scratches to deal with ... and they're young. They were here earlier, but we didn't know when you'd come round, so I told them to go and rest.'

'How long have I been here? Am I OK?' Shuna's body didn't feel like her own. 'It hurts to move.'

'You've been unconscious for nearly six hours,' said Simon. 'And yes, you're going to be fine. You've got a nasty gash in your shoulder and smaller cuts on your feet and legs, but nothing to worry about.'

He reached down and cupped her cheek in his hand. 'I can't believe I came that close to losing you all.' Shuna managed to focus her errant vision and saw that Simon's eyes were shining wet. 'I heard the blast from half a mile away and knew straight away that something was wrong. If it hadn't been for that museum guard ...'

'The taxi driver?' said Shuna, seeing Jim's face loom in front of her. Random images were bursting in her mind like popping candy, but she couldn't seem to tie them together.

'Yes. Him. The girls told me he was there.' Shuna could remember the way the old sad man had transformed in a microsecond. As soon as Zoe had spoken, he'd flipped into action like a freshly wound clockwork toy, the clarity of his gaze and the sharp, clean snap of his words demanding instant obedience. 'Well, according to the police,' Simon continued. 'If it hadn't been for Jim Pritchard, none of you would have survived.'

'Is he OK?'

Simon shook his head and looked away.

'What happened?'

'Are you sure you don't want to wait?' said Simon. 'Rest a little?'

'No,' said Shuna. 'I'm fine. Tell me what happened.'

As Shuna leant back against the soft pillow, her shoulder twisted slightly and she couldn't hide the gasp of pain. A lightning bolt of agony more intense than anything she'd ever experienced flashed down to her fingertips and straight back up to her left temple. She squeezed her eyes tightly shut and lay still, waiting for her breathing to slow.

'Are you sure you're all right?' Simon had moved closer and his voice oozed panic and helplessness. 'Should I call the nurse? Don't you think it would be better to rest some more?'

'No,' said Shuna, opening her eyes. 'I'm trying as hard as I can, but my memories are all mixed up. Tell me what happened. I need to know.'

'OK. But I only know what the police told me and they've only just started their investigations. Apparently an MI5 officer arrived just before the explosion and saw what happened.'

'And they weren't hurt?'

'I'm not sure,' he said. 'I think she may have been injured, but she was obviously well enough to make a report.'

'Lucky her,' Shuna grunted. 'So, tell me.'

Simon pulled the chair closer to the bed and sat down. 'The bomb was apparently quite sophisticated. Some sort of plastic explosive or dynamite. The sort they use in mining or quarries.' Shuna could see that he was choking up and struggling to speak. 'Apparently it's a miracle that there weren't more casualties. The suicide belt was packed full of steel ball bearings'

'Oh my God,' said Shuna. 'How many people were hurt?'

'There were only two deaths apart from the bomber himself and another thirty-two injuries, mostly fairly minor. Somehow, the two men shielded the blast and funnelled the force upwards. Most of the injuries actually came from falling dinosaur bones.'

'Which two men?'

'Sorry. I'm getting ahead of myself,' said Simon. 'Just before the blast, your taxi driver had got quite close to the bomber and there was another man who'd seen what was happening and come up from behind him. Apparently they'd persuaded the young guy not to detonate the bomb. He'd taken his hands out of his pockets and was surrendering to them.'

'I don't understand,' said Shuna. 'So, what happened?'

'No-one knows exactly. They believe there was some sort of back-up in place – in case the bomber changed his mind. It'll take weeks to do the forensics, but it's likely there was a secondary mobile-phone trigger. I'm pretty sure they're not telling me everything they know. What was an MI5 officer doing there, for instance?'

Shuna didn't really care. 'So, Jim? And the other guy?'

'They were leaning over the bomber and, between them they took the brunt of the shock wave and the shrapnel. They didn't stand a chance.'

Shuna could remember the way Jim had spoken to her, the calm and strength in his words. He'd known what he was doing and had probably also known what he was risking. He'd protected them, and everyone else, because it was the right thing to do. She felt the sadness settle on her like a damp, heavy blanket, softly easing out the tears.

Simon was holding her good hand and laid it carefully beside her. 'You need to rest,' he said. 'I'll finish later.'

Shuna didn't know how long Simon was away. There were vague memories of a nurse coming in and giving her more painkillers and then she found herself drifting in and out of sleep, her dreams a mishmash of seemingly unconnected, half-remembered images: she was back on the beach again, but a London Taxi was careering towards her over the South African sands; two men were running towards her from opposite directions, Jim and a man with no face, his head smooth as a boiled egg; the sun was falling from the sky like a burning stone, getting closer and closer until the roar of its flaming tail was pounding on her eardrums; her two precious girls were curled up on the beach like sleeping dormice while Shuna frantically scrabbled sand on top of them in a desperate attempt to build a protective dome.

However long she'd actually slept, she felt much better when she woke up. Her ears were still ringing but the cotton wool feeling was less. She still couldn't remember anything about what had happened, apart from what Simon had explained. Who was the mystery second man?

And then, as though conjured by a fairy godmother's wand, Zoe and Anna were standing beside her bed.

Shuna had already learnt not to make any sharp movements, but the impulse to leap up and wrap them both in her arms was almost unbearable.

'Hi Mum,' they said together, awkward and shy in the unfamiliar setting.

'Oh, darlings,' said Shuna. 'I'm so happy you're all right.'

'We're fine,' said Zoe. She managed a poor smile. 'You've looked better though.'

'Cheeky minx,' said Shuna. 'You just wait ...'

'Does it hurt?' said Anna.

'A bit,' said Shuna. 'But I'll be fine ...' A picture of Anna sitting alone on a wooden bench flashed in front of her and she gasped. 'Oh my God. I'm sorry I didn't come and get you sweetie. The guard said he would help and ...'

Anna looked so small sandwiched between Simon and Zoe. 'Don't be silly, Mummy,' she said. 'The policemen told me that, if you hadn't done what the guard said, you'd both be dead.' Tears started to flow down both her cheeks and she buried her face into Simon's jumper.

'... And you sheltered me from the blast,' said Zoe. 'There wasn't anything more you could do.'

Shuna's mind was gradually starting to connect thoughts and memories in logical sequences, synapses now firing in co-ordinated salvos rather than the random bursts of drunken revellers at a Mexican wedding.

'But who was the mysterious man?' Shuna said. 'The one who crept up on the bomber from behind.'

Simon moved to one side, and a woman stepped forward. She was late sixties, a little frumpy, but with a generous smile.

'Hi. I'm Rachel,' she said. 'He was my husband, Dan. Your little girl was sitting with us when Dan figured out what was happening. The two of them protected us all.' Her voice was clear, but her eyes were red and filled with pain ...

Nadia

Nadia felt the bandages being pulled away and opened her eyes. The light was too bright – like staring straight into the sun – and she squeezed her eyes closed immediately.

'Try again,' came the disembodied voice of Dr Hill. '... Slowly.'

Nadia had known the doctor for five days and was keen to see if his face matched her imagined version. She opened her eyes again, only a fraction this time. Slowly, but surely, the burning sun dimmed until she was able to open them wide. It took even longer for shapes to begin to appear within the white haze.

The face looming over her wasn't the mysterious Dr Hill. It was

240

Ed, a semi-bearded Ed.

'Hey Nadia,' he said. 'Good to see you back. It's been weird talking to a lump of bandages.'

'Good to see you too,' she said. 'The bearded mountain-man-look works.'

Ed scratched his beard. 'It's been a busy few days,' he said. 'You know how it is. Press and politicians running around looking for scapegoats while the rest of us are trying to get stuff done.' He shrugged. 'After Karachi, I'd almost forgotten what it's like. Anyway, we've identified the coded call used to set off the bomb and tracked down the phone used to send it. Burner phone, no fingerprints, dumped in a bin outside the tube.'

'Was it Unicorn?'

'Ninety-five per cent,' said Ed. 'There's CCTV footage of a man throwing something in the bin five minutes after the blast. It looks like him, but he was wearing a hat and keeping his head down. He got in a cab which we tracked to White City. The driver confirmed it was probably our man.'

'Do you have eyes on him?'

'Not a chance,' said Ed, looking over his shoulder to see if anyone was in earshot. 'This guy's a ghost. Seems to know exactly where every camera is pointing. He went into the Westfield Centre five days ago and he's still there as far as any of us can tell. Truth is, he's probably back in Peshawar by now.'

Nadia didn't know what to say. Ed was spitting out the words between clenched teeth and, as her vision improved, she could see that he looked terrible – his whole body sagging with exhaustion and dark rings circling his eyes. Everything was pointing to yet another successful coup for Unicorn and Ed had reason to be taking it personally. All the world's security services looking for a single man and he was still able to appear and disappear at will.

'I'm sorry, Ed,' she said, once the silence had grown unbearable. 'On the positive side, we now have confirmation that Snowflake didn't actually press the trigger. His conscience did get the better of him.'

Ed glared at her. 'I'm going to put that down to the drugs they're pumping you full of,' he said. 'Snowflake did everything Unicorn needed him to do. What difference does it make if he had a crisis of conscience at the last minute? The bomb still went off, didn't it? ….. Maybe the stupid idiot was just afraid to die.'

Nadia could tell Ed was frustrated, but did he need to be so cruel? 'It makes a difference to me,' she snapped back. 'I'm convinced he wasn't a bad man and, if we demonise all the weak people as well, where do we stop? And, yes, I'm happy that my judgement wasn't completely wrong.'

Ed looked at her and managed a weary smile. 'Fair enough,' he said. 'I didn't mean to be so sarky. I'm just tired.' He handed a plastic evidence bag to Nadia. 'What do you think of this? The forensic guys think it was in Snowflake's back pocket.'

There was a black-and-white photograph inside the transparent bag, one corner burnt black and torn, but largely intact. From the white creases which quartered it, the photo had been folded and unfolded many times. Nadia could tell from the tight focus that it had been taken with a telephoto lens.

A black Mercedes was parked outside some metal gates on a dusty street. A well-dressed woman in dark sunglasses was stepping out of the back, a small baby wrapped in her arms. The image was crisp and clear and, even with her sore eyes, Nadia could see the happy smile on the woman's face. She was gorgeous.

'Beirut?' she said, looking up at Ed.

'Cairo,' he said. 'Maadi district. We haven't identified her yet, but we will.'

'Why would he have this in his pocket?' asked Nadia.

'Have a look at the back.'

The pencil writing was smudged and hard to read. As Nadia pieced together the words, she gasped.

'Always remember! We know where to find her.'

'I don't understand,' said Nadia. 'You don't think …?'

'… Our working assumption is that the woman is Mona El Masry.'

'… And if it is, Snowflake was blackmailed – coerced rather than convinced?'

242

'Yup,' said Ed. 'It seems that Unicorn threatened to kill Mona and her child unless Hassan carried out the attack … It looks as though you were right about the man, just missing some other key facts.'

Nadia handed back Mona's photo and slumped back onto the soft pillow. The poor young man had still been in love with her even after everything that had happened to him. And he'd been prepared to do the unthinkable to protect her and another man's child.

'Bloody hell,' she said. 'Luckily it wouldn't have made a difference this time, but I should have been professional enough to step back and see the bigger picture, shouldn't I?'

'Maybe,' said Ed. 'That's why it's good to work in teams. Helps add objectivity.' He put the photo back in the evidence bag and smiled. 'Anyway, even though no-one else is aware of this, you'll be happy to know there's a lot of sympathy for Snowflake out there.'

Nadia winced as she tried to raise her eyebrows; she'd forgotten about the stitches. 'How so?' she said.

Ed handed her a small folder. 'Have a read,' he said. 'I'll be back later.'

After Ed left, Nadia took a few moments to look around her; she was in a boring white hospital room, screaming functionality and antiseptic cleanliness. That was fine by her. Anything was a bonus after five days in total blackness.

The doctors had told her that her vision should make a full recovery, although they'd taken great pains to emphasise that she'd been extremely lucky. Apparently one of the ball bearings from the bomb had ricocheted off the pillar next to her and hit her in the cheek. It had been a glancing blow, but enough to send a small shard of bone up into her eyeball. Because of the unusual angle, the surgery had been particularly complex, and they'd been worried she might lose the eye.

Although Nadia had known for a couple of days that the surgery had gone well, she felt her body sagging into the soft mattress as relief coursed through her. Being told her eyes would recover was one thing but, for once, seeing really was believing.

She noticed a vase of white roses on the table next to her with a small card leaning against the vase and recognised the writing straight away - *Get well soon. Good job. David.* Another reason to be relieved; he wouldn't have written that if he intended to make an issue out of her ignoring his order.

She was still holding the folder Ed had given her. It was full of newspaper clippings – dozens of them – divided into two sections, Snowflake and Heroes. She decided to leave Snowflake until last and began to flick through the second section.

Most of the articles were predictably not much more substantial than their blocky, punchy headlines – the typical hand-wringing sensationalism she would have expected. Populist, opinionated and preaching simplistic solutions to horrendously complex problems. All powered by 20:20 hindsight.

However, almost all of them were proclaiming the two old men as heroes and Nadia had the sense that an entire nation had taken them to its heart. There was one article in a respected weekly magazine which stood out; the journalist had taken the time to research his piece properly.

Unlikely Heroes.

The terrorist attack of 10th July 2016 at London's Natural History Museum was well planned, ruthless and aimed to cause maximum harm to a "soft" civilian target. The Dinosaur Bombing, as it has been labelled, would undoubtedly have resulted in significant loss of life if it hadn't been for the selfless acts of two brave men.

Although Jim Pritchard (62) and Dan Bukowski (78) never met, they both made independent decisions to risk their lives in order to protect others. Witnesses have confirmed that both men must have known what might happen to them.

The men came from totally different backgrounds but, with tragic irony, both had already been linked to terrorism earlier in their lives.

Jim was an Eastender, born and bred. He served for twenty years in the British Army before retiring at the age of forty, having reached the rank of sergeant. During his service, he experienced three tours of Northern Ireland during the worst of the Troubles and was injured twice in Republican attacks. Although his own injuries were not severe, eight of his friends and colleagues lost their lives in those attacks.

Having taken early retirement, Jim trained to become a London taxi driver which had been his childhood dream and he worked as a cabbie for the following twenty years. It was only after losing his taxi license in 2014, that he took a job with the Natural History Museum. Jim was one of the two museum guards on duty in the Hinke hall when Hassan Qureishi entered the room.

As soon as he realised that Hassan was behaving suspiciously, we understand from eye-witnesses that Jim's army training kicked in and he took charge of the situation, walking towards the suspected bomber, trying to calm the situation and to prevent the attack.

Nadia had been one of those witnesses and would never forget the way the old man had held himself straight and tall as he'd approached Snowflake, even though he must have known what might happen. Would she have had the courage to do that? Hopefully, she would never be put to the test.

She'd been told a little about these two men as she'd lain in her enforced darkness over the previous days, but this journalist had dug deeper into their backgrounds and she was almost in tears by the time she finished the article.

Dan couldn't have been more different. Born in Toronto to academic parents, he lived and studied at the University of

Texas in Austin, where he started his career as a leading expert in the works of Russian writer, Fyodor Dostoevsky. Dan was the author of several acclaimed academic textbooks, notably including "The Devil Inside: Dostoevsky and Modern Terrorism".

It was during his time in Austin that Dan became a tragic victim of one of the worst mass shootings in American history. Dan's young wife, Rosa, and his unborn child were shot dead in the Texas Tower massacre of August 1st 1966.

Former US Marine, Charles Whitman shot 44 people from the main building tower at the University of Texas in Austin, killing 16 of them. Like so many subsequent US shootings, he wasn't apparently motivated by religion or by politics, but rather by a frustration with society, fuelled by easy access to high-performance firearms. Many experts would say that killings such as these can't be classified as terrorist attacks, but this newspaper struggles to see where the difference lies.

Dan's book, which explores the origins and motivations behind modern terrorism, is already topping best-seller lists worldwide.

Even though Nadia had only seen Dan Bukowski from behind, he'd held himself with a similar purpose as Jim Pritchard – or at least as much as a man of nearly eighty could manage. Apparently he'd had terminal cancer, but that didn't detract in any way from his bravery and the lives he'd saved. From the early forensic results, there was little doubt that the frail old man had saved Nadia's own life along with many others.

Ed had made a point of separating out the articles discussing the two heroes from the ones discussing Snowflake. Nadia could remember the sense of relief which had overwhelmed her as she'd seen the young man take his hand out of his pocket and sink to his knees. Ed and David's warnings were unnecessary and overcautious. It was all going to be all right.

She'd barely had time to register the – slightly smug – satisfaction of knowing she'd been right all along, before the world had turned white. Inside the memories of burning light, she couldn't stop seeing Unicorn's face staring at her out of the flames. His green eyes were filled with triumph and he had one eyebrow arched as if to say, 'Really? Who do you think you are, little girl?'

She began to leaf through the Snowflake press cuttings and quickly understood what Ed had meant. Of course there was plenty of criticism of Hassan Qureishi, but the writers were mostly voicing disappointment at his weakness and naivety, and trying to understand how an Oxford-educated Brit could have been brainwashed so completely. Every article made a point of emphasising the fact that Hassan had actually surrendered and much of the anger and vitriol was reserved for Ibrahim and the Pakistani Taliban.

... Oxford-educated bomber – why did he change his mind?

... mother says he must have been brainwashed.

... Tragic love story. Who was the mysterious Egyptian girl who broke Hassan Qureishi's heart?

... bomber was victim of class divide and snobbery as much as race. Austerity creates vulnerability!

... Three witnesses say that the museum bomber had chosen to give himself up. Police have confirmed that the bomb was detonated remotely.

... Bradford-born multi-millionaire donates £250,000 to anti-radicalisation programmes.

Nadia had to read the final article twice. The Bradford-born multi-millionaire was, of course, Hassan's drug dealer uncle. Who would have expected that?

247

Although the press coverage was still full of anti-Moslem, anti-immigration sentiment, it was more balanced and more focused than might have been expected. The fact that fatalities had been limited helped, but there was something more; for whatever reason, many people – of all backgrounds – seemed to have identified with Hassan and, like Nadia, to choose to focus on the tragedy of a young life, with so much potential, being wasted.

If they only knew about the threats to Mona's life ... but they never would ...

One mainstream right-wing tabloid had gone as far to say:

Let's make an end to division. People of all faiths must come together to protect our youth from the evil influence of a small group of fanatics. We all let this young man down. Let's make sure it never happens again.

Only words, but it was a start. Maybe there was some hope for the future, after all?

And then, as the weeks and months of stress finally began to catch up with her, Nadia slumped back into her pillow, rough cardboard folder clutched to her chest and warm tears running down her cheeks.

Best Eaten Cold

by Tony Salter

The Bestselling Psychological Thriller you can't put down.

Imagine that someone wants to do you harm. Someone you once knew, but have almost forgotten.

Now, imagine that they are clever, patient and will not stop. They'll get inside your head and make you doubt yourself.

They'll make you question who you are, and ensure that everyone you care for starts to doubt you too.

***** "Fast-paced, terrifyingly believable, chilling at times... the kind of book that's hard to put down"

***** "I admire any author who can hold my attention so thrillingly from beginning to end"

***** "Much superior to Girl on the Train."

Best Eaten Cold is AVAILABLE NOW in paperback or eBook format from Amazon and most booksellers.

The Old Orchard

by Tony Salter

The family thriller that will grip you until the last page.

Finance Director, Alastair Johnson, is in trouble. He needs a lot of money, and he needs it very soon.

Alastair's solution is unorthodox and completely out of character – the fallout leaves his family torn apart.

But everything is not what it seems ...

***** "What a cracking story! Loved the way it all unfolded at the end. Really clever and credible and I didn't see the twists coming."

***** "FLIPPIN' BRILLIANT!"

***** "The Old Orchard is a pacy, tense, domestic thriller which builds an original and satisfying plot around real characters we can believe in. The prose is light and evocative with vivid descriptions and many moments of real insight and human wisdom."

The Old Orchard is AVAILABLE NOW in paperback or eBook format from Amazon and most booksellers.

Cold Intent

by Tony Salter

The Thrilling Sequel to Best Eaten Cold.

It was always too good to be true.

Finding her, arresting her, proving her guilt … that should have been enough.

It should have been, but a small voice, deep inside him, refused to be silenced. The voice which whispered the same words over and over – how even a jail sentence wouldn't stop her.

And then Sam looked at Julie, standing tall in the dock waiting for the verdict. He watched her smile and knew that it would never be over. She would always find a way to reach out for him and the nightmares would become reality once more.

***** "Sleep isn't an option. You have to know what happens next."

***** "Utterly compelling."

***** "A masterclass in page-turning - thrilling!"

Cold Intent is AVAILABLE NOW in paperback or eBook format from Amazon and most booksellers.

Acknowledgements

Writing novels is a solitary task but I don't think I could enjoy it without some company along the way. Feedback, encouragement and patient support are essential emotional props, but so are the sweeping blows of honest criticism which help to remind me that I am writing for readers and not only for myself.

Sixty Minutes was a difficult book to write for many reasons, not least because of the sensitivity of the subject matter. It is entirely a work of fiction, a story about ordinary people thrown together in extraordinary circumstances.

I need to thank all of my friends and family for their help and encouragement – in particular, Sue Brown, John Cronley, Di Cronley, Stephen Garwood, Aliki Radley, Emma Newman, Annie Eccles, Dana Olearnikova and Kath Watson. Special thanks are due to my editor, Claire Baldwin.

Finally, I must thank my wife of thirty years, Gro. Without her love, support, patience and tolerance, none of this would have been possible.

47372694R00155

Printed in Poland
by Amazon Fulfillment
Poland Sp. z o.o., Wrocław